A NEW RESOLUTION

Book 3 of the Resolution Series

ROSE DEE

HOLE IN THE WIND PUBLISHING

A New Resolution - Copyright 2016 – Rose Dee

Re-edited for the US eBook market.

Formatting by: Wild Seas Formatting (RikHall.com)

ISBN EBook: 978 – 0 – 9944011 – 7 – 5

ISBN Print: 978 – 0 – 9944011 – 8 – 2

Hole in the Wind Publishing

ACKNOWLEDGEMENTS

Thanks first to my Heavenly Father who inspires every story. To my family who are ever supportive and understanding. Thank you to my readers, particularly Mullum Stone. I am grateful to the professionals who shared their expertise - Wendy Noble and Iola Goulton.

This book is dedicated to my late husband, Terry, whose life experiences on the ocean have been a great inspiration for my 'Resolution' series. Thank you for sharing your stories with me. And for the unending support and love you gave me.

For My Late Husband, Terry
(16.03.1953 - 30.12.2019)

PROLOGUE

The darkness was closing in. Anika's legs were moving, running, pumping as fast as they could. It felt as though she was wading through a sea of quicksand. Every muscle ached as she willed her body to push ahead. Her forward motion stalled with every feeble attempt to escape the dark shadow looming behind her.

The debilitating black mass was close. Her heart beat so hard, she was certain it would seize her at any moment.

She reached out frantically, knowing the bright light she had been chasing would overcome the darkness, but the white brilliance faded before her eyes.

It grew to a dim hue and then disappeared. She dropped to her knees. Despair overcame her and she opened her mouth, but her attempt to scream was futile. Not even a squeak came from her parted lips.

She sank into a lifeless heap, knowing the impenetrable darkness would gradually envelop, then suffocate her. It would squeeze the life from her in an unrelenting and overwhelming pressure.

She curled into a ball and braced for impact.

A sudden shake, a motion unexpected in this scene she knew so well, forced its way into her subconscious. The ominous evil faded. Another shake came, then another, followed by a distant voice.

"Ani."

Although the voice was muffled by layers of sleep, it was vaguely familiar.

"Ani. Wake up."

Anika's eyelids fluttered and then inched open. She was still in the cupboard, curled up at one end. Her mother's dresses formed a barrier between her and the old wooden door hanging wide open. It groaned as it swung precariously on one hinge.

The dresses were pulled to one side and the owner of the voice had her upper arm in a vice-like grip.

The reality of discovery forced her upright. A surge of fear, far more terrifying than her dream, flooded her body.

She had been found.

Her safe place had been compromised.

A shiver ran through her and, despite the humidity in the cupboard, she shook in uncontrollable spasms.

The noise of the party forced its way into the bedroom. She recognized the drunken octane as it reverberated off the thin walls. Loud music thumped in harmony with the slurring symphony of inebriated men, the squeals of the women, and the clattering and clinking of glass and tin. Ani threw herself against the wall of the cupboard and prayed for invisibility.

"It's okay little one. I won't hurt you."

The voice was slow and sure. The man withdrew his hand to squat at the door and as he did so, light from the hallway spilled onto his face.

"Uncle?" Ani rubbed her eyes and squinted through the blackness. The light illuminated one side of the man's face and, even though his complexion was dark, the reflection was enough to confirm his identity.

She clambered through the assortment of clutter to get to him.

"Uncle Amos?"

He held out his hand to help her. His strong arms enveloped her little body.

"I'm here, Ani." His voice was reassuring. "I'm going to get you out of here. For good."

A tidal wave of relief washed over her. She melted into the safety of his arms.

CHAPTER 1

Anika Deumer looked at the white stick on the bathroom vanity. She couldn't believe her entire future hinged on a piece of nondescript plastic.

She was late. Three weeks late. *What am I going to do if it's positive?*

The thought she hadn't yet dared to contemplate entered her head. She sat down on the edge of the porcelain bathtub and put her head in her hands.

Seventeen was too young to be a mother, even though she was twelve months older than her own mother had been when she was born. *And that's gone great, hasn't it?* Her mother had been absent for a large part of her life.

A knock sounded on the door. Anika held her breath, fearing discovery.

"Ani, I need to brush my teeth."

It was Ronald. The shy six-year-old was the most recent addition to the clan of foster children that included three girls and four boys. Ani was the eldest. She forced her breath out in a relieved rush.

"Give me a few minutes," she said. "I'm almost done."

The brush-off seemed to work. Silence fell on the other side of the door. Ani looked at her watch. *Two minutes gone, three to go.*

She perched on the edge of the bathtub and hid her face in her hands. A peek through her spread fingers. The stick hadn't magically disappeared.

With a heavy sigh, she straightened up and tried to avoid its overpowering presence by focusing on the framed photo above the laundry basket. It was an old picture of Aunty's family.

A long line of brothers and sisters, ten in all, stood outside the family home in Kiisay Point, around nine hundred kilometers south of Aunty's home here in Cairns. The face of one brother stood out. Uncle Amos. Her unlikely hero. He had a mass of curly hair, a wide grin, and he wore nothing but a pair of faded shorts.

But Amos, Aunty's older brother, was indeed Ani's knight in shining armor. He had rescued Ani from her mother's partying lifestyle. Despite being only distantly related, Ani had always referred to the members of her Pacific Islander family as Aunty and Uncle.

Another soft thud at the door interrupted her thoughts. Ani bit her lip and waited for further communication from the other side.

"Aunty says I need to clean my teeth now. She says to tell you your hair looks fine. I think it looks good, too."

She couldn't help but smile at Ronald's shy compliment. "Thanks, Ronald. I'll be two more minutes."

She stood up and looked in the mirror. Her hair was the bane of her existence. Any other day she would have been standing there, brushing, clipping and applying any and every product available in an effort to tame the dirty blonde corkscrew curls that fell below her shoulders. Aunty's assumption that she was holed up in the bathroom doing her hair was usually accurate. Today she was barricaded in due to a life-changing matter which entirely trivialized her hair issues.

Ani picked up a long-toothed comb and did her best to run it through her curls. Her bright blue eyes stared back. She lost count of how many times people commented on their brilliance. Perhaps it was because the color was so unexpected for her Island heritage. Her dark olive complexion and curly hair were the only Island heritage features she possessed.

Her physique was also different from her peers. Ani envied her friends with their curves and womanly hips. She always thought her curves were more lumps than bumps.

"Eat up, Ani. Got to get some meat on those bones." Aunty used to say when Ani first came to live with her. She had been a scrawny ten-year-old at the time.

"You take after your father," her mother would spit at her. "We're all cursed." Ani hated when her mother spoke of the family curse. Fathers without faces had been the fate of each woman before her. Left pregnant and abandoned by her rich married lover, her mother believed no Deumer woman would be cherished by a man.

Ani was convinced it was all rubbish and nothing but bad choices had placed her family in this recurring historical predicament. She was determined to be the one to break the curse.

Now, here she was, one drastic mistake later, wondering if she would end up being part of the cycle. Young, pregnant, rejected, desperate, traumatized, substance dependent. A family tradition passed down from generation to generation.

Ani looked down at the white stick. She closed her eyes, taking a few deep breaths. *Please, don't let it be positive.* She sent up a silent prayer to the God Aunty told her existed, hoping He had a moment to hear her plea.

She inched her hand towards the stick. Her heart pounded in her ears. She picked it up without showing the result and then flipped it over to the viewing space.

There was no mistaking the two blue lines: positive. She closed her eyes as tears welled behind her lids.

What are you going to do? How could you be so stupid?

She opened her eyes and stared at the stick, willing it to magically change as hot tears streamed down her face.

"Ani. Thank goodness. I've been yelling at you to open up. What's wrong with you?"

Anika looked up to see Aunty's ample girth fill the doorway. She'd broken into the bathroom. Her greying afro framed her face like a halo, and the ever-present tropical flower, picked from the garden, sat above her ear. Aunty gave her a questioning gaze before her eyes settled on the test in her hand.

Her eyes widened and her mouth dropped as horror replaced her annoyance. "Oh, no. Ani. No."

Anika stood stock still. It was as though the whole world had stopped. She stared at Aunty through the blur of her tears.

"Can you please let him know Anika called again?" She poked the tip of the pen into the wooden table with a heavy thud.

There was a pause on the other end of the line, followed by a short-tempered huff. "I'll pass on the message but you won't get him on this number after today. He goes back to school this afternoon and I don't expect him back to stay with me anytime soon."

Anika didn't blame the woman for being short. She had lost track of the number of messages she had left for Heath.

"Please let him know it's vital I speak to him before he goes back home." She was desperate. Heath had avoided her for weeks now.

"Like I said, I'll pass on the message." The lady, who she assumed was Heath's aunt, paused before repeating the news Ani had already been privy to. "You do know he has a girlfriend, don't you?"

She felt her heart drop and rage rise at the confirmation. "Yes. I do know. It would have been nice if Heath had told me that himself before he professed his undying love for me and convinced me to have sex with him." She could feel the anger boiling over.

"Don't you get nasty with me. I know your type, little girl. You're a money-grubbing lowlife with dollar signs before your eyes. Nothing more. Don't call me again or I'll get the police onto you." The line went dead.

Ani threw the phone on the table and slumped back in the old worn chair. Heath had stopped answering her calls and had cut all contact with her since she'd told him she was pregnant.

It was a complete contrast to the boy who had pursued her with unlimited energy for weeks. She shook her head when she recalled the fancy restaurants, expensive presents, and the intense way he looked at her.

Heath Mayfield was rich. He'd been visiting family in Cairns for the school holidays and had set his sights on her early in the eight-week hiatus. Heath was unlike anyone Ani had ever met. Suave. Sophisticated. His good looks were only surpassed by his intelligence, cultivated by his posh private school education. They had fervent conversations about her favorite books and, to her surprise, he had an extensive knowledge about the sea creatures of the reef, one of her main interests.

She loved listening to him recount stories about the countries he had visited. She had also shared her secret with him - she had saved her money for months to get her passport. To her, the fact that he had visited all the countries she had dreamed about made him special.

Unfortunately, it was nothing but an elaborate act. He had thrown out a lure and she had taken the bait without a suspicion of the truth. Heath was a player, with a girl in every port. She was the flavor of the month.

When Ani had confronted him two weeks ago, his handsome, boyish face had collapsed in horror before becoming quiet and reflective. She breathed a sigh of relief when she saw his silent contemplation. Heath would have the solution, she was sure.

"No problem," he said. "Just get rid of it."

It wasn't the answer she had anticipated from someone who professed to love her. Ani had sat in stunned silence for a moment before deciding to be completely honest.

"I don't know if I can do that, Heath."

"Why not? You don't want it. I certainly don't want it. What's the problem?" He cocked one eyebrow as he stared at her. Ani couldn't believe she'd never seen this side of him.

"I don't know if I could go through with an abortion. It feels wrong to me."

She recalled what Aunty would tell her in those moments when she felt abandoned and unloved. Aunty had always insisted God had a purpose for each and every person. There were no mistakes. He was invested in every life from the moment of conception, regardless of the circumstances.

Heath had scoffed and curled one side of his upper lip. "You have got to be kidding me. You can't seriously be thinking of having it?"

Am I seriously thinking of having it? Do I really have a choice?

He had reached into his pocket, and pulled out his leather wallet. "Here." He threw a wad of cash at her. "Do what you have to."

Ani had stared at the money in her lap as anguish set in. Heath must have seen her distress because his face softened.

"Look. It's been real fun, Anika. Well, up until now anyway." He paused to run a hand through his blond hair. "I'm back at school in a few weeks and, to be honest, I'm far too young to be this serious about anyone. Maybe this is a sign that we should call it off before it gets unpleasant."

She had reeled back. *Unpleasant?* How much more unpleasant could it get? But before she could collect herself, Heath was up and heading to his car.

'Thanks for the memories." He closed the door and was gone before she realized he had moved.

Ani was left wondering if she had dreamed the entire exchange.

After several unanswered phone calls, she had received a call from one of Heath's friends. He relayed his friend's message - She should get an abortion and leave Heath alone. Heath's girlfriend was visiting from Sydney for the last week of the school holidays and Ani had been nothing but a fun distraction.

She was a fool. How could she have fallen into this trap? Since she had come to live with Aunty, she had worked hard to get an education and make something of herself, and now it looked as though she wouldn't even finish high school.

Heath had convinced her that he loved her. Ani had been firm from the start - she wasn't interested in an intimate relationship with him. She was a virgin and vowed to remain that way, determined the family curse would stop with her. She'd thought Heath's acceptance of her decision was evidence that his feelings for her were genuine. But when the kissing and touching intensified, she was left in no doubt as to what he wanted to see happen between them.

The night he professed his love for her on the beach as they walked in the moonlight was the final attention that shattered her resolve. He had told her he wanted her, over and over.

It was the first time anyone had said those words to her. She had spent her entire life feeling as though nobody wanted her. It wasn't hard to give in to him. After all, he had professed the very thing she so desperately needed to hear.

Unfortunately, the scenes in movies where the actors make passionate love on the sand as the waves roll in were a big farce. Lying on sand was uncomfortable and the salt water stung. It was an awkward scenario consisting of Heath getting what he wanted and neglecting any aspect of her comfort. Ani had a feeling she had been used.

Now she knew she had.

She had no idea what to do, but he wasn't getting out of his part so easily. She had to find a way to see him before he left for Sydney.

Cairns Airport was packed with passengers. Anika had trouble negotiating the throng. A mass of faces merged as she scanned the departure lounge for Heath. She had been here for hours. There were four flights to Sydney every afternoon. She knew he would have to be on one of them, and this was the last flight of the day.

A shock of white-blond hair stood out from the crowd. Heath was tall, moderately muscular and boyish. As the movement of the passengers shifted, Ani caught a glimpse of expensive designer clothes. It was him. She was certain.

He was trailing an equally classy entourage. Ani could see his private school mates and three girls, two blonde and one brunette, each with an air of privilege and sophistication. Visions of American socialites flashed before her eyes.

Great. She hesitated, pulling back out of view to decide her next move. As she stood in the shadow of a dividing wall, she watched Heath swing an arm around one of the blondes. The girl playfully slapped him on the chest and laughed as he kissed her neck.

Resentment and bitterness bubbled up as she watched the exchange. *Who does he think he is? Just because he's got money doesn't mean he can treat me any way he wants.*

Ani stepped forward with determination and made her way towards the group.

One of the boys saw her coming and she heard him curse as he thumped Heath and indicated her approach. As she stopped in front of them, Heath dropped his arm from the girl's shoulder. His eyes widened.

Angry tears brimmed and a hard lump moved up and down Ani's throat with every swallow. "Who do you think you are? What makes you think you can treat me like something that can be used and thrown away?" She could hear her voice cracking.

Heath put up his hand and drew back. "Settle down. I'm sure we can talk this through."

His arrogance further stoked her temper and she felt her nostrils flare.

The blonde cocked an eyebrow. "Is this the local girl? I thought you said she was pretty?" The other two girls snickered.

Heath gave her a withering look. "You're not helping, Amy."

Amy screwed up her face. "How do you expect me to act? Some lowlife has an obsession with you and you think it's hilarious?"

Ani shook her head, her eyes never leaving the group. Whatever he had divulged about their relationship, it hadn't been the truth. She set her gaze on the blonde. "You have no idea do you? He never told me he had a girlfriend. If he was so into you, why did he sleep with me? You're being used just as much as I've been."

Amy placed her hands on her hips. "Why don't you go and crawl back into the hole you came out of. Or was it a trailer park bush? Isn't that where your kind reside?" She smirked as her girlfriends moved in around her.

The wrath inside her reached new heights. A deliberate attack on her social status was bad enough, but to come from the likes of this so-called well-bred girl was an insult she could not accept.

She steeled her gaze firmly on the fiend. 'Money isn't everything. It clearly hasn't bought you any breeding or intelligence."

Amy squared her shoulders. "What would you know about breeding? Heath's told me all about you. Fatherless and in Foster Care with a drunk for a mother. You need to accept the fact that you're a loser who's way out of your depth."

The insult hit Ani like a fist to the stomach. She recoiled inside before overwhelming rage took hold.

"I'd rather be a loser than a…" Her colorful insult was muffled by a loud voice on the intercom above their heads as the airline representative's voice announced the boarding of the flight.

Ani finished her tirade and stared Amy down. She could see Heath shuffling back and forth, looking to his friends for help. A horde of passengers milled around them as they made their way to the boarding gate.

Heath embraced the distraction. He turned to his friends. 'Take the girls through, will you? I'll be a minute."

He pushed his friends towards the girls. Heath reached down and whispered in Amy's ear. She turned to give Ani a death stare before picking up her bag and allowing one of the boys to lead her away.

Heath moved to Ani's side, grabbing her upper arm and pulling hard.

"Don't touch me!" She ripped away from his grasp.

He stopped and blew out a short, exasperated breath. "What do you want from me, Anika? Is it money?" He pulled out his wallet. "How much? I can give you three hundred now. Any more, and I'll have to transfer to you." He fingered through the hundred-dollar bills in the bifold.

She couldn't believe it. He still thought he could buy her. "I don't want your money. I never wanted your money. Who do you think you are? You can't go around telling girls you love them so you can have sex, then dump them the second it backfires on you."

Heath looked down at his shoes before reestablishing eye contact with her. "Look, I thought maybe I did love you. At the time it seemed real." He shrugged. "I have responsibilities. My father has my life all mapped out for me. You're not acceptable."

Suddenly the penny dropped. Heath's

overbearing, controlling father wouldn't be happy with a low-class addition to the family. Heath was too weak and unwilling to step up. His playboy persona was a farce.

She stood in silence and stared at the pathetic emotional cripple in front of her. Heath was trapped playing the role of successful son, and his privilege had entitled him to buy his way out of any unpleasant consequences. She had to face the facts. She was on her own. The quicker she accepted it, the better off she would be.

She shook her head. "I don't want your money. I don't want anything from you." She turned to walk away.

"What about the baby?" His voice sounded behind her. "I've been told to offer you whatever it takes to get rid of it. Name the price and I'll transfer it to you."

Ani turned back. Aunty's favorite Bible verse echoed in her head. "Do unto others what you would have them do unto you, Heath."

She turned and walked away, and didn't look back.

CHAPTER 2

Anika could hear the wails before she even got one foot out of the car door. The night light beamed off the porch of the old, run-down cottage, anticipating her arrival home. She pulled her foot back into the vehicle and let her head thump onto the headrest.

"I do not want to go in there." She wondered if she would have been so honest without the cheap wine she had consumed earlier in the night.

Her friend readjusted the volume of the stereo. "I don't blame you. What a drag."

Ani rolled her eyes. None of her friends had any idea how much of a drag a three-month-old was. She sighed and put her foot back onto the ground. Sitting here was only delaying the inevitable.

"Thanks for the lift." She pulled herself from the car.

"Pleased it's you and not me." Her driver offered the unhelpful comment as she shut the door.

Ani wished it wasn't her either. She had decided to take the year off school. Trying to juggle her final year of schooling with the life-changing event of motherhood wasn't a good idea. Considering pregnancy wasn't something she could suspend, she had opted to leave school. She hadn't anticipated how lonely it would be, stuck in the house all day with a newborn.

Although Aunty expected her to fulfil her maternal duties, she had conceded that Ani had to have a social life. However, each time Ani left her little boy she enjoyed great relief. She had skipped out the door four times already this week. Not that he was a difficult baby. He was good. She was just scared of doing something wrong, of not being capable of loving him the way a mother should.

The wails got louder and louder as she dragged her feet to the door. She took a few deep breaths before walking up the three steps to the weather-beaten door.

Aunty looked up as she entered. She sat in the ancient rocking chair, pushing back and forth, with the little boy splayed over her shoulder, legs stiff and lungs in fine form.

"Where have you been, Anika? This child's been screaming for over an hour."

Ani took the baby from her and settled on the sofa, giving him his bottle before addressing her angry foster mother.

"I had to wait for a lift home. Dinner was more expensive than I thought. I didn't have money for a taxi." She wasn't about to tell the truth — that she had delayed coming home for as long as she possibly could, and had spent her money on wine.

"I'm not his mother. You are." Aunty's statement of the obvious did nothing for Ani's frayed nerves.

"I know that. Can't I have a life of my own?" Ani looked up from her nursing duty to give her Aunty a glare.

"No. You gave up your life the day Kye was born. He's your life now. Babies come first, Ani. It's not about you anymore."

Ani sighed and rolled her eyes. She had heard it

all before. The action inflamed her Aunt further. "How many times have I heard you say that this family curse would stop at you?"

She huffed in a show of exasperation. "In case you hadn't noticed, Aunty, the horse has bolted. The kid's here. Curse fulfilled. Life over. The end." She used her free hand to cut through the air like the drama queen she wasn't.

Aunty sighed. "You're wrong. This is just the beginning. You may have the baby, but you still have the choice to put him first or not. You can be the mother to him that you didn't have yourself."

Ani looked down at the little boy and voiced the question she had wanted to ask since the day he was born. "Why don't you be his mother? You always wanted children. Now you can have one from birth."

She loved her son dearly. But motherhood wasn't something she was ready for, prepared for, and she was certain she would fail him like her mother had failed her.

Aunty stopped rocking and sat up. Her grey eyebrows furrowed in the middle and brown eyes grew even more intense as she focused on her. "God has placed this little boy here for a reason. Just like He placed you here, Ani."

Ani sat watching her baby fed. Aunty had always spoken about her faith, but Ani had never understood it. A personal relationship with God seemed like hard work. Besides, if God did exist, why would He be interested in her? He never had been before. He hadn't given her a father, a happy home, or a decent mother. She was clearly insignificant. It was time she spelled it out.

"God, whoever He or she is, is not interested in me. So don't give me that whole, 'God is love' line, because I can tell you I haven't see any of it in my life."

Her words came out far more aggressively than she had planned.

Aunty looked hurt. Her mouth drooped to the side, and tears welled in her eyes.

Ani concentrated on Kye. She stroked his head as if it were the most important task in the world. Regret burned within her. *Why didn't you keep your mouth shut?*

"You're wrong, Ani. He does love you. I wish you could see how much."

The comment quashed the regret and a fiery indignation stirred in its place. *How much He loves me?*

"Well, He's got a real funny way of showing it. I spent most of my childhood either cleaning up after my addict mother, or dodging drunkards. I never knew when I would eat next. My mother only kept me around because she didn't want to lose her childcare benefit. She didn't even know I was there most of the time." Ani couldn't help her scoffing words any more than she could help her angry and bitter tone.

"I'd hide in cupboards to avoid the people my mother invited in. Sometimes I'd hide under the house in the dirt, where I got bitten by rats. And the best thing in my life was when my mother was so out of it that she couldn't party or sell herself. Not one person gave a toss about me. I may as well have been dead. So, now you tell me how much God loves me."

She steeled her gaze at Aunty, waiting for the rebuff that would no doubt come. But the older woman said nothing. Not one word to counteract her aggression. Not one explanation of her past existence. Not one preachy utterance, just a steady flow of tears streaming down her face.

A great sadness threatened to overwhelm her. This was the first time since coming to live with Aunty that she had spoken honestly about her childhood. She had always kept the emotions to herself, bottling them up so she wasn't a burden to others. It had only ever come out in her dreams. Sleep was the only release for her pain.

Ani looked around the shabby lounge as tears filled her eyes.

"I am so sorry about what happened to you." Aunty's voice shook.

Ani swallowed hard in an effort to stem the flow of her emotions. "Why should you be sorry? You didn't do it."

The minute the words left her mouth she realized how true they were. Aunty hadn't done those things. Instead, Aunty had given her a loving home and security she never knew could exist in life.

Uncle Amos had done more than save her that day. He had given her a family.

Maybe God does think of me now and then.

A blowing noise came from the rocking chair. Aunty had retrieved a handkerchief from her pocket and was clearing her nose. "You do know that God didn't do those things to you either? People did. Your mother had choices. She didn't make many good ones, but she did choose to give you a life. You have choices as well."

That's right. And I've made the exact same mistakes she did. She looked down at her baby boy. Aunty was right about one thing. There was a difference between being unplanned and unwanted. She had been both. Like her, Kye had no father to affirm him. It was up to her to make sure he was loved. Her instincts told her she wasn't up to the task.

I guess you only get one knight in shining armor experience per lifetime. She recalled her childhood nightmare and the way she would shout to the white light to save her. *Or maybe God could send another one?*

Please God, please. Give Kye the father he deserves. Don't let him grow up without a Dad. Please let Heath want to know Kye, want to come back into his life. Please.

"Ani!" Aunty's call to attention sounded from the vicinity of the lounge.

"I'm in my bedroom," she yelled back.

A thud of little feet sounded down the hallway. Kye pushed open the door.

"Kiki." He ran in and jumped into her arms, accepting the multitude of kisses planted on his chubby little face.

At two years of age, he was a real combination of genes. There was no mistaking the bright blue eyes and olive complexion, both of which were an obvious inheritance from her. His physique was clearly his father's, tall for his age with broad shoulders and big feet. The only other feature he shared with his father was lighter blonde hair. Ani took great pleasure in the fact that, although the color was Heath's, the corkscrew curls were a clear sign of her dominant gene pool.

"Kiki, Aunty want you." Kye pointed a stumpy finger towards the door. He had recently taken to calling her Kiki. He had picked up on the 'k' sound in her name and emphasized it to produce his own pet name for her.

At first Ani was affronted by not being called mum, but Kye persisted and his own term of endearment soon grew on her.

"Okay, let's go." She got to her feet and allowed him to take her hand as they walked out the door.

Aunty was sitting in her rocking chair, watching television.

"Sit down for a minute. I think there's something on the news about Heath. I couldn't hear very well because someone…" she gave three children on the couch a stern look, "was making too much noise. But I could have sworn it was his name."

She waved her arm towards the children. "You three get off and go and clean your room, like I told you to."

They reluctantly relinquished their position to Ani and Kye.

The advertisement break ended and a female announcer commenced the news segment. She launched into general greetings before a photo of Heath appeared to her right.

"Police have released the name of a man who died in a high speed crash in Sydney last week. Heath Mayfield, son of prominent Sydney solicitor Mitchell Mayfield, died of head trauma injuries sustained in the crash. Heath was the driver of a

BMW that collided with a semi-trailer in Sydney's north-west suburbs. The crash also claimed the lives of three passengers in the vehicle."

Ani glanced at Aunty, whose eyes had doubled in size. A sick feeling stirred inside as a picture of the mangled vehicle replaced Heath's photo.

"Toxicology reports reveal a blood alcohol reading five times the legal limit." The announcer looked down. "In other news ... "The screen went blank.

Ani stared at the black box for what seemed like ages, trying to comprehend the report. She was distracted from her numbness by Kye. His legs were thumping repeatedly on the sofa.

A babble of soft murmurings accompanied his methodical action.

This is it. All hope of Kye ever having a father faded to nothing. The hope she clung to was gone. A tear trailed down her cheek.

"Ani?" Aunty sat forward in her seat, her elbows on her knees as she leaned towards them. "Don't be discouraged."

Aunty's gentle words evoked a painful realization.

"How could I not?" She stared at the older woman, feeling the bitterness of defeat in every fiber of her being.

"God has heard your prayers. He won't let you down. You have to trust that He has a plan for you, and for Kye. A good plan. A loving plan."

Anika shook her head. "You don't understand, Aunty. I've done everything I can."

Aunty looked briefly at her slippers before

meeting her eyes once more. "Everything but trust."

The words cut through her. *Trust? Trust? Now I have to trust?* It was too much. How could she trust in a God who wasn't listening to her? It was confirmation of a fact she already knew: she wasn't important to Him. She never had been.

The mid-afternoon sun cast shadows on the street as Anika stepped out the door of the police station.

The cop turned to her as she made her escape. "I hope you've learned your lesson." he said. "Don't drink and drive."

His somber face penetrated her consciousness and, for the first time, Anika felt a pang of guilt over the seriousness of the situation. "Don't worry. I won't."

It was a promise she would have no trouble keeping, certainly not in the near future. The driver's license she had held for over twelve months had been taken from her and she wouldn't know her fate until a court date was set.

The bus ride home was excruciating. The few drinks she had consumed that afternoon at a friend's barbeque were nowhere near the quantity she would normally pour down her throat.

For the last four months she had been on a bender, to use Aunty's term.

It had all started with the news of Heath's death. The incident had no end. She left the room each time Mitchell Mayfield's face appeared on the television. Eventually she had given up watching television, listening to radio, and reading online news articles.

Ani knew she had never loved Heath. She'd been attracted to the thought of him, the romance of him and the freedom he represented.

This knowledge did not stop her from wanting him as a father for Kye. The fulfilment of her fatherless heritage proved she was nothing but a failure.

She had forced away her sorrows by drinking, partying and indulging in a string of meaningless one-night stands.

Looking back now, Ani realized she had fallen into each one without thought.

Pregnancy had seen the end to her boyish figure. Where she once had a moderate chest and thin hips, she now possessed full breasts and a curvier shape.

This fact alone drew attention from men. But she also had an aura of vulnerability and a need to be loved. She was a willing and easy target. After being starved for attention from the opposite sex for well over two years, all it took was some strategically placed compliments and a significant consumption of alcohol for a man to bed her.

Now her drinking had forced an all-time low. The long walk home from the bus stop purged her system of any remaining alcohol.

She popped a few mints into her mouth before opening the door. The household was frantic. It became apparent that the occupants were on their way out the door. The noise accompanying eight children, all making preparations to leave a tiny house, was enough to do her already-throbbing head in.

"They're my shoes."

"Where's my cap?"

"Did you take my lip gloss?"

"I'm thirsty."

The wall of noise made her want to turn back around. She was stopped from doing so by the appearance of Aunty.

"Ani, I expected you home hours ago." She squatted in order to place shoes on Kye's feet.

"Kiki." The little boy thrust his body forwards for a cuddle. He was stopped by Aunty's hold on one foot.

Ani took the luxury of a long pause, wondering how to recount the day's events. Aunty clearly wasn't in the mood for conversation. "Well, don't just stand there. Get some of these kids to the car."

The car? She wants the car? Oh no.

The old Holden station wagon was still parked on the side of the road where she had been breath-tested and found wanting.

She deflected with a question. "Where are you going?"

"I told you, Bruce is coming by with the van to pick us all up and take us to the church meeting."

Ani was confused. Despite having a strong faith, Aunty wasn't a routine churchgoer. Aunty's brother, Bruce would take them to a Sunday morning service on the odd occasion, but this was Saturday night.

Aunty must have seen her frown. She put her hands on her hips, the action freeing Kye who now ran to her and threw his arms around her legs.

"I told you all about it this morning. There's a visiting speaker. You told me you would be home in time to come with us."

Oh, this morning. That explains it. Ani nodded her head, knowing she had paid no attention to Aunty's instructions as she lay, hung over, in her bed that morning.

"Well, come on you lot. I want you all out the door, and waiting for Bruce." Aunty shuffled them along the narrow corridor.

Anika allowed herself to be led by the throng, silently thankful for the reprieve that bought her some more time.

As they collected in a group at the front door, Aunty checked over each child and then stopped to take a deep breath.

Anika stood quietly, holding Kye as the children chattered around them. She sneaked looks at Aunty out of the corner of her eye. If only the van would arrive now without Aunty noticing the absent car, she would have a chance to retrieve the vehicle and keep the day's incident under wraps.

The older woman scanned the front yard.

She left the group to walk around the side of the house, returning with a deep furrow on her brow.

Oh, no.

"Anika, where's the car?"

Church was held at a community hall each Sunday. Most weeks it was moderately attended, but tonight it was packed to overflowing.

Ani made her way in behind Aunty, her head hung low and avoiding eye contact as they took their seats. She had been forced to relay the entire story on the way. Aunty had said little in reply and Ani knew this was the worst possible reaction.

She felt like a fool and a liar and a traitor.

Ani thought back to her mother and how one bad decision had led to another and another and another, until one day she had woken up an alcoholic and all alone.

Is that where I'm heading? The question scared her to death.

The service started and she allowed herself to be distracted by the predictable singing.

The guest speaker was one of the darkest men Anika had ever seen, much darker than the Indigenous and Islander people who lived around here. He had to be African. As he started speaking, she sat up and gave him her full attention.

His message had two main themes. One was the Good Samaritan, and the way God can use the most unexpected person to bless you. The second was the role God had played in his life as the loving parent he had never had.

Anika was captivated.

The tall African paced the stage as he spoke. "I wanted a parent. I needed a parent. But it was the one thing I did not have." His broken English faltered as emotion strained through his words. "

"My mother and father were killed when I was only five. I had nothing. And because of this, I became nobody. I had no identity. I only existed." He stopped to scan the congregation. Ani could see the pain in his eyes.

"I had no direction, so when the soldiers came and took me away, I thought I finally had a purpose.

But they did not care about me. They only wanted to use me. We were told we were fighting for freedom, but I was not free. When I was lying in the hospital, close to death, unable to talk or see because of my wounds, I listened to the words the missionary said at my bedside. His words freed my heart, made me cry, and fill me with hope. These were his words." A list of Bible verses appeared on a projection screen as he read them:

"You are my child and I am your father.

I knew you even before you were conceived.

I determined the exact time of your birth and where you would live.

You were not a mistake, for all your days are written in my book.

I have been misrepresented by those who don't know me,

For I am the perfect father.

I offer you more than your earthy father ever could.

And it is my desire to lavish my love on you.

For you are my treasured possession.

Because I love you with an everlasting love.

I am your Father, and I love you even as I love my son, Jesus.

I am able to do more for you than you could possibly imagine.

If you seek me with all your heart, you will find me.

My question is…Will you be my child?

I am waiting for you."

Tears trailed Ani's cheeks one after another in a silent stream. The realization broke through. This is what she was missing.

The words on the screen pierced her heart. Could the love of this heavenly Father—the one who claimed to know her before she was even conceived—surpass that of an earthly father?

She looked up at the stage and saw the small wooden cross—the symbol of death, faith, and new beginnings.

I'm done, God. I accept that Kye doesn't have a father. It's so hard. I've been trying to cope on my own and I've failed. I'm in a bigger mess than ever. No more men, no more partying. I'm done with expecting you to answer me the way I want. Please forgive me. Show me your way, whatever it is. Without your help I will fail my son.

Yes. She would take a chance on God and trust in His promise to love her.

CHAPTER 3

Not much had changed in Nate's old bedroom. The brown blanket still lay over his bed, high school football trophies took pride of place on the bookshelf, and college paraphernalia adorned the walls.

Outside the double windows, the sun shone out from beyond the sprawling Texan hills.

Being home again was bittersweet. It was over three years since he had been back to Running Brook Ranch.

Nate sank into the shabby sofa that sat against one wall of the room. It was the perfect length and width for his body. At just short of six foot, finding a couch that accommodated him was rare.

He stretched out and allowed the emotions he had been sucking back all day to surface. Being back at the ranch to attend his mother's funeral had been a huge shock. If only he had followed through on one of his many promises to visit her over the last three years. But work had kept him away. He only saw his mother when she made the trip to Dallas. Now he knew he'd let her down.

"Here you are. I've been looking all over for you."

Nate looked behind to see his Uncle Braden enter the room. The tall, aging man was never normally out of his standard uniform: jeans, Stetson, and boots. It was strange to see him dressed in a black morning suit, even if he did still wear the black cowboy hat atop his greying head.

"I needed a break." He sat up. "Aunt Lane was introducing me to too many people at once. It was doing my head in."

Braden laughed. "That's our Lanie, all business to keep from falling apart." He took off the hat and slipped the brim between his hands in unconscious motion. "Well, you'll be happy to know the wake's finished in your absence. I've been sent to find you for the reading of the will."

Nate let his head fall back against the soft cushion. He closed his eyes and sighed. *Another event to get through.* His knew his mother had requested her will be read, but he hadn't given it a second thought during the day.

Braden placed a hand on his shoulder. "It'll all be over soon enough, son."

Nate shook his head. "It should never have happened."

Braden gave a heavy sigh. "I know. I told her that stallion had a mean streak. If only I had insisted she go see a specialist after that fall. But she didn't look badly hurt. The knock on her head was nothing more than a bit of a bump."

Nate had already gone through all the "what if's" of the situation. It was hard to understand how one tiny bump had resulted in an aneurism that had taken his mother's life.

Nate gave his uncle's hand a pat. "You have no fault in this. Don't take it on yourself."

Braden moved to take the seat next to him on the couch. He sat his hat on the end of his knee. "It was as though the Lord decided He wanted her home."

His uncle repeated the statement he had made earlier in the day as part of his eulogy for his younger sister.

The statement confused Nate as much now as it had then. "What exactly do you mean by that? What God would want to see a woman of fifty-two die? Why now, when she finally found some joy in life?" Nate stopped to huff. "She had to live though marriage to my father, with all his mistresses. Then the divorce. I may have only been seventeen, but I was old enough to see what it did to her. In the last few years she seemed to be happy. She loved the challenge of the breeding program and the charity work. It's like she was cut down." He glanced at his uncle. "What God would do that?"

Braden rubbed his hands on his thighs. "Son, I'm not the one to be explaining the purpose of the Almighty. I can only be thankful your momma knew Him, and I know she's with Him now."

Nate didn't know how to answer his uncle. His mother had been raised in a God-fearing home, but had only discovered faith for herself following her split from Nate's father. She had told him often enough in the past few years that her faith had turned her life around.

There were times he envied the joy she possessed. Nate wasn't quite sure where he fit in on the spectrum of spiritual belief. He was raised in church, but he didn't practice faith. And, like his father, he had certainly never denied himself the pleasures of the opposite sex. He was aware women found him attractive, and never had any trouble in that department. Although he didn't consider he had his father's wild ways, he didn't have his mother's quiet, unshakable faith either.

Braden must have sensed Nate's reluctance to continue the conversation because he sat up straighter in his seat. "I had a call from your Daddy today. He wanted to know if there was any way he could help. He told me he's doing much better."

Nate stared out the window opposite them. Three years ago, his father had been diagnosed with a rare, but not terminal, form of leukemia. Against his mother's wishes, Nate had agreed to move to Dallas to oversee the running of his father's family law firm. His father had agreed to his terms—Nate would stay only until his father's health improved sufficiently for him to take over again.

"I suspect he's doing much better than he's making out. He's back in his office, and has a new woman on his arm each week. But he keeps avoiding my questions about the state of his health." Nate shook his head at his father's evasion. "Momma said he would find a way to manipulate me into staying on at the firm."

Braden gave a low chuckle. "He certainly is good at working things out his way, that's for sure. I remember when you were deciding what to do at college. He was dead set on you following him into law."

Nate couldn't help the grimace. "Yeah, and look at what a waste that turned out to be. I hate it. Every second I spend in that place I can feel a little more life being sucked out of me."

Braden swung around to him. "Well, why don't you leave and go back to writing? You loved it."

The few writing classes Nate had taken at college

had spurred his love for the written word. When he had finished college he had had some success with his writing career, gaining exposure in a few magazines as a freelance journalist. Back before his father had called him for help.

"Maybe I will go back to writing."

He added this thought to the list of things troubling him. Lately he felt as though his life was travelling a path that had been planned for him, and he had no control over it.

Braden pulled out of the couch and moved across the room to survey the array of football trophies. He picked one up. "Wasn't this the game where you got that break in your nose?"

"One of the games." Nate smiled and touched the awkward bend of his nose. His father had often told him it was ugly, and he needed to get it fixed, but his mother had always counteracted by proclaiming that it gave his face character. The broken nose was one of his prominent features. The other main feature, a dimple sitting directly in the middle of his chin, was an inheritance from his father.

His cell phone rang out and Nate moved to retrieve it from his pocket.

Braden replaced the trophy and slapped his Stetson back on his head. "I'll let you get that. See you downstairs?"

Nate nodded then glanced at the caller ID. Caroline.

He contemplated letting the call go to voice mail but she had already left over ten messages, so he decided he had better take it – she would continue to call him if he didn't.

"Hello?" He made no attempt to disguise his annoyance.

"Is that any way to greet your girlfriend? I've been trying to contact you for days." Caroline's shrill voice rang out through the receiver. "Did you lose your phone or have you been deliberately avoiding me?"

Nate smirked at her last assumption. Had he been avoiding her? Certainly he had fallen into a causal relationship with Caroline, an associate at the firm. It had proven to be a very poor pairing. Perhaps this was the opportunity he needed to break up with her — something he had decided to do weeks ago. He didn't get the chance before his mother's death had brought him back home.

Before he could answer a beeping noise echoed through the connection.

"I'm going to have to put you on hold. I've got another call. It's Jack." Caroline hit the hold button before he could tell her not to bother keeping him on the line.

Nate hit disconnect and turned off his phone before she had the chance to call back, and wondered why his father was calling such a junior colleague. Never mind. What he had to say to her would have to wait until he returned to Dallas.

Time to get this over with. He reluctantly got to his feet and moved to the mirror to straighten his tie before going downstairs for the reading of the will.

Nate moved to leave, turning to scan the room one last time. A photo frame on a shelf caught his eye, and he went back to pick it up. It was a picture of him as a young boy sitting proudly on his mare, Ginny. His mother was holding the reins and smiling her bright, beautiful smile. He could see they shared many of the same features—light brown hair that streaked when he spent time in the sun, high cheekbones fitting the same sharp contours as hers, and green eyes that flashed with the same brown flecks. He caressed her face with his finger before tucking the photo under his arm and leaving the room.

"I, Rosalind Eve Ewing, being of sound mind and body, do hereby proclaim this, my last will and testament." The elderly family attorney read the proclamation in low tones.

Nate ignored protocol and slouched in the leather armchair.

People were in tears all around him. Aunty Lane had cast aside all pretense of courage and sobbed into her husband's shoulder. Uncle Connor held her close as they sat together on the three-seater sofa. Their daughter, Tammy, sat on the other side of her mother.

Nate's other cousin, Daniel, took a chair beside his father. His tailored attire suited his position as caretaker of the family's mining concerns. At thirty, Daniel was only one year older than Nate, but the differences in their natures had dictated they would never be close.

Braden was the only other person present. His wife, Aunt Rayne, had died four years ago after a courageous battle with cancer. They had never had children, although Braden had always claimed Nate as his surrogate son.

It was an accurate assessment as far as Nate was concerned. His father had been absent for most of his childhood and Uncle Brae had stepped into the role of parent. He was the one to teach Nate to ride a horse and a motorbike, to fish, and to shoot. The time they had spent sailing on the family yacht had contributed to Nate's education. It had inspired a love of the ocean he shared with his Uncle.

"To my ex-husband, Nathanial Jackson-Hollingsworth the Fourth …"

The mention of his father's name made Nate sit up and pay attention. *What on earth did my mother leave him?*

"I leave the Alberto Missoni vase we received as a wedding gift."

Nate couldn't stop a chuckle from escaping. The mourners all stopped their blubbering to look at him. He was met with a variety of expressions from confusion to disapproval. The attorney peered from above his spectacles.

Nate shook his head and chuckled again, more to himself than to those around him. He signaled for the attorney to continue, deciding to keep the reason for his outburst to himself. It wasn't the right time to explain that the vase was the only thing his parents had fought over in their divorce. It was the most disgusting object he had ever laid eyes on.

His cantankerous grandmother had insisted her wedding gift be returned to her son. Rosalind had succeeded in keeping the ugly ornament and rejoiced at seeing his grandmother get her comeuppance.

The attorney took some time to regain his place. "To my niece, Tammy Walters, I leave my engagement ring and diamond bracelet."

Tammy let out a small sob.

Nate was happy for Tammy. Even though his mother didn't have an exceptionally close relationship with his cousin, Tammy had a sweet nature and they were all fond of her.

The attorney waited for quiet before continuing. "The remainder of my estate, including all business interests, property, cash on hand, and personal effects I leave to my son, Nathanial Braden Jackson-Hollingsworth the Fifth. With the following proviso …" the elderly man glanced up for a second, adding to the suspense of his words. "… that he spend one full year, a full twelve months following my death, living and travelling on the Savannah."

A wave of confusion set in. Why would his mother dictate he spend a year on the family's motor yacht? She was aware of his love for the vessel, but why be so specific?

He looked over at Braden, who slanted his eyebrows and shrugged his shoulders.

The gravelly noise of the attorney clearing his throat drew their attention.

"That's not all." He looked back down at the page. 'Should Nathanial refuse to follow my wishes, my entire interest in the breeding program on Running Brook Ranch, including all stock and charity programs will be transferred in its entirety to my nephew, Daniel Alexander Walters."

A murmur of unrest echoed around the room.

"What did she do that for?"

"I don't understand."

"What was it, exactly?"

Nate remained silent before locking eyes with Braden. His uncle's mouth tipped at the ends, the slow ascent finally ending with an enormous grin.

What is he thinking? Nate squinted at him in an attempt to read his expression.

Braden took off his hat and slapped his leg. "Well, I'll be." His laughter echoed off the walls of the study.

Nate declined his father's offer of a drink and continued flicking through his mother's will.

"If you fought it, you'd win. Eventually." Jack Hollingsworth sat forward to pour himself another Scotch. "The problem is you'd be stuck in a mass of legalities for months." He took a long drink. "Your mother was one smart lady, Nate. I'll give her that."

Jack stopped to pick up the Alberto Missoni vase sitting on the coffee table next to the carafe of Scotch. He chuckled and shook his head. "I can't believe I'm stuck with this horrible thing. She knew how much I hated it." He set it back down. "If I was smart, I'd break it. But I might keep it to remind me of her."

He gazed out the window of the penthouse. The Dallas city skyline threw bold shadows of grey through the sunlight. Nate noticed the depth of the breaths his father was taking, and the faraway look in his eyes.

"She certainly was one of a kind, that mother of yours. I never knew what I had until it was gone." His father glanced back at him. "If there's one piece of advice I could give you, it's don't take the love of a good woman for granted. There's no pleasure in the world that can replace devotion." He looked into his Scotch, swirling the ice cubes in the glass. "Trust me, I know."

Nate studied his father's face. His chiseled features were hard, but the emotion in his words softened his usually rigid countenance.

When his father had appealed to him for help after his diagnosis, Nate knew he had to step up, as his father never asked anyone for anything. It was as much a compliment as it was a duty. "Family responsibility," his father had said. But his father's emotional plea for help was what had eventually swayed his decision to move to Dallas.

This time, Jack Hollingsworth's show of emotion made Nate uncomfortable. His father was one of the best lawyers in the state but he had one flaw, and it cut too close to home. He may have loved his ex-wife in his own way, but he was unable to reciprocate the devotion and fidelity she had given him.

A bubble of anger surfaced. There needed to be a change of subject. He shifted his weight in the uncomfortable designer chair and contemplated his next question. This may be the opportunity he had been waiting for, a chance to discover the true state of his father's health. "So what's your advice concerning the conditions of the will? Should I take the trip?"

Jack leaned back in his chair. "I don't see any way around it other than for you to take the time off and go."

"What about your health? A few weeks ago you

told me you still couldn't do without me. I won't leave unless I know your health has improved." Nate observed his father's body language.

Jack gave nothing away. "I can't see you lose out to that sniveling cretin of a cousin, Nate. Daniel will not get his hands on anything of your mother's. She did this to force my hand. She knew I'd send you off before I let that happen."

His father's ability to avoid a direct question was an undeniable gift. It was one of the traits contributing to his great success.

Nate eyed his father carefully before trying a more direct approach. "What did the specialist say at your last appointment?"

"Don't think for a second that Daniel will relinquish his claim to the breeding program to keep peace in the family. It's a profitable business and he knows there's money to be made."

Jack didn't need to point out Daniel's materialistic nature. Nate knew a diversionary tactic when he saw one.

This could go on forever.

His father looked into his glass and swilled the ice cubes further, pretending to be distracted by his own thoughts. Nate knew better. Jack Hollingsworth never missed a thing. He finally looked up to meet his gaze.

Jack lifted the glass and pointed a finger at him. "And you can forget about the charity program your mother set up. The riding for autistic children and the camping for those disabled kids. Daniel will dump the lot. All the work she loved will be scrapped."

After the reading of the will, Daniel had assured

Nate that he was not interested in taking over the breeding program. But he had shown some concerns over the costs of the charity portion of his mother's work. From the conversation, Nate was certain Daniel's business nature would override his sense of community service. Jack was right. If Daniel had the chance, he would drop the charity work.

Nate looked down at his lap and allowed a small smile to form. Clearly his father was coaxing him into making the decision to leave on his own. It was a clever way of avoiding any wrongdoing. Nate knew his father had manipulated him to stay on in the firm. Getting him to admit this was nigh on impossible.

Well, two can play at manipulation.

"I've made up my mind. Momma had concerns about me coming to Dallas to help you, but I came anyway, because you needed me. You've told me you still need me and I'll not let you down." He looked his father squarely in the eyes. "I'll put aside her last wish so I can be by your side." He got to his feet. "I gave you my word that I would be here for you until your health improved and I will keep my promise. The children Momma helped will have to find another venue for their therapy." Nate turned to walk out of the room. His hand reached the door knob when his father stopped him.

"Oh, come on back. I know when I've been beaten." Nate turned to see his father shaking his head.

He walked back and stood in front of him. *Thank goodness.* His bluff had paid off.

"The specialist has given me the all clear. I'm in full remission and he's happy for me to take on the workload at the firm."

Nate wasn't happy with that. "When exactly did you get this news?"

"That's not important. What it means is that you're free to take the trip your mother wanted you to. Your obligation to me has been fulfilled." Jack placed his glass onto the coffee table and stood to face him. They were the exact same height.

"Your last specialist visit was months ago. You've had this information all this time, haven't you?" Nate may not have had his father's killer instinct, but he did have his mother's ability to read people. "You do realize I could have spent the last six months at the ranch? That's time I can't get back."

His father frowned. "Oh, come on, Nate. If I had known your mother was going to die, I would have sent you back to her in a second. You're not being fair to me, throwing that in my face."

Nate shook his head in disbelief. "Not fair! You just admitted you cheated me out of six months and you're claiming I'm being unfair?" He could feel the bitterness of betrayal bite at him.

Jack looked furious for a second before turning away. "You have to understand my position. I wasn't there for you when you were growing up."

Nate snorted. His father gave him a steely look. "Hear me out. Then you can judge me."

There was honesty in his request. Nate softened enough to give him his attention.

"For generations, the firstborn Hollingsworth son has followed in his father's footsteps. I don't want this tradition to stop with me. When I was diagnosed, I realized everything my grandfather, my father and I'd worked for was going to end when I died. And it was all my doing. I was too busy to get to know my only child. These last few years with you here has given me a new lease of life. I can see there's hope for the firm, and I've enjoyed getting to know you. I haven't wanted it to end."

Nate could see that for once, his father was genuine. The barriers were down for a brief second and Jack was being honest. Nate couldn't help but be drawn to his honesty.

"I understand. But we had a deal. I told you from the start that following in your footsteps wasn't going to happen in the long term."

His father scoffed. "So what are you going to do? Be a two-bit writer when you have a multi-million dollar legacy at your disposal?"

Nate shook his head. "I don't know what I'm going to do, but you forget that, apart from your legacy, I also have my mother's. It's a multi-million dollar concern as well, but she never pressured me to follow in her footsteps and breed horses. She was willing to see her dream die in order for me to find mine."

His father ran one hand through his hair. He looked past Nate to the window for some time before turning back. "Well, I can't blame you for wanting that. And I can't blame her for wanting it for you." The resignation in his voice made Nate smile. "And as much as I want you to take over the firm, I can't help but be proud of you for wanting to forge your own way. It takes great courage." He placed one hand on Nate's shoulder. "Go and find your own way. You have my blessing. I hope you can forgive me for keeping you past your time. Don't ever think I don't appreciate it."

Nate grabbed his father's arm and pulled him into an embrace, slapping him several times on his back, before letting him go.

The older man sat back down. "So when do you leave on this boating trip?"

"Good question. I'll have to get the yacht ready first." It was a discussion he needed to have with his uncle.

"I remember the last time I took your mother on the Savannah. It was just after her divorce." Braden stretched his legs and scanned the horizon from their position on the porch of the main house. The last of the sun's rays peaked from around the distant green plains. It had been a picturesque Texan sunset.

"Your Momma was living in a huge black hole. I told her she needed a change of scenery to snap her out of it, so Rayne and I packed her up and we set sail to regions unknown." Braden grinned. "We felt like a group of kids running away to the circus. Don't you remember the three months we spent away?"

Nate searched his memory. "I do recall a dozen or so postcards I received from her in my first year of college. The Caribbean, I think?"

Braden let out a booming laugh. "I remember that first day, when we were deciding where to head to. Your mother told us to take her somewhere hot, so the Caribbean it was." He paused to shake his head. "It was some trip. We had a ball." A downcast shadow appeared on his face. "We hadn't been back long before Rayne was diagnosed. The divorce of your parents was horrible, but I don't know if Rayne and I would have had that time together if your mother hadn't been going through a bad time. Her trouble became a happy memory for us all. The good Lord used that time to give your Momma His peace, and He gave Rayne and me a darn tooting holiday together. Calm before a storm. It's amazing how He works."

"And how exactly does He work?" Nate couldn't get his head around all the talk of God and His plan. "I mean, how does God allow something bad to happen to us, and then turn it into something good? If it's bad, doesn't it remain so? It makes no sense."

Braden rubbed the stubble on his chin for a long time before answering. "Well, Nate, my boy, I suspect it has everything to do with love. God claims to love us, and He's not about claiming anything He doesn't mean. Life's always going to have its ups and downs. God doesn't dispute that. He doesn't stop us from experiencing the bad things any more than He stops us from experiencing the good things. What He does promise is that He'll love us through all of it, if we'll let Him. Your Momma told me she realized this during her time on the Savannah."

Nate was surprised. His mother had never confided in him. But as he pondered what his uncle had said, he understood the changes in his mother the first time he returned home from college. She was happier than she had been in years, exuding calm and a sense of peace that he was relieved she had found.

"I wonder why she never talked much about her

time on the Savannah when it had made such an impact on her?"

"I couldn't rightly say. Maybe it was too precious to her. Maybe prompting you to go and have your own experience on the ocean is her way of telling you all about it."

Nate smiled at the thought of his mother's subtle manipulation. "Well, I hope God can give me some direction, like He did for her."

Braden reached over in his crudely-made wooden chair to pat him on the shoulder. "As a little blonde Aussie friend once told me, ask and you shall receive, my boy."

Nate shook his head at his uncle's vague comment before the purpose of his visit came back to him. "By the way, where is the Savannah docked at the moment?"

"Sydney, my boy."

CHAPTER 4

"Sydney? You mean as in Sydney, Australia?"

"That's right." Nate stopped short to acknowledge a sense of déjà vu in the conversation. He'd said the exact same thing to his uncle after finding out where the Savannah was docked. When he looked up from his packing, he saw Caroline hadn't moved. She stood in the doorway, mouth hanging open, and eyebrows high. Nate raised one corner of his mouth at the sight before she recovered from the shock.

"Are you seriously telling me," she said, 'you are leaving today, for Australia, to sail up the coast of said country in a sailing boat, for a total of twelve months non-stop?"

Nate shook his head at the summary. If someone had told him he would be doing this a month ago, he would have thought them crazy. As it was, he was in the process of packing essentials for the trip he had lovingly termed his 'saving grace'.

"Yep," he said.

Nate noticed her arms had moved from hanging limp by her side to balance firmly on each hip. Her two hands were splayed, the fingers of each hand almost touching, such was the tiny span of her waist.

"So, tell me," Caroline's voice changed from a high-pitched flutter to direct interrogation. "When were you going to tell me about this? Was it before or after you had gone? Because I would have thought

I was someone you had a vested interest in filling in."

Nate rolled his eyes as he stuffed another t-shirt into the duffle bag. He predicted this scene would be unpleasant.

Caroline had clearly targeted him for husband material. The fact that he was disinterested in entering into a matrimonial state hadn't stopped her from playing the fiancée-in-waiting.

He abandoned the packing to address her pouting face. Caroline was an attractive woman. Her blonde hair and perfectly-sized fake breasts had once been a magnet for his sex drive. But Nate had soon discovered that no amount of pretty on the outside could make up for the ugly on the inside.

Caroline had proven to be a racist, bigoted, manipulative social climber. Nate had heard several rumors she had a spare in the wings should all fall foul with him, and he was certain those rumors held more than an element of truth.

"Caroline, if we were both honest with each other, we would admit that we were over long ago. You've hung on because you enjoy the social position I give you, and I've hung on for the sake of convenience." His words came out sounding harsher than he planned.

She reared up like a cornered snake. "That's a fine thing to say to someone you've had a two-year relationship with."

"It's been eighteen months, actually, and during the first four we weren't even exclusive."

"I should have known you were a dead loss when you wouldn't even clear a drawer in your bathroom for me. I can't believe I allowed myself to become so invested."

"Oh, come on, Caroline, you've done very well out of this relationship. Thanks to me, you've got a good job, you drive a nice car, and you've climbed a few rungs on the social ladder."

The perfect 'O' formed by her perfect lips gave away her exasperation. She closed her mouth before pulling away from his gaze. Her jaw softened and a pained expression flickered through the indignant purse of her lips.

Nate recognized the imminent change in her demeanor before she had committed to it. Whenever things weren't going Caroline's way, she played what he secretly called the 'damsel in distress' card. Her eyes became doe-like, and after a long wetting of her lips, the corners were dragged downwards into a mournful crescent.

Her hands left her hips. One arm grasped the doorway of his bedroom, while the other was placed strategically across her breast, fingers probing her collarbone. The whole act was designed to draw attention to her surgically enhanced attributes, while expressing an unmitigated need to be pandered to. Caroline had missed her calling–she should have been an actress.

"I can't believe you would leave me like this. Not after all we've been through." Her expression was a perfect faux-pout.

Nate noticed her voice taking on a southern huskiness when she played this part. If the situation wasn't so serious, he would burst out laughing.

"And what exactly is this 'all' that you claim we've been through?"

"You know full well." She stopped to ponder the 'all'. "Your father's illness, for one."

Nate shook his head. "You joined the firm two years ago. My father had already undergone treatment. Find another one."

She broke character for a second to frown at him and puff up her chest before launching back into the character. "Your mother's death?"

"Yeah, great support. You didn't even come to the funeral. Does 'not good at dealing with grief', ring a bell?"

Caroline's excuses not to attend the funeral had prompted him to wait until he returned to break up with her. Now he wished he had made the break when his instincts told him to.

Her arm dropped from her chest and snapped back to her hip. The damsel was fading. "Nate Hollingsworth, I have invested a good deal of time on this relationship and I'm not about to let you walk away from me. My parents—everyone, in fact—expect us to get engaged. Are you telling me you are going to leave me waiting for you for over twelve months while you gallivant around some godforsaken place in a boat?" She waved her hands as she spoke. "That country is nothing short of barbaric. The people eat worms, Nate. Worms!"

Her voice raised several octaves as she recalled the documentary they had seen about the Indigenous people of Australia, and the bush food that formed part of their diet.

Nate rubbed a hand along his forehead and rolled his eyes. "How did you ever pass the bar?"

How did someone so stupid get accepted into college?

And law school? What did I ever see in you? One look at her cleavage gave him his answer. *Nate, you are a fool of the highest order. A fool in a mess with another fool.* He shook his head at his own indulgence and a vision of his father's womanizing ways flashed before his eyes. *What was that?* He didn't have a chance to explore the picture further because Caroline had sidled up to him, placing her hands around his waist and thrusting her hips into his.

"Tell me you don't love me." She looked up at him with a far more sensual than loving expression. The gentle gyrating of her hips distracted him for a second before he came to his senses and pushed her away.

He took a moment to focus on her green eyes. "I don't love you, and you don't love me. You love the thought of me, the prestige I can give you, the money you will have, and the life you have planned for yourself. I'm sorry, but you know as well as I do that this relationship was purely circumstantial and convenient for both of us. And it ran its course long ago."

She huffed in a rage and stomped back to the doorway as quickly as her high heeled shoes would allow her. Turning back, a large rush of air snorted through her nostrils.

"Fine, have it your way. You'll be sorry. I'll make you sorry. You can't dump me. I'm dumping you first." She made a sharp turn and disappeared down the hallway of his condo. The slamming front door signified her undignified exit.

Nate took a moment to collect himself. "Well, that went well," he told his refection in the ornate mirror opposite his bed.

It was a huge relief to see her gone, but he did wonder at the part he played in the relationship. He had certainly had his needs met. Caroline was an expert lover. This alone had kept him in the relationship. Now, with the acknowledgment of this fact, he realized every one of his past relationships had followed the same pattern–a beautiful girl giving him what he wanted, finally expecting more from him than he was prepared to give, and it ending badly. His love life was a long line of classic use and be used.

Nate stared at his reflection. "Is that how you want to live your life?" The face staring back at him screamed the answer.

No.

That was how his father lived his life. The one trait he hated most about his father was the trait he was repeating. He flopped back on the bed in defeat.

Was this something his mother had seen? Was it one of the reasons she insisted he be alone? Nate knew what he had to do.

No more women. No relationships. No more repeated patterns. Just me, the Savannah, and the Pacific Ocean for twelve months. The resolution was firm.

He zipped up the duffle bag and threw it over his shoulder. *Next stop, Down Under.*

The Savannah was finally ready to sail. The month Nate and Braden had spent preparing the yacht for sea had paid off. The hull was clean, repairs had been undertaken, and a new set of sails blew wildly in the Sydney Harbor wind.

Braden had brought the Savannah over from Galveston to Sydney five years ago with the notion of sailing around the famous harbor. Unfortunately the plan wasn't fulfilled, and Braden had purchased a new yacht in Cairns. His sailing appetite was fully satisfied exploring the tropical coast of Australia. Now the Savannah would have her opportunity.

The boat had been docked for years at a marina close to the harborside house Braden owned. It had undergone all preparations at the marina. Then, yesterday they had sailed her around to the floating pontoon adjacent to the house.

"She's a beauty, all right. A real lady." Braden surveyed the hull, running his hand over the snow white steel with pride. "My Daddy knew his sail boats."

Nate stepped back to appraise the vessel. He had grown up on the Savannah. There was a variety of family photos taken of him aboard the vessel as far back as infancy–sitting on the bow, eating in the galley, and fishing off the duckboard.

His grandfather had taken him sailing at every opportunity. He had died when Nate was seven. Braden had then continued with adventures aboard the Savannah with him.

Braden boarded the boat from the pontoon, calling back as he entered the galley, "You coming, Nate, my boy?"

Nate surveyed the boat's length, admiring the way the vessel moved in perfect harmony with the lapping waves. Was it any wonder his mother had a life-changing moment aboard the boat? There was something magical about the Savannah, something that didn't exist with other boats of her kind. Perhaps it was because she was a tried and tested old lady of the sea, or maybe it was due to her colorful past, rescued and lovingly restored by his grandfather. Or perhaps it was because she was their family boat, and they all loved her. Whatever magic it possessed, Nate sensed the Savannah pulling him in for an adventure, just like she had when he was a boy.

Braden stuck his head back out the doorway. "Nate, you've got to come and see these electronics. This new gear is something else."

Nate succumbed to his uncle's enthusiasm and boarded the yacht. He spent the following hours going over the boat with Braden. The new additions in software and electronic devices were designed to make solo sailing as trouble free as possible. In spite of the updated safety equipment, Nate could tell his uncle held some reservations at allowing him to undertake the journey alone.

"Now, are you sure you can handle this girl?" Braden made his way to the back of the boat.

"Uncle Brae, you said yourself that I've been sailing since before I could walk. Don't worry about me."

Braden took off his Stetson and wiped the sweat from his brow. "If you say so. It's still not too late to hire a deckhand, you know?"

"But then I'd have to share my space with him." The last thing Nate wanted was to be stuck on a boat with a stranger. This was his trip, the trip his mother wanted him to take alone.

"Fair enough." His uncle stepped off the boat

and back onto the pontoon. "Now, promise you'll spend some time with my friends up north."

Braden had relayed, several times, the story of how he had met his Aussie friends. Years ago, when he was sailing the tropical waters of North Queensland, he was saved from drowning by Dutch, the owner of Resolution Island. As payment for saving his life, Braden set about finding Dutch's missing daughter, Bay. He eventually found Bay in Cairns. Bay met her husband, Flynn, on Resolution Island, and worked with him and her father to rebuild Resolution Island Resort and transform it into a spectacular ecotourist destination.

Nate smiled in memory of the tale. "I promise to visit them."

His uncle nodded. "Well, I suppose you best be off."

Nate turned to take the helm while his uncle cast the ropes. He turned back to bid his uncle farewell as the boat pulled away from the pontoon.

"Godspeed, Nate my boy," Braden yelled, removing his hat and waving it in salute.

Nate resumed the task of steering the yacht through the harbor traffic. The shadow of the Sydney Harbor Bridge darkened the deck as he passed under it. The ferries honked their horns signifying their direction, and the sails of the Opera House flashed white against a clear blue sky.

The salt spray on his face produced an overwhelming happiness and a heightened feeling of anticipation. For the first time in years, Nate felt truly alive and free.

CHAPTER 5

The New Year's Eve party was in full swing by the time Anika arrived. She took a seat as far away as possible from the throng. This was the first time in ten years that all of Aunty's family had come together. Every member of the family from Thursday Island to Victoria had descended on her uncle's house in Cairns. She estimated there would be at least seventy people filling the back yard for the reunion.

Anika caught a flash of her son as he ran by and smiled. He had deserted her the second they arrived, and was now playing with the other children. A growth spurt had coincided with his birthday a few weeks ago. It meant his seven-year-old legs were now longer and thinner, helping him keep pace with his older friends. He was in the second grade at school. His teacher had recently described him as a bright, energetic and happy child.

She looked across the room and waved to Amos through the crowd of unknowns. His eyes met hers, and he threw her a brilliant smile.

He ambled over to her. She stood to greet him, returning his affectionate hug and kiss.

"How you been, Ani?" He took the vacant seat next to her.

"I've been good, Uncle. How's island life?"

Amos lived on Resolution Island. It was one of the largest in a group of seven islands sitting directly off the coast of Kiisay Point, approximately nine hundred kilometers south of Cairns. Amos visited them often. His interest in her welfare hadn't ceased from the moment he plucked her from the cupboard at the age of ten. The nightmare that had plagued her childhood had mysteriously ceased when Amos had rescued her. However, in its place, she had developed frightening dreams of isolation and failure.

When Amos visited, her anxiety seemed to decrease. She had often wished he would move to Cairns permanently, but, despite having family in the area, he preferred to stay close to his Kiisay birthplace along with several other family members including his cousin, Neville.

"The resort's busy now. Lots to do." Amos nodded.

The last time he had visited he had detailed all the changes to his island home. The old resort had been completely transformed. The weathered fibro huts had been removed and it was now a thriving ecotourist resort with new one and two bedroom cabins. Each cabin was set off the ground on stilts in order to protect the natural environment. A combined reception and restaurant area was built in the style of a Balinese hut. A pool oasis, floating pontoons and moorings completed the first-class amenities.

It was hard for Anika to envisage the improvements to the island she had last visited over eight years ago. She couldn't wait for the chance to see Resolution for herself.

The owner of the island, a man known as Dutch,

along with his daughter Bay and son-in-law Flynn, had ensured Amos and Neville were well looked after during the rebuilding. Each man had a cabin around the corner from the main resort, replacing the makeshift shacks they had been living in.

"So you finished your course now, Ani?" Amos asked.

She nodded. The Marine Biology degree she had undertaken, mostly by correspondence, had been a challenge. She had finished study six months ago and had graduated at the top of her class.

"Yep. I'm still working on the reef boat, but they put my wage up a bit because I'm qualified now." She pulled her shoulders back with the sense of achievement.

It had been hard work juggling university studies with her job explaining sea life on one of the many boats taking tourists on day trips to the Great Barrier Reef. But now that she had graduated, the pay rise was a huge bonus for her hard work.

"So you plan to stay put for a bit?" Amos gave her a sidewards glance.

"I have to, Uncle. I don't earn enough for us to get our own place, as much as I would love to. Besides, I'm lucky that Aunty looks after Kye when I'm working."

It was hard work being a single mother, and she wouldn't sacrifice Kye's security to have her own space. She had spent most of her childhood fending for herself while her mother did her own thing. She didn't want that life for her son.

"I got an idea." Amos reached in his pocket and retrieved an envelope. He slowly unfolded a piece of paper.

"Dutch's wife, Yvette, is a marine biologist. She's set up a research station on Resolution to study dugong. The government's given her some money for it. She wants a helper, but can't afford much. I thought maybe you might be interested."

He handed her the piece of paper.

Anika looked over the detailed job description, turning it slightly to better catch the light. It was only part-time but it sounded terrific. She could feel her excitement building over the thought of using her training for more than educating tourists. Collecting data and samples, analysis, and research. The tasks were perfect, but the salary was a significant amount less than she was currently being paid. Ani sighed with disappointment, handing the paper back to Amos.

"I'd love the job, Uncle, but I couldn't even afford a cheap rental place on that wage, let alone childcare for when Kye's not at school."

Amos took the paper from her. "We've all talked about that too, and we got a plan."

Anika leaned in to hear him above the noise of the party.

"Neville's got a job with the National Parks." He stopped to nod towards his cousin who sat on the opposite side of the gathering. "He knows the area like the back of his hand, so I think he'll be good at it. If he can shut his trap long enough."

Ani smiled. Neville was well known for his penchant for gossip.

"His new job comes with a house in Kiisay Point, so he won't need his cabin. It's right next to mine, and it's got two bedrooms. Be perfect for you and Kye."

Anika listened with interest as he continued.

"It would come with the job, so no rent to pay, and Bay says the resort'll pay for all your meals too, so you won't have any living costs. You could save a lot of the wage."

A sense of excitement flared. This could be a great move for them—a way to start a life of their own. Living on the island would also mean no transportation costs to get to work like she had now. Dreams flashed into her mind. She could save her wages and finally get a stamp in her passport. Each dream destination popped into her head, one after another. *It could finally happen.* Then another thought occurred to her. *What about Kye's school? Who would look after him when I'm working?* All her plans came to an abrupt halt.

"I can't. Kye needs to go to school." The excitement flare fizzled.

"I thought of that, too. He could do his schoolwork by correspondence, and I can look after him when you're working. I could teach him some traditional ways. Time he learnt to spear fish and live in the bush. Kids these days have too much TV and computer games. Not enough life learning."

Anika couldn't agree more. The few years she had spent on the Islands were a bright point in an otherwise traumatic childhood. Learning the customs and practical traditions of her ancestors was as valuable to her as what she'd learned at school. She also was confident, considering the correspondence courses she had taken, that she could supervise Kye's schooling. She knew there would be times when this sort of arrangement would be hard, but she knew she up to the challenge. This was the out she had been waiting for. There was still one problem.

"Are you sure you want to have Kye that much?"

Amos gave a wide grin. "Oh, I'm sure we can find plenty for Kye to do. There's lots of work around the resort. Besides, we all spoke about it and everyone's happy about him coming. Bay and Flynn's already got jobs lined up for him. Be good to have a kid about, and plenty of other kids come to the resort for school holidays. He won't be lonely."

Anika considered what Amos had said. It wouldn't be any adjustment for Kye to have to live with others. He was already growing up in a large mixed family. It was also a great advantage for him to have male influences in his life. Ani had no doubt Amos would take him under his wing. With all her concerns addressed, the flare of excitement ignited again. She turned to Amos and gave him her best smile.

"When do I start?"

The wake from the tinny created small waves that lapped into shore in rapid succession. From her position on the patio, Anika could see her son's capped head as he bobbed along with the motion of the small boat. Uncle sat at the back holding the tiller of the outboard, and Cousin Neville was seated beside Kye in the front. They were doing a run to one of the small fringing reefs across from Resolution Island Resort.

Anika took her seat on Bay's patio and watched their progress across the span of water to Turtle Island. It was a beautiful day, and she would have gone with them if there had been any room in the tinny. As it was, the alternative social event—coffee with Bay—was a welcome substitute.

"Look at that blue sky! You wouldn't have thought we'd have seen it so clear today considering the rain we had last night." Bay waved her hand at the sky as she spoke.

Anika nodded her agreement as she looked sideways at Bay. Her hair had fallen out of its plait, leaving loose golden wisps blowing around her face. Bay was one of the most beautiful women Anika had ever seen. She had serious model looks that complemented her sweet nature.

Bay and Ani had clicked immediately upon her and Kye's arrival on Resolution, four months ago. Kye had been a little overwhelmed at first, being the only child with the attention of many adults. But he had soon discovered that the recreational aspects of island life were managed along with the work. Eventually, they had settled in and now it felt as though they had always been there.

"How's the research going?" Bay offered her a plate of biscuits.

Ani selected one before answering. "Slow. It's proving difficult to pinpoint the movement of the dugong. We've targeted some areas of their habitat, but we still don't have enough knowledge about them to conduct further study. Yvette's looking into funding for a monitoring device."

"I know how hard it can be. I've been trying to

get some decent photos of them for years."

Ani's anxiety rose at her friend's comment. The travel patterns of the large grey mammals had been difficult to track.

"We know a family of them feed close to Kilmore Island, but we need to pinpoint their exact location." Ani had seen dugong activity close to the most northern island in the group. The seagrass growing on the mud flats had geometrical feeding patterns, a clear sign of dugong activity. The grazing technique had long ago given them the nickname 'sea cow"'. It was also thought that the dugong was the creature responsible for mermaid legend. Their curious nature often led them to danger such as collisions with boats and being trapped in shark nets.

Bay took a sip of her coffee. "Keep looking. You'll find them."

She hoped Bay was right. Yvette's research required further knowledge about the numbers and movements of the animals. If Yvette was going to be successful in proving her theory — that boating activity and development in the area had negatively impacted the mammal's population — she needed to know more about their declining numbers. The gentle animal was in danger of extinction if their habitat wasn't protected. Yvette's goal was to have the non-fishing zones in the area, the green zones, moved to accommodate the dugong population.

Ani closed her eyes and listened to the soft thud of the waves as they collided with the sand. She couldn't think of a place she would rather be.

A happy whistle broke through her semi-slumber. There was no mistaking the red-streaked head of hair rounding the corner. She knew it was Flynn before he jumped the three stairs to cuddle and kiss his wife.

Bay squealed in protest, and then laughed as his wet hair dripped down onto her. "You're soaking me."

Flynn dropped his bottom lip. "Don't you want a kiss from your husband?"

"Not when you're wet." She giggled.

Flynn looked over at Ani. "You know, once upon a time she never complained when I was wet."

"Well, I do now." Bay grabbed a towel hanging over the patio railing and thrust it at Flynn.

Ani smiled at the exchange. She had never seen two people so in love. It amazed her that, despite being opposite in so many ways, they complemented each other and shared a sense of oneness. For a moment she despaired at her single status.

"Did you tell Ani our news?" Flynn looked at Bay, rubbing his hair as he spoke.

"Not yet."

Anika frowned. "What news?"

Bay looked sheepish. "We're going to have a baby."

Ani's mouth dropped before she jumped to her feet to hug them both. "That's awesome. How far along are you?" She retook her seat.

"About fourteen weeks." Bay patted her flat stomach.

"We waited until the danger period was over before we told anyone." Flynn had the sort of grin only an expectant father could display.

Bay looked up at her husband. "We could

probably tell Neville now." Flynn nodded and Bay turned back to her. "We kept it from Neville because if we hadn't, everyone would have known long ago."

Anika laughed. Neville couldn't keep a secret. "Well, I'm so excited for you. And it also explains the longest case of stomach flu I have ever seen."

Bay and Flynn laughed. Bay had been complaining about a stomach upset for weeks.

"I'd better clean up." Flynn excused himself and went inside.

Bay reached for another biscuit. "Kye's such a terrific boy, Ani. I'll be relying on you for some parenting tips."

Anika squirmed in her chair. She felt completely unqualified to give any advice on raising children.

Bay went to take a bite then stopped. "Ani, I hope I'm not overstepping the mark with what I'm about to say. You're a great mum, but what about you? I know some of the girls at the restaurant have asked you to join them in town for a night out. We're more than willing to look after Kye if you want a break from the Island."

Anika could see Bay's offer was genuine. "Thanks, but I decided years ago that Kye came first. No romantic entanglements for me. When I was with my mother, she had one man after another. I never had much of a childhood. Kye's not going to suffer that."

Bay bit her lip again. "That's not what I was suggesting. It's just that you're so young. Twenty-five is too soon to decide you're never going to get married. What about dating, or spending time with some friends your own age?"

Anika shook her head. "Not interested. I can't afford to slip up. I've got responsibilities. Besides, every man I've ever known has let me down. Every man except Uncle."

Bay opened her mouth as though she was going to say something further, then just as quickly closed it and gave a small nod. "Fair enough."

"Here you are. I've been looking all over for you." Dutch climbed the steps quicker than expected for a man over sixty. Ani had often marveled at the way Dutch seemed to have a part of every aspect of running the resort. The non-stop activity must help to keep him fit.

Bay smiled up at her father. "Where else would we be on a day like this?"

"Up here, mate." Dutch called out to someone over the rail of the veranda, then looked back at the women. "Some suit's here, looking for Ani."

Sure enough, a man in a tailored suit rounded the corner. He had a satchel in one hand and was wiping his brow with a handkerchief in the other.

"What would he want with me?" Ani said softly to Bay. Suits and ties were an oddity on the island. Even shoes were optional in parts of the resort.

Bay shrugged in reply.

As the man walked up the steps he reached into a satchel and pulled out a large envelope, then looked her up and down. "Anika Deumer?"

"That's me."

He thrust the envelope towards her. "Sign here please." He presented a delivery form and pen.

"What is it?" she asked, as she accepted both from him and scribbled where directed.

The man placed the signed documentation in the satchel before answering. "Legal papers."

"What type of legal papers?"

"Don't know. I just deliver them." He nodded to them before walking back towards the pontoon.

Ani frowned at Bay as she broke the seal on the envelope.

Her breathing labored as she read further and further down the page. Although her mind reeled from the legal jargon, the purpose of the document was clear.

A heavy fog of shock fell over her as a hand clasp her shoulder.

"Is everything okay?" Ani heard the question, but it was as though Dutch's voice was muffled by cotton wool. She looked up at him, then at Bay.

"I think Kye's grandfather is suing me for custody."

The splashing that had drawn her attention increased as Ani maneuvered the tinny through the mangroves. She had been through this section of the estuary so many times in the last four months that she knew every twist and turn by heart.

The mangroves on the sheltered side of the islands formed a spectacular honeycomb of waterways. The larger sections were open and relatively easy to negotiate, with boating beacons signifying the course. However, the section where dugongs were known to live was a less travelled path.

Anika knew the creatures were there. Amos and

Neville had both given her the advantage of their local knowledge about the dugong. Generations of their ancestors had caught them in the area. Dugong were vital to Island culture. In recent years those with local knowledge had worked closely with the government to foster the sustainability of the species. But fishing them was one thing. Tracking and monitoring their population was another.

"There it is again." Kye pointed in the direction of the spray.

"I see it." Anika ducked to avoid being hit by a mangrove branch as they navigated through a narrow section of creek.

"Is it a dugong, Kiki?" Kye sat up high on the front seat of the aluminum tinny. The canopy of mangrove trees moved in harmony with the breeze inches from his head.

"Sit back down. You're going to get hit by a branch."

With this new discovery, she regretted allowing Kye to come with her. Since she had been informed of Mitchell Mayfield's intention to seek custody, a court date had been set to determine his access to Kye. Ani had been assigned a legal aid solicitor. The process was taking forever, and it could be years before a final decision was reached.

The whole custody suit was like a heavy weight hanging over her. She had a permanent sickness in her stomach, a constant headache, and every night was passed with either sleeplessness or nightmares. Her dreams were full of distressing scenarios—nightmares of Kye being taken from her or having him disappear, followed by her frantically searching for him. The pictures were so vivid she was becoming reluctant to leave Kye.

That day she had been certain her dugong tracking would amount to nothing. With her failure to find the creatures in mind, she had brought Kye with her. Now, his enthusiastic proclamation earlier that 'today was the day' looked to be a good prophesy.

They went through the last narrow waterway and entered a wider section of the estuary. Ani looked up to see an illegal fishing net secured to either side of the bank. Only professional fishermen with a specific license could set nets, and there were strict conditions to the license. The holder had to remain with the net at all times, and they could only fish in certain parts of the estuary, at the risk of losing their license. Ani and Kye were deep in a green zone, meaning no fishing of any kind was allowed.

"What is it?" Kye leaned over the side of the boat, his mass of sandy blonde curls falling over his face.

"It's a net. Something's caught in it." She looked around for the owner of the net as she maneuvered the boat closer. A grey tail broke the surface of the water and flapped in panic.

"It's a dugong. It's trapped." She leant over the side of the boat and pulled the float on top, trying to ascertain how far down the creature was tangled.

"We have to save it." Kye threw himself over to the same side of the boat as Ani. The weight of both their bodies caused the edge of the tinny to lean dangerously close to the water's edge.

"Kye, you're going to tip us out. Stay on the seat." She directed him to his place at the front of the boat.

He scurried back. "What are you going to do?"

Anika weighed up her options. It was difficult to tell how long the dugong had been there, but she knew the creature couldn't stay under the water for too long before needing to breathe. If she waited for help, it could drown. She leant back and opened the tackle box, retrieving a knife.

"Don't move."

Kye nodded in agreement.

She began the slow process of cutting through the thick net. The twine was messy and tangled. A mass of leaves and debris lay thick in the twisted knots. She soon realized the only way to free the animal was to jump into the water and work her way around its body.

After securing the anchor and giving Kye instructions to stay put, she jumped in.

It seemed to take forever. The tide had turned and Ani could feel the force of the water on her chest as it ran through the net.

She held onto a float at the surface for a moment to rest, noticing the floats had distinctive red crosses on each side.

Ani took a few deep breaths. Fighting the tide, as well as the effort it took to cut, was beginning to take a toll on her stamina.

She estimated, from the size of the animal, that it was an adolescent, and the constant thrashing suggested it hadn't been trapped for long. That, at least, was a welcome relief.

"Are you okay, Kiki?" Kye called from the boat.

Even though he was only a few meters away, Ani

hated being separated from him. She took some comfort in the fact he was well trained in handling a tinny.

She gave Kye the thumbs-up. "Not long to go." Most of the net was now loose, and she could see the remainder of the problem was underneath the creature.

"Kye, I'm going to have to dive down to cut the rest. Stay where you are and don't move," she called, her voice competing with the lapping of the water and the whistling wind. The slight breeze that had been present all day had increased dramatically at the change of tide.

"Okay," he called back. She could see him frowning.

Ani took a deep breath and pulled on the net as she sank under the muddy brown water. At first she could only make out bits of brown debris as it swirled before her eyes, but then the distinct figure of the dugong became clearer.

She was right. The net was a mess underneath as well as on top. One big eye stared at her as she made her way down the body of the creature. It amazed her that the animal didn't move an inch as she cut the net from underneath. It was as though it knew she was there to help. She made one final strategic cut before she pushed herself to the surface for a breath.

"Kiki. Kiki!" Kye's frantic call drew her attention as she rubbed her eyes to clear them. She looked back at him.

He was standing up in the tinny, his bright yellow life vest thrashing around as he waved his arms and jumped up and down.

"Get out. Get out," he yelled. "You got to get out. Now!" He pointed to the side of the bank.

An enormous crocodile had appeared. Ani felt her eyes grow wide and her stomach do flip-flops at the sight. It was a fair distance away from them, but its body was high off the ground, and it was plodding its massive bulk in the direction of the water's edge.

She glanced back at the dugong, knowing they were both in serious danger. There was no time to think it through. Ani frantically slashed at the net.

"Kiki!" Kye's hysteric call broke her action and she let go of the knife. She threw herself back towards the tinny and pushed with all her might through the water.

A heavy force pushed behind her as she reached the side. She lifted her arm up to the edge and swung herself over. The superhuman strength she possessed could only have come from being chased by something very big.

Kye jumped on her as she lay in the bottom of the boat. His cheek rested on hers for a second before he got back up.

"You got in the boat right as that croc's tail went under the water." He looked down and smiled.

Ani sat up and tried to control her breathing. She smoothed her wet hair back from her face, relieved the crocodile had been in no hurry to get into the water. It would be heartbreaking to witness the predator devouring the creature she had worked so hard to save.

But the water was calm apart from a ripple running over the remainder of the net. Ani had fully expected to see the thrashing of the massive crocodile as it claimed its dinner.

"Where's the dugong?"

"You did it, Kiki. It got away." Kye's eyes were as wide as his smile.

"It did?" She couldn't believe it.

"Yep." Kye nodded. "It swam past you so fast. I saw its tail flap as it went through there." He pointed to a fork in the mangroves a good five meters away from them. "He was saying thank you."

Ani allowed herself to smile as relief flooded through her. Her efforts hadn't been in vain.

She looked at the bank to see the slide in the mud where the crocodile had entered the water. It was massive.

"We'd better get out of here. That croc's bigger than this boat." Ani reached over to pull up the anchor. Kye caught the slack in the rope and coiled it.

They made their way back to the main creek where she idled the outboard and pulled out her mobile phone.

There were several rings before Neville answered. "It's Anika, Neville."

"Hey, Ani. What's happening?" Neville was a younger version of Amos, the major difference being Neville's wide smile held a beaming full set of teeth.

"I'm over behind Kilmore Island. There's an illegal net set up across one of the side creeks."

"No worries. I'm about ten minutes away." The change in his voice signified Neville was all business. "Can you stay and show me where?"

"Yep, I'm out on the northern side of the main

waterway."

"Cool. Oh, hey Ani, be careful. I saw a big croc up there recently."

Anika rolled her eyes and shook her head. "Thanks for the heads-up."

She set about securing the tinny to wait for him.

It didn't take Neville long to reach them and investigate the illegal net. He would have to follow National Parks' procedure in order to remove what remained of it. Considering the presence of the crocodile, they would wait until low tide and an appropriate lookout would have to be present.

Ani was relieved that she didn't have to assist Neville. One close call with that reptile was enough to last her a lifetime. They both headed back to Resolution.

Kye related the day's events to Amos as she and Neville secured their boats to the floating pontoon.

"You should have seen my Mum, Uncle. She was so fast in the water. That croc was huge. Bigger than a car. Bigger than a bus. Bigger even than a train!"

Amos grinned at the boy's exaggeration, before turning to Neville. "I wonder if it was the same croc that ripped up three of my crab pots not far from there. I've never seen him there before. He must have moved into the area."

Ani grabbed her bag and they made their way up the beach towards the resort.

"This is the first time I've seen that croc, too," she said.

Amos gave her a lopsided grin. "The bank he

come across is real narrow. He must've come through from the other side. Probably out wandering, chasing a girlfriend. Don't think he would've got you. Sounds like he was a fair way up the bank."

"But how on earth did someone get away with setting up a net there?" It didn't make sense.

Neville shook his head. "Don't know. It's a shame he didn't teach the fisherman a lesson. A good scare might have stopped him netting in a green zone."

"The dugong got away. That's what counts." Ani was relieved with the positive result.

Neville stopped to stare at her. "What counts is that you're all right, Ani. And not only with the croc. Whoever set the net could be watching it. Illegal netters are dangerous. It brings in lots of money. Can't imagine they'll be happy you cut their gear to bits. You've got to know the place real well, but you have to be careful. If you find anything else call me right away."

Ani's gut dropped as she nodded. For the first time that day she thought of what could have happened — not only to her, but to her son. There was no way she would put him in that sort of danger again.

CHAPTER 6

Nate's sea legs were well established as he made his way to his laptop. The motion of the waves had increased that afternoon, and the once semi-calm mooring had become choppy as the afternoon progressed.

"Here it is." He spoke as clearly as he could into the cell phone whilst keeping steady on his feet and opening the e-mail message. "I'll read it to you, Uncle Brae."

"Go ahead son."

"The magazine wishes to offer you a weekly column, which will appear in both our printed edition and our online site. We will begin printing the column this week, proceeding each consecutive week with the six articles you have already sent us. Please find attached a contract to run for twenty-six weeks. After this point we will review this arrangement."

Nate stopped short of reading the formalities at the bottom of the message. "It's an awesome opportunity, Uncle Brae. It's the best travel magazine in the States." Nate couldn't contain his excitement.

"That's great news. I always told your Momma you were a storyteller. Doesn't surprise me in the least that you'd become a writer."

"I thought blogging would be a good way to keep in touch with friends and family. I didn't expect a publication to show interest and ask for exclusive rights." Nate was still in shock over the offer.

"Well, I don't know much about publishing, but what I read was mighty entertaining." Braden's chuckle made Nate smile. "The bit you did about the family of seven travelling around in a tiny catamaran was unbelievable. And the dog that wouldn't step foot off its boat ... I haven't laughed that hard in years."

Nate chuckled along with his uncle at the memory of the dog's antics. His adventures so far had certainly made great subject matter.

"Unfortunately, I won't be blogging any more. If I take this offer, I'll have to give the magazine all my material."

"That doesn't matter," Braden said. "I'll just have to subscribe to the magazine to find out what my renegade nephew is up to."

Nate smiled broadly at his uncle's description.

"Where are you now?"

"I arrived in the Resolution group of Islands yesterday afternoon. I've dropped anchor south of the resort where your friends live. It's a beautiful spot. I think I'll stay here a while."

"That's a good idea. They're great people, Nate. You'll love them. Tell them all I say g'day." Nate rolled his eyes in amusement at his Uncle's pathetic attempt at an Australian accent. "Who knows, if you stay there long enough I might pay you a visit."

"I'd love that, but give me a while to decide what I want to do. I may continue up the coast a bit further. I've still got four months on the Savannah. Then I guess I'll have to decide what I want to do next." Nate hadn't given his life after sailing much thought.

"Well, looks to me as though you may have a future in writing," Braden said.

"I'm definitely going to sign this contract. I still can't believe it's fallen into my lap like this. I guess it's luck."

"It's not luck, Nate, it's divine intervention. You told me you asked for direction for your life. I'd say this is an answer to your prayer."

Nate closed the cover of the laptop. "You're right, Uncle Brae. Something this extraordinary isn't luck."

"I'd better go, Nate. I've got thirty executives waiting for me in the boardroom. Thirty minutes is long enough for a pack of wolves to wait."

"I'll talk to you again soon." Nate pressed the disconnect button on the cell phone.

He picked up the red leather-bound Bible on the stateroom table, recalling the last time he had spoken to his uncle. It had been over a month ago, and Nate had confided the decision he had made to seek divine direction.

"I wanted to know Momma better, so I've been going through the highlighted passages and notes in her Bible," he had told his uncle. Each highlighted section had various notes scribbled in the margin. "She had so many hard times."

Each major struggle his mother had endured, every hurdle she faced, was documented along with the answer she had been given.

"Your Momma didn't always have a strong faith, Nate. She went through years of hardship before she realized she couldn't do it on her own," Braden had said.

"I can see that now." Nate had found the testimony of his mother's life in the pages of her Bible, and he marveled at the way the answers his mother received weren't always what she expected, but still worked to comfort her, empower her and help her grow.

"I think I'm starting to understand who God is," he had told his uncle. His Christian upbringing had ensured he knew every Bible story, the important passages, and even the appropriate hymns, but it hadn't given him a clear perspective of who God was.

"I've decided if He could give my mother the direction she needed in life, then He could also show me."

"That's the best news I've heard all day, Nate my boy. Now, trusting in God doesn't assure you an easy ride, but it does mean you won't have to go it alone."

Even though his uncle couldn't see him, Nate had smiled at the statement, and at the obvious joy in Braden's tone.

Nate had always thought the Christian faith was a group thing, a religion everyone participated in. After reading his mother's Bible, he realized God wanted everyone to have a personal relationship with Him. Being a part of a group was important, but God also wanted know each person, and to communicate with them, as an individual. He had discovered God was in fact completely interested and invested in him as a person, even if he currently wasn't a member of a religious congregation.

Since his decision to ask God's opinion he had gained a whole new sense of God's presence. It made everything around him feel different. All of a sudden, the uplifting feeling he enjoyed from being on the water was heightened.

Even the solitude held an overwhelming comfort. And when he finally got over the feeling of talking to himself, the time he spent sitting and talking to God as the sun rose over the watery horizon became the best part of his day.

The loneliness he had experienced in the last few years disappeared. In its place was the incredible feeling of wholeness. Nate was having the time of his life, exploring a newfound faith that drew him like a magnet.

He opened the Bible to his favorite passage.

Trust in the Lord with all your heart and lean not on your own understanding; in all your ways acknowledge him, and he will make your paths straight.

Nate realized his life still had no direction. He didn't want to revert to going through the motions when his trip ended. Didn't want to get to the end of his life not having experienced the fulfilment his mother had.

He placed the Bible back on the table.

God, please give me a purpose apart from writing. Something that will fulfil me after this trip is over. I don't want to finish back where I started.

A clanging noise at the side of the boat drew his attention.

"Hello, anyone there?" a deep male voice called out.

Nate got up and made his way to the deck.

A large man in a small tender was pulling up to the duckboard. As Nate stepped out of the cabin, he put a hand up to his forehead to shelter his eyes from the glare reflecting off the water. He recognized the tinny as the one tied behind a shrimp boat or, as the Aussies called it, a prawn trawler that had shared the island mooring spot with him the previous night.

He estimated the man to be well into his sixties, overweight, with scruffy white hair and several days' growth on his face. He was decidedly unkempt. He wore the standard uniform for most Aussie fisherman—torn t-shirt, faded shorts, and bare feet.

"G'day," the stranger called from his tinny. Despite his bulk filling the small boat, he managed to keep stable in the choppy sea. "It's come up a bit rough this afternoon, hasn't it?"

"Yes, the weather man didn't forecast this change until tomorrow." Nate knew he would have to move for the night.

The man nodded in agreement and reached out a weathered hand. "Bert Johnson."

Nate reached over to reciprocate. "Nate Hollingsworth. Come aboard."

He held the boat stable while Bert negotiated the tricky step onto the duckboard.

Nate had no qualms inviting him onto the Savannah. He had met many others in the same manner during his journey up the coast. He soon discovered it was standard practice in Australian waters for boats sharing a harbor to socialize with each other.

"Whereabouts in Yankee land you from?" Bert leaned back against the side.

"Texas."

He tipped his chin. "I hear they got some big

steaks in that part of the country."

Nate smiled. "Everything's big in Texas."

Bert transferred his weight, sticking one foot out to balance. "I got a bit of a problem. My decky's crook. I told him not to eat the leftover Chinese from the fridge but he ain't got much between here." Bert pointed to each one of his ears. "He's been throwing up all night and he's useless. The prawns are on the run and I can't afford the time to take him into port. Don't want to miss out on tonight's load. Thought I'd see if you wanted a night's work." He looked around the back of the Savannah. "Not that you look short of a quid."

Nate took a moment to decipher the slang. He reached the conclusion that he was being offered a job. He considered it for a moment. It would certainly give him some new material for his column.

"I haven't worked on a prawn trawler before."

Bert shrugged his shoulders. "Well, it ain't rocket science, mate. You obviously know your way around a boat. The rest's just muscle."

Nate smiled. Bert was a character he couldn't pass up. "Okay. When do you want me?"

Bert looked back at his boat. "I'll come back over and pick you up in 'bout an hour's time, eh?"

Nate nodded. "Sure."

He helped Bert back into his boat.

"See you soon," the skipper called as the old outboard puttered its way through the choppy water.

Nate stayed to watch his progress back to the sky-blue trawler. The stabilizers hanging off each side of the vessel were working overtime to level the boat in the swell. On the side, the name *Sweet Mary-Jane* was written in elaborate white letters.

Bert was almost at the trawler when an ominous backfire from the outboard halted his progress.

Nate could hear colorful cursing as Bert pulled at the starter cable, finally succeeding in bringing the ancient motor back to life.

Nate couldn't help but laugh. He looked forward to the night's activity.

Anika knew she was in trouble when her legal aid solicitor began shuffling through his papers in nervous succession. It was a disjointed action he had repeated continuously during the last five minutes of the family court hearing.

"Your Honor, my client simply requests access to his only grandchild. Considering the death of the child's father, it is quite feasible Mr. Mitchell Mayfield would want to foster a relationship with his only living relative." The well-dressed opposing counsel presented an air of superiority, as though he were above such proceedings.

Ani clenched her teeth and felt her jaw pop. *How dare he intrude upon our lives?*

She watched Mitchell Mayfield as he sat next to his solicitor. *Who do you think you are?*

He was a distinctly older version of Heath. His aristocratic profile was enhanced by a smattering of grey amongst his dark brown hair. He could have been classed as a handsome man if his expression hadn't been so stiff. His perfectly manicured fingernails had most likely never seen a hard day's work. It was yet another aspect of the man to loathe.

Ani stared him down as hard as she could without blinking. He didn't baulk, nor had he looked at her since the court session had started.

She leant over to whisper to her solicitor. "Ask why he wants this relationship now. Kye's seven. They've never offered a thing towards his upbringing, nor made any attempt to get to know him."

The young man gave her a frightened glance. He had worn a distinct deer-in-the-headlights expression from the moment they walked in the door. He opened his mouth to speak but no sound came out.

The distinguished judge on the raised platform looked his way. "Do you have anything to say, Mr. Waysal?"

Ani cringed. Weasel was most likely a better name for the small, pale-looking man.

"Ah, yes. Waysal shuffled more papers. "My client would like to ask why Mr. Mayfield is seeking contact with the child at this time considering he hasn't in the past, and the child is seven years of age. Um ... also ... there has never been any financial support of the child."

Waysal slumped in his seat, as if the question sapped him of all his strength. The judge looked to Mayfield's counsel. "Can you answer this, Mr. Peterson?"

"Your Honor, as I have already detailed, Mr. Mayfield is without an heir. He has no other significant relatives. He believes he can offer the child a chance to connect with extended family. This is particularly important for the development of the child considering Ms. Deumer does not have contact with her mother, who is currently detained under drug charges. And her father has not been a presence in her life. Ms. Deumer has never sought child support, either officially or personally. Had she done so, an agreement regarding support would have been made." Peterson paused to wet his lips. "Considering the child's father is deceased, is it not reasonable Mr. Mayfield should have a chance to replace that paternal tie in the life of this child?"

No, it is not reasonable. Ani wanted to scream. Instead she turned to Waysal. "Tell him Kye has family. Tell them about his Aunty, Uncle, cousins." She poked him hard on the forearm. "Tell him."

Waysal turned to glare at her. He spoke through clenched teeth. "I've already told you, you cannot prove the link those people have to the child. At the most they are distant relatives."

He turned back to stare at the front of the room. Ani sat back in shock. It was unfolding like a bad dream.

Waysal had turned into a sniveling idiot the second Mitchell Mayfield and the self-important Mr. Peterson had arrived at the court. Even though today's proceedings were only to establish Mayfield's rights to gain access to Kye, Ani knew she was completely out of control of the situation. She couldn't believe he was going to win this vital step to custody.

"Do you have anything to add?" The judge looked at Waysal.

"No. Um. No." Waysal slumped further in his

chair.

Ani ground her teeth in sync with the pen she clicked in and out at a frantic pace. Her solicitor was a complete idiot.

She jumped to her feet. "I have something to say."

All eyes turned to stare at her. Waysal muffled 'sit down', in a hushed tone.

"Go ahead." The judge waved at her in a non-committal way, almost as if he was reluctant to listen to her.

"This man has never once acknowledged Kye." Ani gestured towards Mayfield. "Not from the second he was born. In fact, Heath told me when I was pregnant, that his father would prefer Kye not to be born at all."

Mr. Peterson jumped to his feet. "Your Honor, these sort of comments are complete hearsay and defamatory. I think Mitchell Mayfield's standing in the community, and in this country for that matter, is testimony to his respect as an upstanding citizen who does not deserve this kind of unprovoked attack."

"Quite right." The judge nodded his agreement. "Please keep defamatory comments out of your little speech, Ms. Deumer."

Anika couldn't believe what was happening. The judge was clearly biased. She was being ganged up on.

"You don't understand. Heath told me his father would pay any price for me to have an abortion, and now he's trying to take my child away from me."

Peterson lifted one hand towards the platform. "Your Honor, please. This young lady is clearly misguided. Mr. Mayfield has simply asked to spend some time with the child, to get to know him and provide a positive influence for the boy, one which he could clearly benefit from." Peterson cast a withering glance in her direction.

The judge raised his bushy grey eyebrows at her. "Hmm."

An explosive heat swelled inside. *Now who's being defamatory?*

Mayfield sat stone still, as calm and emotionless as a statue.

She couldn't believe it. This judge was quite happy for his colleague to defame her family, but when she tried to tell nothing but the truth she was shot down in flames. She didn't stand a chance.

"Do something." She appealed to Waysal. "Please," she added in desperation.

Waysal shrugged.

"I find that Mitchell Mayfield has the right to access visits with his paternal grandson, Kye Deumer. These visits will take place at a location close to the child's current residence. That is all." The judge stood up to leave.

Ani slumped back down in her seat. She looked over at Mayfield as a slow tight-lipped smile appeared on his face. He stood to shake Peterson's hand before turning and walking out the door.

Peterson turned to Waysal. "We'll be in touch regarding the dates and times for access." He held out his hand for Waysal to shake.

The younger man stood and nodded several times. "No problem. Let me know what you want."

Anika sat in shock. *Did that all just happen?* She

had to be trapped in a nightmare she would wake up from any second. She stared at her hands splayed on the table top. She was vaguely aware of Waysal gathering papers next to her.

"I'll be in touch regarding the arrangements." He turned to leave.

Ani snapped out of her stupor. "Hang on one minute." Her voice was louder than she had planned. "You totally sold me out. Why didn't you do something? He has no rights to my child. He didn't even want Kye to exist."

Waysal waved his hand at her. "You are so lucky he didn't take your accusation further. Do you have any idea who that man is? Mitch Mayfield's one of the country's leading barristers."

Anika wanted to hit him, hard. "I don't care who he is. He doesn't have the right to take my child."

"Anika, this was an access case. He deserves access to your son. He is the child's grandfather." Waysal raised his eyebrows at her.

Ani shook her head in disbelief. Even her own solicitor was against her. "He's a complete stranger who has never sought one second with Kye. Besides, you said yourself he intends to pursue full custody." She closed her eyes, feeling as though her whole world was falling in around her.

Waysal looked at his watch. "Sorry, I've got to run. Got a drink-driving case next door."

Anika sat in her seat and stared at the vacated platform. *Why is this happening to us?*

She put her head in her hands. *God, please don't let this man take my child. Please.*

CHAPTER 7

Nate leaned back in the deckchair on the back of the *Sweet Mary-Jane*, watching the first beams of sunlight break over the horizon.

His second night helping Bert had been grueling. Prawn trawling proved to be hard work. Between negotiating the nets, sorting the prawns from the catch, and dodging angry sea snakes, he was exhausted.

He fingered the rip in the inner thigh of his jeans. A crab had caused the damage. Thankfully he had successfully avoided a more serious injury above the tear. *Who would have thought you could be castrated by a crab?*

"Here you go. Get that into you." Bert emerged from below deck handing him a mug of coffee. The skipper held a beer as his preferred choice of morning beverage. "You sure you wouldn't rather a beer?"

Nate took a sip of the steaming liquid. "Not a chance."

Bert shrugged and took a deep swig before reaching into his pocket and handing Nate a wad of cash. "Here. You earned every cent. I haven't had a catch like this in months. If I wasn't stuck with Coot, I'd ask you to stay permanently."

Bert had introduced the skinny deckhand when Nate had first come aboard. At the time he had assumed Coot to be a nickname.

"So why is he called Coot?"

"It's short for bandicoot. Don't you think he looks like one?"

"I'm not sure what a bandicoot looks like."

Bert positioned one leg on an upturned container. "I guess it's a bit like a rat. Long nose, lives in the bush. You could eat them back when I was a kid. Tastes like chicken."

Nate considered Coot's exceptionally long nose and small slouched-back stature. He did look somewhat like a rodent.

Bert leaned in and lowered his voice. "He's a crap deckie but I'm stuck with him. I married his sister a few years ago. She hasn't got the nose, you see."

Nate grinned into his cup.

Bert lowered his tone further "Between you and me and the gatepost ..."

Nate wondered briefly what a gatepost had to do with the conversation. He shook it off as another Aussie expression he didn't understand.

"... marrying her was the biggest mistake I ever made," Bert said. "She spends money quicker than I can make it. It's driving me into an early grave. I wanted to retire, but I got too much debt." He sat back and took a swig on his bottle.

"How long have you had the trawler?" Nate sought to change the subject.

"Ever since I was in me twenties. She was a mess when I bought her. Took me a few years to get her into shape. I renamed her after my daughter Mary-Jane. She's all grown up now with four kids and no husband." Bert shook his head. "My girl, she's a hard worker, but her youngest was born with Down's syndrome. It's one of the reasons I keep working. I do what I can to help her out. Not that my missus knows anything about it."

"Don't worry. I'll keep it to myself." Nate didn't anticipate he and Coot would be sharing meaningful conversation in any case.

"Good. The wife's been at me to sell up. I came close a few times but this boat's like another child to me. It's been my home for so long. And then there's this." He lifted his shirt and turned around to reveal a tattoo running across his shoulders. It was Mary-Jane in the same elaborate lettering as displayed on the side of the boat.

Bert turned back. "You see, I'm marked with her for life. Besides, I know the missus wants the money. She's got her eye on a new car."

He felt sorry for the old skipper. The machinations of his wife were clearly causing him some grief.

"So where you headed now?" Bert asked.

Nate swallowed before answering. "Actually, I think I'll stick around here for a bit. Visit the resort over on Resolution. I'd like to do a bit of fishing on the reef."

"This is the spot to do that. Flynn, the bloke who co-owns the resort, runs charters. He's the best in the business."

Nate had heard as much from Braden. He gulped the last of the coffee and stood up, moving to place his empty mug back in the galley. "Best be getting back," he said. He was halfway across the deck when a call came from the opposite side of the boat.

"Ahoy there." A female voice called out. "Bert? You there?"

Nate turned to see Bert make his way to the back of the boat. He peered around the edge of the huge deck freezer to see a girl in a dingy. A mass of blonde curls poked out from underneath the back of her cap. Nate suspected she was cute underneath the sunglasses and nondescript polo shirt and shorts.

"Hey there, Ani. What doin'?"

Nate turned to enter the cabin. He could hear Bert discussing the weather with his guest.

Coot surfaced from below deck as Nate was about to step back onto the deck.

"How are you fairing today, Coot?"

The pale, skinny man had an ugly scowl on his face.

"I hate this boat." Coot grumbled as he grabbed a beer from the fridge.

Nate considered he couldn't be too sick if he was drinking alcohol. "Well, you'll have your job back tonight."

Coot lifted one side of his lip in obvious distain. "You can take over soon if you want. I've found a much better way to make a buck. Just waiting for my investment to mature, so to speak." His lip straightened into a tight-lipped smirk.

Nate decided to leave the conversation rather than pursue it. Coot was a strange character, one Nate didn't fancy having too much involvement with.

He heard the conversation between Bert and his guest lull as he made his way to the back of the boat. The topic of the weather had clearly been exhausted.

"So who's Richie Rich over there on the fancy yacht? Shouldn't it be in a marina, not hanging off an anchor here?"

Nate knew she must be talking about the Savannah. It was the only other boat in the bay.

"That would be me," he said as he joined Bert and the girl. She was now standing with Bert on the back of the trawler.

Nate saw her jump at the sound of his voice. She clearly didn't expect anyone to appear from behind the huge freezer taking up a large part of the deck.

"Sorry to startle you."

The girl gave him a heavy frown.

Bert indicated to him. "Ani, this is Nate. He's been helping me the last few nights while Coot's been crook.

The girl abandoned her disapproving stare to glance from Nate to the Savannah, and back again.

He could only assume, by her one raised eyebrow, that she was having trouble making the connection between the opulence of the yacht and the job he had been doing as a deckhand.

Normally, he would produce a hand in greeting, but considering both hands were rough and cut from the work he gave her a nod instead. "Nice to meet you."

Ani gave a curt, "Hi," before turning back to Bert. "You haven't seen any sign of illegal netting, have you? We found one set in a green zone a few days ago. It had a dugong caught in it."

"You don't say?" Bert rubbed his chin, then shook his head. "Sorry, can't say I've seen anything suspicious, although I saw a few blokes camping over on Tanner Island a week ago. Don't know what they were up to, but there was a lot of coming and going from the campsite."

She nodded. "Thanks. I'll get Neville to check it out. If you see anything else can you let us know?"

Bert gave a firm, "No worries."

She turned to retrieve her tinny hanging off the back of the trawler.

"Hey, Ani, could you could give Nate a lift back for me?" Bert asked as he helped her into the dinghy.

She looked back from her position at the tiller. "Okay. But I'm in a bit of a hurry."

Nate turned to retrieve the bag he had brought over the previous night. As he bent down to pick it up the wad of cash in his pocket bulged into his thigh. He retrieved it and quietly handed it back to Bert. "Here. Give this to your daughter for me."

"What?" The old man reeled back. "No way. You worked for it. I didn't mean to give you no sob story."

Nate paused, knowing he had to choose his words carefully. "I know, but I don't need this, and Mary-Jane sounds as though she does."

His eyes met the old man's. They stared at each other for a moment before Bert reached out to accept the money. "That's a mighty fine thing. I'll make sure she gets it."

Nate stepped over the side and into the tinny. The driver didn't wait until he was properly seated before she revved the outboard, and he almost fell. Nate planted his feet and held on. They made their way back to the Savannah at high speed.

He wasted no time getting out of the boat and onto the duckboard in case she decided to take off on him again.

"Thanks for the lift," he called.

She gave him a tight smile then quickly turned and left.

Nate wondered if she was generally unfriendly or plain rude. He stepped inside, happy that at least the experience on the trawler would provide him with new material for his column. He had three articles planned from his experiences aboard the Mary-Jane.

Anika sighed with frustration, partly at her son's confusion, and partly with the situation. The first court-appointed meeting with Mayfield was about to take place and it didn't seem to matter how many ways she had tried to explain the situation to Kye, he didn't understand it. She couldn't blame him, as she didn't understand it either. Unlike Kye, who simply didn't understand the connection between him and a stranger, she didn't understand how a stranger could be legally granted access to her son.

"So he's my grandfather?" he asked again, as they drove to the agreed park in Mackay.

"Yes, he's your grandfather and he wants to see you."

"What if he's mean?"

Ani wished she could allay his fears, but she considered Mitchell Mayfield to be nothing but a meanie.

"Just be yourself, Kye." She knew if her son was genuine, he would feel all right about the unusual situation.

"Cool." With that, he went back to looking out the window.

The drive was a long one and Ani was thankful Bay was with them to provide moral support.

Not long after they arrived, Mayfield and a well-dressed woman in tailored pants and white blouse approached them.

As the pair reached them, Bay placed a hand on Ani's shoulder as a silent support. "Don't forget, he'll be in your sight the entire time."

Mayfield had conceded to meeting them in a public place. It was one stipulation Anika had insisted upon. To her surprise, Mayfield hadn't challenged the demand.

Mayfield acknowledged them with a stiff nod, while the lady reached out her hand. "I'm Sarah Rhodes, Mitch's personal assistant." She shook both her and Bay's hands.

Mayfield squatted down to Kye's level and held out his hand. "You must be Kye."

Kye looked up at her. Ani forced a smile. "You can shake his hand."

Kye looked back at Mayfield and placed a small hand in his. "I'm Mitchell Mayfield. But you can call me Mitch if you like."

Kye screwed up his nose. "But aren't you my grandfather?"

Mayfield looked him in the eyes. "Yes, I am."

'Then I should probably call you Grandad, seeing as that's what you are." He nodded his little head.

To Ani's surprise, Mayfield grinned. "That's fine with me."

"Hey, Kiki, can I go over to the monkey bars now?" Kye looked for her approval.

Ani didn't get a chance to respond before Mayfield did. "I'd love to see how far you can go along those bars."

They both made their way to the play equipment.

Ani and Bay stood watching them walk away. Sarah Rhodes looked briefly at her polished shoes before lifting her head. Her blonde ponytail swung with the sudden movement. "I know this situation is a bit strained."

Ani snorted. "A bit?"

"Okay, it's horrible." The woman fiddled with the strap of her handbag. "I want you to know that Kye is in good hands. Mitch just wants to get to know him. He's had a hard time dealing with Heath's death and it's changed him."

Ani studied at the woman. Her face was genuine enough, but the attempt to pacify did nothing but stir up the big, angry giant within her.

"Boohoo for Mitch." She glared at the woman. "Please forgive me if I have trouble mustering up compassion for a man who didn't want Kye to exist in the first place. Kye's never had a father because that man's son didn't step up to the job." She pointed at Mayfield. "And he had a lot to do with that. Now he wants to ease his loss by creating one for me?"

Sarah was clearly taken by surprise. She shuffled her feet as her eyes darted from Bay back to her.

"Do you have children, Sarah Rhodes?" Ani could feel her body lean into the woman as she asked the question.

"No, I don't." Her voice was shaky.

"Well, until you do, don't try to tell me it's okay for someone to come along and steal mine." Ani turned and stomped away.

She didn't stop until she had reached the car. Opening the door, she slumped into the passenger seat. Tears of frustration burst out before she could close the door behind her. Bay was with her as fast as she could maneuver her five-month bump behind the steering wheel. Ani cried while Bay held her.

Marlee Jones had a spectacular head of cornrow plaits. She was also the most trendsetting Island heritage lady Ani had ever come across. Despite being a little overweight, her attire was slim-fitting, hugging her curves in all the right places. Her fishnet stockings and brightly beaded necklace were both surprising style choices for a middle-aged solicitor. As were the yellow, pink, and blue beads swinging on the end of selected braids.

Marlee had been appointed to Anika after she had insisted on another solicitor. After being informed legal aid representatives were in short supply, and she may be stuck with Waysal, she recalled that some cases could be subject to specialized representation.

After learning of her heritage, the woman assigning cases was thrilled to place her with Marlee.

"I've been looking through the documents they gave me and I have to say they've done their homework." Marlee peered over her glasses. They were sitting in a stuffy consultation room in the Legal

Aid building in Mackay.

"What do you mean?" She didn't have a clue what this homework consisted of.

Marlee flipped through several papers on the desk. "Here, for instance, they have every detail on your childhood. Your mother's record. Your grandmother's record. They've even dug up a drink-driving incident on you."

"What? That was years ago."

Marlee peered over her glasses again. "Doesn't matter. They'll use anything. Any slight mistake or slip up." She moved in closer to the table. "Anika, now is the time to fill me in. I need to know any and every detail of your life. Even if you think it's insignificant."

She racked her brain. "Apart from the drink-driving, I've never been in trouble with the police."

"What about relationships? Apart from Kye's father who else have you been with?"

She cringed. "A few one-night stands. I kind of went off the rails for a bit after I found out Heath had died. But no one since then. Seriously, it's been years."

"Hmm." Marlee moved her mouth to one side while she scribbled in a note book. "If they find out about it, which I'm sure they will, the fact they were one night stands will work against you."

The anger possessing her during the hearing erupted. "This is completely ridiculous. Kye is my son. Why should I have to defend myself against a man who has no right to claim him?"

Marlee set down her pen and gave Ani her full attention. "You're right. This should be a no-brainer.

In any other instance, this claim would have never progressed this far. But this is a very powerful man. He's rich, he's respected, and it looks to me as though he's determined to get your boy."

Ani felt sick. "But how? How can he possibly take him from me?"

She didn't understand how a system priding itself on keeping children with their mothers could consider taking her son and giving him to a complete stranger.

"He's going to try to prove you're an unfit mother. But looking at you, I know he's got his work cut out." Marlee reached over and took her hand. "You're a good mum, Anika. From the second I met you and Kye, I knew he was a very lucky, well-balanced child. That's the good news. The bad news is that Mitchell Mayfield is going to pull out every trick he can to prove otherwise. He's an absolute master at the legal game and we can't drop the ball for a second."

Ani tried to control her chest that heaved with the burden of the enormous fight she was set to endure.

"Don't let this discourage you. This has got me riled up, and I'm not a pretty sight when I get angry." Marlee squinted. "I will do everything I can to ensure Kye stays with you."

Ani could see Marlee was a force to be reckoned with. For the first time, the weight of the problem lifted a little.

"Now, can you tell me anything else?" The solicitor held her pen poised above the paper. "Any instance where Kye was unintentionally put in danger or any trouble he has been in?"

Anika paused for a moment before a thought occurred to her. "Oh, no!" She rubbed her palm on her forehead.

"What?"

She took a deep breath before relaying the dugong rescue story. "I'm certain Kye told Mayfield during his first access meeting last week." She closed her eyes for a moment.

"What makes you think that?"

"I didn't hear him, but the arm actions were clear. He loves to tell the story." Ani couldn't believe she had been so careless.

"Well, we'll have to do some fancy problem solving on that one." The tip of her pen made a thud as Marlee placed a heavy full stop on the page. "By the way, how did the first access visit go?"

Anika relayed the details of the last week's meeting.

Marlee took off her glasses and set about cleaning the lens on the hem of her shirt. "Sounds like it went smooth enough."

Anika sighed. "Not quite. There was a bit of an incident afterwards."

"What kind of incident?" Marlee replaced her glasses as Anika summarized her meltdown at Sarah Rhodes.

"I kind of lost it." She looked sheepishly at Marlee.

"I can't blame you. If it was me I probably would have punched them both out."

The solicitor's honesty softened her confession.

"Thankfully, Kye was so busy showing off he

didn't even notice how upset I was."

"You haven't told him about the situation?"

"Not yet. He's going to be forced to spend time in this man's company. I don't want him to feel bad about it. The funny thing is, if Mitchell Mayfield had set about making an effort to get to know Kye without this legal stuff, I would have given him a chance. He refused mediation, and I suspect he pulled a few strings in order to bypass it." Ani knew she would have been open to Mayfield if he had gone about everything the right way. Custody disputes and child access cases were generally settled with communication and mediation. Mayfield had avoided both. There was also the Waysal factor. Ani was sure her previous representative would have bowed to all of Mayfield's demands without question.

"He's not a man to compromise, that's for sure." Marlee picked up her folder. "Just be aware of what you're doing. From now on, be super alert. Don't put Kye in any situation that could be interpreted badly. You don't want to provide them with any more ammunition."

Ani retrieved her hand bag and stood up. "Thank you so much. I can't tell you how relieved I am that you've taken this on."

Marlee gave her a broad smile. "Well, it won't be short. Mayfield has to establish a relationship with Kye before he can pursue full custody. That's going to take time."

They made their way to the door. Marlee stopped short of exiting. "I noticed you mention Neville as a caregiver for Kye."

"Yes. One of Neville's cousins is my foster mother." She explained the connection.

"Say hi to him for me," said Marlee, avoiding her eyes.

"No problem. So how do you know Neville, if you don't mind my asking?"

Marlee swished a hand in the air, clearly attempting a casual gesture and failing dismally when she almost dropped her folder. "Oops." She saved it from hitting the floor. "We, um ... we went to high school together. We kind of had a bit of a thing going for a while."

Anika was taken aback. Neville had never mentioned a teenage romance.

"Actually, it was so long ago he probably won't even remember me. It was only a brief ten-month thing. We broke it off when I went away to university. My parents were determined to see me fully educated." She lifted her gaze towards the ceiling. "On second thoughts, don't bother saying hi."

"Ten months isn't brief, Marlee. I'm sure he'd remember you."

"Well ... if you think so." She grabbed Ani's arm. "But don't make a big deal of it, okay?"

Anika couldn't help the smile spreading across her face. This old flame was clearly still burning.

"I promise," she assured her new friend.

CHAPTER 8

Nate looked out at the gap between the islands that created a channel through to the open sea. He had dropped anchor in Resolution Harbor a few weeks ago. The yacht was moored around the corner from the little beach he was now walking along.

He had previously sailed along the coast of Mexico and through the Hawaiian Islands, but Resolution was one of the most beautiful tropical islands he had ever seen.

Not only did the resort entirely complement its natural surroundings, the sheltered island was close to the mainland. The resort sat on the southern side of the island, and the Savannah was moored only a short distance away from the floating pontoons providing easy access to the resort.

But Nate had to admit it wasn't only the environment that made Resolution so attractive. He had never felt so welcome and at home anywhere. From the second he met the family who owned the resort, he had an uncanny sense of knowing them.

Flynn had taken him to the reef twice in the last few weeks—once on a fishing trip, and another time to explore some dive spots. The Great Barrier Reef was every bit as spectacular as he had anticipated.

Amos had accompanied them on both trips. Nate had taken an immediate liking to the older man, who never spoke unless he had something specific to say. He grinned when he recalled meeting Amos's cousin,

Neville, who was the complete opposite. Neville didn't stop talking. But his constant chatter about the history of the area and his family traditions made for interesting listening.

Nate had initially kept his family connection to himself, but when he met Bay, her father Dutch, and his wife Yvette, he had conveyed the greeting from his uncle.

"Welcome, Nate." Bay had thrown her arms around him, her protruding bump getting in the way.

"You should have told me you were Braden's nephew. You're next to family here." Flynn chastised him.

Nate had shrugged. "Sorry, it just didn't come up."

Flynn's broad smile assured him that he didn't consider it an insult.

"How is that crazy old cowboy?" Dutch had slapped him on the back.

"He's thinking of visiting while I'm here. But I'm not sure how long I'll be staying."

Bay swung an arm around her husband. "Well, we'll have to find some way of keeping you with us for a while."

Flynn nodded. "That's for sure."

That was over a week ago, and as Nate made his way along the short sandy beach he considered how the family had been good to their word.

Neville had given him a tour of the estuary. Flynn had taken him crabbing. He had accompanied Dutch into town for supplies, and Bay had insisted he dine with them on several occasions. But the majority of his time had been spent with Amos. The more he got to know the man, the more he liked him.

Amos lived a simple life. He loved his home, caught his own food, and from what Nate could see, didn't even own a pair of shoes. But there was something raw and honest about him. He possessed an almost spiritual aura, a wisdom surpassing understanding.

Nate had accompanied Amos on several bush walks, had helped with turtle hatching, and sat with him on the beach as the tide came in. He had found himself confiding in the man who shared his faith.

Today Amos had offered to teach him to spear fish. They had planned to meet on the beach around the corner from the resort where an old traditional fish trap still remained. Amos had explained the trap had been built long ago by arranging rocks in two semi-circles jutting off the shore. It allowed the fish to come in on the high tide, and trapped them as the tide receded. It was the perfect area to learn to spear.

Nate could see Amos and another small figure sitting on the short rocky outcrop. As he made his way towards them he saw that it was a child who was fishing while Amos rifled through the little tackle box.

"Hey there, Amos!" Nate called out, as he picked his way over the rocks to reach them.

The small figure was a boy with olive skin and a head of curly, blond hair sticking out at all angles from underneath the edges of his cap.

"We'll have to put the lesson off till tomorrow. I got my nephew, Kye, to watch this afternoon. We're going to do some fishing. Come and get yourself a line." Amos looked down at his charge, who was squinting up at him.

"Kye, this is Nate."

"G'day." Nate tried his Aussie accent and failed dismally.

"Hi." Kye gave an enthusiastic wave before turning his attention back to his hand line.

"Are you on holidays, Kye?"

"No, I live here."

"Kye usually spends a lot of his time with me, but he's been with his Mum these last few weeks," Amos said.

"She's gone crazy." The boy screwed up his nose as he spoke.

Amos grinned. "He's a bit sick of hanging out with women."

Nate laughed. "I don't blame you, Kye."

"Hey, Nate, any chance you could watch Kye for me while I run back to the cabin and get some sinkers?"

"No problem."

Amos squatted down to the boy. "Don't move or your mother will kill me."

"I won't. I don't want to be stuck in that office anymore." The child gave an over-dramatic sigh.

Nate took a seat on the rocks next to the boy as Amos made his way up the beach. The outcrop they were on was around five meters above the water line, and the waves thudded with a crash underneath them, sending salt spray into the air.

"What sort of fish do you catch here?" Nate shifted his weight to a comfortable sitting position.

"A bit of everything. Cod, sweet lip, sometimes

a trout. I got a huge trout here a few months ago." The boy sat up in obvious pride.

"How long have you lived here?" Nate could see Kye was different in looks to both Amos and Neville.

"A while." He turned to look at him. "You talk funny."

Nate smiled. "That's because I'm from Texas. Do you know where that is?"

Kye nodded. "In America. My Mum's got a big map in her bedroom and there's a big red circle around all the places she wants to go. It's full of red circles."

"Have you ever travelled overseas?" Nate picked up Amos's line and tossed it into the water.

"No. I want to. My grandad lives in Sydney. He says I can visit him there one day. But most of my family lives here."

"Do you have any brothers or sisters?"

"Heaps." Kye paused to shake his head. "Ronald, Netty, Mary, Bridget, Peter." He checked them off his fingers as he spoke.

"Wow. Big family."

Kye nodded. "And I've got hundreds of cousins. I don't even know all their names."

Nate chuckled.

Kye began reeling in his line. "Are you staying on the island?"

"No. My home's that yacht anchored out in the bay."

The child abandoned his task to give him a wide-eyed gaze. "You mean the big sail boat."

Nate nodded. "She's called the Savannah."

"Wow. You live on it?"

"Would you like to come aboard for a tour one day?" Nate was overwhelmed by the child's enthusiasm.

"Would I what? That would be way cool."

"Kye!"

A female voice yelling from behind them cut through their conversation. Nate turned around to see a girl standing at the end of the rocky outcrop. Her patterned sun dress ruffled in the wind, and she wore a large white wide-brimmed hat.

Nate was distracted by her silhouette. The sun shone right through the fabric of her dress. She had dangerous curves.

Kye stood up, still holding his line. "What?" he yelled back.

"What are you doing?" It sounded more like an accusation than a question.

"I'm fishing."

The girl placed her hands on her hips. "What have you been told about wandering off on your own? Get that stuff packed up and get over here." Her severe tone gave away her frustration.

Kye groaned. "Aw, Kiki. I'm not on my own." He glanced down at Nate.

She shook her head and walked a few paces towards them. "You're sitting with some strange bloke. What have I told you about staying away from people you don't know?"

Nate could almost see the fumes coming out the top of her head.

"He's not a stranger. That's Nate." Kye pointed to him.

The girl raised a hand to her ear. "What? Get up

to the cabin."

Nate could see she was having trouble hearing Kye. He made swift work of reeling in his line and got to his feet. "I'd better go introduce myself."

Kye finished pulling in his line. "It won't do any good."

"Even so, your sister hasn't met me. I'll go and explain." Nate helped the boy secure the tackle box.

"She's not my sister. She's my mum, and she's gone complete loopy loons." Nate almost laughed as the child circled the air with his finger on one side of his head.

Nate was still too far away to ascertain the girl's age, but he never would have guessed she was old enough to be Kye's mother. He wondered where all the siblings fit in. Kye must have been exaggerating.

They picked their way over the rocks. Nate noticed Kye deliberately dragging his feet.

As they approached, her attractiveness waned under her expression. They were met with flared nostrils and pursed lips. Nate recognized her as Ani, the girl he met aboard the Mary-Jane.

He bent down to whisper to the boy. "Is she always mad?"

"Nah, she's just gone mad lately." The child rolled his eyes in dramatic fashion.

Ani threw out her arm, pointing towards the top of the beach, while keeping the other hand firmly on her hip. "Go!" she yelled at the boy, who bowed his head and inched his way in the direction of her finger.

Nate stepped forward. "Look, I think I can clear this up. We've met before." He presented one hand.

"I'm Nate Hollingsworth, remember. Is it Ani, or Kiki?"

She turned to glare at him, ignoring his peace offering. "I don't care who you are. Why don't you get some friends your own age?"

He took a step back. "I don't think you understand ..."

She didn't let him finish. "No, you don't understand. What is a grown man doing hanging out with a seven-year-old?"

Her glare was so wild Nate considered Kye may be accurate in his diagnosis. *Perhaps she is mentally unstable.*

She placed the other hand back on her hip. "Well? Are you dumb as well as stupid?"

Indignation replaced his shock. Who did this woman think she was? He certainly wasn't going to let her get away with unfounded character assassination.

"You are one nasty piece of work, lady. If you stop throwing accusations around, I'll explain what's going on." Nate had had enough of being the target of her displeasure.

She took a step towards him and pointed her finger at his chest. "Stay away from my kid, or I'll report you to the police."

Nate opened his mouth to let her have it when Amos appeared by her side.

"What's wrong, Ani?" A bewildered look crossed his face. "Kye says he has to go home."

Nate noticed the boy was sitting at the top of the beach.

The girl turned to Amos. "I found him fishing off

the rocks with this random bloke."

Amos looked between them. "That's Nate. I asked him to watch Kye for me while I got some sinkers. He's a friend of Bay and Flynn's, and he's a mate of mine."

Nate smiled for a moment at having been classed as Amos's friend, then looked back to Ani. She seemed to deflate before his eyes. Her mouth dropped open and she stood there looking between them.

Ha. Not so feisty now, are you? He placed his hands on his hips in the same style as her and stared her down. "I think now might be a good time for an apology."

She closed her eyes for a second. "He's your friend? Well, how was I supposed to know? I thought Kye must have taken off on his own again."

Amos's frown showed obvious concern. He put a hand on her shoulder. "You've got to stop this worry, Ani. It's too much. Not good for you or him."

Her bottom lip started to tremble as tears welled in her eyes. She nodded and Nate saw her swallow hard.

His indignation evaporated. She was distraught, and possibly borderline unstable.

She wiped her eyes. "I'll send him back down." She turned without acknowledging him and walked back up the beach.

Nate raised his eyebrows and looked to Amos for an explanation.

"Sorry about that. She's been under lots of pressure." Amos dug into his pocket and retrieved a packet of sinkers. "Let's go."

Nate lifted one corner of his mouth as Kye rejoined them. "Sure."

CHAPTER 9

The phone rang several times before Anika answered it. "Hello."

"Ani?"

"Oh, Aunty, it's so good to hear your voice." She sank into the cane sofa. She had been missing Aunty so much lately. Hearing her voice was the best thing to have happened all day. "How are you?"

"Not so great. I wish you were here."

When they had left Cairns six months ago, the overwhelming excitement of starting a new life had overridden any sadness she had suffered at leaving Aunty's care. Now Anika wanted nothing more than to feel the safe, strong arms of her foster mother around her.

"I was talking to Neville," Aunty said. "He told me you've been a bit emotional."

She sighed and closed her eyes. A bit emotional was the understatement of the year. No doubt Amos had retold every one of her meltdowns in minute detail.

"It's all getting to me. The legal stuff, the access visits, keeping Kye out of trouble. I can't sleep and, when I do, I have nightmares." She acknowledged the ever-present tears pricking the back of her eyes.

"Anika, this is a horrible situation. I know it's hard for you, but you're a good mother. Kye is a lucky boy to have you."

She couldn't stop the sobs from escaping. "I

don't feel like a good mother, Aunty. I'm so strung out. Kye hates me and I can't blame him. I hate me."

"Ani, you have to remember that God loves you both. He always has and He always will."

"Does He, Aunty? I don't know any more."

"Yes, He does. He will never give you more than you can handle. He will provide you with the strength you need. It's only when you try to go without Him that you're going to run into trouble."

A drop in her stomach revealed her conviction.

"You're right, Aunty. I don't have anywhere else to turn. I need help." The last time she was this discouraged was when Heath died. Her life had been out of control and she had asked for help. God had provided the strength to carry on. He would give it to her again.

"I know it's hard," Aunty went on. "But God's not going to let you or Kye down, no matter how hard it is, or how bad it looks. He may have lessons for you to learn in this place you are in. But you're not in it alone."

Anika wiped the tears streaming down her face. "I know, Aunty. I know." She couldn't stop the occasional sob from escaping.

"How are the visits going?"

She took a deep breath before answering. "Surprisingly well. Kye seems to like him. It's strange, Aunty. He comes across as so hard. He still hasn't said one word to me, but Kye's taken to him, and he's always been a good judge of character."

"Maybe Mayfield isn't as tough as you think he is."

Ani had no capacity to contemplate the notion.

"What about Kye's school?" Ani told her aunt about her son's schoolwork, and the recent test revealing he was advanced for his age.

She also told Aunty about the embarrassing incident ten days ago with Amos and the American.

"Kye's done nothing but talk about this bloke, Nate, for the past week. Apparently he goes everywhere with him and Uncle." She had managed to avoid any further contact with Nate Hollingsworth. She didn't know which was worse—that Kye genuinely liked the man, or that she found herself thinking about him. A lot. From the moment they had met on the Mary-Jane, the man had made her nervous. Now, his presence in Kye's life had her concerned.

"You sound as though you don't like him"

"He's heir to some huge fortune in the States. He's also apparently a lawyer, and he's left it all behind to have a holiday up the coast on his million-dollar yacht." She could feel the resentment rising up within her like bile. "I don't think that sort of life is a good example for Kye. I don't want him to think that having no responsibilities and doing whatever he wants is a good way to live."

"Has this man said something to upset you?" She noticed real concern in Aunty's voice.

"No, I've only met him briefly, twice." It riled her that Nate Hollingsworth had impressed her son, especially when her first impression hadn't been a good one. Sure, he had worked as a deckhand on the Mary-Jane, but Bay had told her he had used the experience in a column he wrote. His humorous account of the job had them all rolling with laughter.

But Ani was convinced Nate was doing nothing but mocking those he thought inferior to him.

Then there was the way he had thrown the money he had earned back at Bert. She hadn't heard their exchange of words, but she wasn't impressed with his lack of respect for the older man.

"I know he's nothing but a playboy, Aunty." Ani was certain of her assessment.

"Are you sure? If Amos has befriended him, how bad could he be? My brother certainly doesn't suffer fools, and he would never allow this man to be in such close contact with Kye if he didn't trust him. You shouldn't make assumptions about someone without getting to know them."

Aunty had a good point, but Ani wasn't about to let reason enter into her consideration. She had decided Nate Hollingsworth was doing nothing but having a laugh at them all. Besides, he had also been witness to her biggest meltdown. No doubt he would use it in some way to belittle her. His type always did.

Ani bristled at the thought of his high-and-mighty status. "I guess it doesn't matter. He'll be gone soon enough. I just hope Kye doesn't get too attached to him."

She had decided she would wait out the situation instead of confronting it. Hollingsworth was the sort who didn't stay at family resorts. His ship would sail soon, and hopefully she would avoid having anything to do with him in the meantime.

Although they spoke frequently, she and Aunty still found it easy to while away the time over the phone. When Ani hung up, she looked up to see they had been speaking for well over an hour.

She lay down on the sofa and closed her eyes, listening to the waves pounding the shore a few short meters outside the cabin.

God, I need your help. I know I've prayed and prayed, but Aunty's right. I'm not trusting in you and the pressure is making me insane. Please show us the life you have for me, and for my son.

Ani nodded as Yvette pointed to the map on the wall of the research station, indicating the waterways around Turtle Island. "Neville is certain something sinister is going on in this area."

"I agree. I can't put my finger on it, but lately, every time I go in there I feel like I'm being watched." Ani sat on the table top and bit her fingernail.

At first she had dismissed the feeling as a symptom of her highly strung state. Then, the last time she had been in the area, she had seen several flashes of bright light. She was convinced it was the reflection from a set of binoculars.

Yvette took a seat behind the desk. "What did Neville say about those men who were camping over on Tanner?"

"Just that they had the proper permit, and when he checked out their camp they had a huge amount of equipment and supplies. No nets, but if they did have nets they wouldn't leave them sitting out where they could be seen. Neville was going to do a sweep of the bush at the back of the campsite and see if they had hidden them somewhere. Apparently, they're planning on staying there a while. He's going to keep an eye on them."

Yvette moved the computer mouse, bringing the screen to life. "In any case, we have a lot of information, thanks to your efforts." She indicated the pile of papers in front of her. "It would have taken me years to collect all this."

Anika felt a sense of pride in her work.

Yvette ran a hand through her short red hair as she fiddled with the computer.

Anika estimated her boss was in her mid-fifties. She had a kind face, and slight middle-age spread that didn't severely affect her figure. She was also a very good researcher with a long history of experience in her field.

Yvette had been tracking the dugong population in the area for years. She was convinced the population had been slowly dwindling, but so far she hadn't been able to produce definitive research to support the argument. Thanks to Anika's involvement, the gap between theory and fact was closing.

"I received an e-mail this morning from the University. They've offered us the use of three monitoring devices. They're the old kind, but they'll do the job." Yvette opened the message for her to read.

Ani scanned it before looking back at her. "This is great."

Yvette nodded. "When we find the target animals, we're good to go."

"Well, now we know where they live, I'll start making a map of their food source areas and try my best to monitor them."

They both looked up as the bell over the door rang.

Ani's stomach dropped as Nate Hollingsworth stood, holding the door open for Bay who waddled in. She was now in her third trimester and looking quite rotund.

The sight of the Texan put Ani on edge. She fiddled with the pen she was holding, clicking the top in and out.

"Hi there," Bay called as she took the nearest seat.

Yvette jumped up to go over and rub her protruding stomach. "How's my little granddaughter today?"

Bay shook her head and looked over at Ani. "She's so sure it's going to be a
girl."

"Well, I already have four grandsons. I'm due for a baby girl." Yvette giggled.

"Nate volunteered to move those shelves for you." Bay fanned a hand in her face in an attempt to cool down.

"Thank you, Nate. Ani and I tried to lift them, but they were too heavy. They're out the back." Yvette turned to her. "Can you show Nate where we want them?"

Oh, no. She was sure her internal groan was accompanied by a pained expression, but she couldn't help it. She had been determined to avoid further contact with him. A rich, privileged, handsome, superior man brought back unpleasant memories. It didn't help that one of his kind was currently attempting to steal her child. She reluctantly got to her feet. "Follow me." She didn't even attempt to hide her dislike for the situation.

The research station was a small building. The main office was located at the entrance, with three small rooms at the back of the building. Yvette had been rearranging her library in one of the rooms.

Ani entered and pointed to a bare wall. "Move them there."

Nate didn't proceed past the doorway. His muscular frame filled the space and she could feel his gaze on the side of her face.

She turned to stare back. At first she was distracted by the strange color of his eyes. They were green with distinct brown flecks, almost like a tiger's. His features were rugged and earthy. The dimple sitting in the middle of his chin gave him a movie star quality. Even his obviously broken nose contributed to his attractiveness. He was a good deal taller than her, and she wasn't short. Ani noticed the ripple along his jaw line. He was clearly displeased.

"You would have to be one of the rudest people I have ever met," he said. "Has common courtesy completely eluded you? If you don't use the words 'please', 'thank you', or 'sorry' for that matter, what example does that set for your son?"

Heat seeped through from her gut to the top of her head. "You have no right to insinuate I'm a bad mother. You don't even know me." He couldn't have picked a worse topic.

"Oh, that's rich. Miss Insinuation herself is going to lecture me on judgement and manners. If I recall correctly, the last time I saw you, you made some nasty judgements about me, and I'm still waiting for an apology."

Anika knew this was true. She really did owe him an apology, but she had hoped he would leave the island before she had to make it. Now, as she looked at his self-important face, her stubborn nature overrode her sense of fairness. There was no way she would give him the satisfaction of an apology, no matter how wrong she was.

"I can't imagine a rich playboy type like you would gain any satisfaction from an apology. Don't you have a multitude of servants already telling you what you want to hear?" She crossed her arms in front of her.

Nate's gaze didn't flinch. If anything the flash of light in his eyes intensified.

"Exactly what have I done to you, lady? Please fill me in, because it must be something really bad to make you so hostile."

"I don't like your type." She spat the words out.

A loud snort escaped his nostrils. "My type, hey? So what is my type? You know me so well."

"Privileged, spoilt, treat people like dirt, and walk all over everyone. That type." Anika could hear her voice rise higher and higher. "Why don't you get on your fancy boat and take your rich brat holiday somewhere else?"

The second the words were out of her mouth she regretted them. This was escalating way past anything she had anticipated.

Nate broke eye contact with her, rubbing a hand through his light brown hair.

Ani blinked several times as silence fell between them. She looked down at her feet.

Somewhere in the back of her mind her conscience was pricked. She was being horrible. A vision of Heath and his entourage of privileged friends flashed before her. It occurred to her that she had put him in the same category as them, for no reason.

Aunty was right. She didn't know him at all. She was being unfair and judgmental.

Great. Now I owe him two apologies.

She looked back up to see his back disappearing down the hall.

Her legs kicked into gear and she took off after him. "Hey, hang on a minute." He ignored her.

"I'll be back later, Yvette." He exited the main door without stopping.

Ani watched him stride away.

"What on earth was that all about, Ani?" Bay's mouth was opened wide.

She looked at the two women. Their faces held a mix of confusion and shock. There was no way they could have avoided hearing the exchange.

She hid her face in her hands. "I'm such an idiot."

"What did he do to you?" Yvette placed an arm around her.

"Nothing. He did nothing."

"Well he must have done something. I've never heard you so angry." Yvette gently rubbed her back.

She dropped her hands and sighed. "No, he really didn't. I'm taking my frustration out on him and I know it's not fair, but I've got a big problem with rich people at the moment."

Bay pulled herself out of the chair. "Nate's a good guy. I can vouch for him. His family may be wealthy but they've worked hard and been blessed with much because they give much, Ani." Bay moved to stand with her. "Trust me. He doesn't deserve that kind of judgement. Besides, Dutch, Flynn, me—we could all be classed as rich. I've never sensed you disliked us?"

Ani's heart began to race. "Oh, Bay, I've never had anything but love and respect for you all."

"So if we're not hateful, then can't you see Nate also may not be what you think? God doesn't look at what we have. He looks at what's in our hearts. It doesn't matter to Him if we have very little, or a lot—we're all on the same footing with Him. It's not fair to dump Nate in with the people who've done you harm."

Ani nodded. "You're right. And maybe Kye's right. Maybe I have completely lost it." She turned to Yvette. "I need to get out for a bit."

The two women nodded. "Take as much time as you need, love." Yvette saw her to the door.

Bay gave her a warm hug.

Nate couldn't make sense of it. No matter how hard he tried to understand, he kept coming back to the same conclusion—she hated him for no good reason.

He eased his pace as he approached the main resort buildings, a few hundred meters from the research station. He had needed every step back to calm down.

Nate knew there was never any chance of him hitting a woman, but if she had been a man he would have had serious trouble keeping his hands to himself. What confused him most was how every person who had spoken about Anika only had good things to say. Based on popular opinion she was sweet, smart, funny, and hard working. Unfortunately, he had yet to see a hint of even one of these traits.

The only attribute he could agree with was the she was a good mother to Kye. Nate had seen the proof of that himself. Kye was a great kid. It had been wrong of him to chastise her lack of manners. He was just so offended by her behavior.

"Hey there, Nate, I've been looking for you." Neville sauntered down the path towards him. He was dressed in his khaki National Parks uniform of long shorts and a button-down shirt. Nate noticed that despite being well dressed, he had never seen Neville wear shoes.

"Flynn told me you're taking a run over to the mainland for him this afternoon."

"That's right. I think I'll leave now." It would be a welcome distraction.

In the month since he had arrived Nate had fallen into the routine of island life. He had somehow been integrated into everyone's day. It was a strangely comforting place to be, considering his year was supposed to be about solitary reflection. But he had to admit he was having the time of his life.

His experiences had also made for great columns. He had received a good deal of praise, both from the publication, and from Bay and Flynn. They loved the free publicity it brought to the resort.

Neville pulled a letter out of his pocket. "Do you

think you could post this for me?"

He accepted it. "Not a problem."

Neville bestowed a toothy smile on him. "You're a real great bloke, Nate."

He managed a slight upturn to the corners of this mouth. "I'm pleased someone thinks so."

Neville's smile turned into a frown. "Someone give you a hard time?"

He shook his head. "No, no. No one."

Actually it was a very angry, crazy someone, but he wasn't going to vent his opinion about her to her cousin.

"Is it because you're an American?"

Nate smiled. "No. Forget I said anything."

Neville tilted his head to the side. "It's Ani, isn't it?"

Nate stiffened at the mention of her name.

"She's under a lot of pressure, Nate. She's not herself."

"So everyone keeps telling me. But I'm the only one she's taking the pressure out on." He shook his head. "I don't know what I've done to the woman."

"You've done nothing. She's a bit wary, that's all."

The explanation only served to confuse him further. "Wary of what? Of me? She doesn't know me. I've met her three times now and each time she was nothing short of hostile."

Neville shifted his weight. "Ani's got a bit of sorting out to do. The business with Kye's grandfather has her all tied up in knots."

"I thought he lived in Sydney." Nate didn't get the connection.

"Oh, you don't know about it." Neville raised his eyebrows as though somewhere in his mind a penny dropped.

He filled Nate in on Ani's difficult childhood, the circumstances surrounding Kye's birth, the hardship Anika faced as a single mother, her hard work to get an education, and the recent development with Mitchell Mayfield.

"We all can see she's having a bit of trouble coping. She's gone off the deep end lately. Been real overprotective of Kye." Neville finished his story.

Nate shook his head. "I don't blame her for being angry. It would be a complete miscarriage of justice if he won custody. But I still don't get why she is taking it out on me."

"Well, that's where I reckon the wary part might come in. She doesn't have a real high opinion of rich people. Thinks they're all no good and out to get her."

Now the penny dropped. That he could understand. She had a history of being taken advantage of by the privileged. The exceptional circumstances she now found herself in could easily have heightened her anger. It also explained the 'type' she had put him into.

"I'm not making excuses for her, Nate. Only, I think she might need a bit of time to warm up to you."

"Thanks for filling me in." He knew he could always count on Neville to do just that.

CHAPTER 10

Judge not that ye also be judged. The Bible verse was one of Anika's favorites. She had referred to it on many occasions when she had experienced the sting of discrimination, except she had always applied it to others, never to herself.

As the tinny skipped along the waterway, she thought about what the verse meant. She realized judgement came in many forms. It was every bit as bad to judge someone based on their so-called privileged status as it was to judge based on their so-called lower class. It all fell under the banner of judgement. It all kept people from accepting one another.

She turned the tinny into one of the small side creeks and killed the outboard. After securing the anchor, she sat back on the aluminum seat and prayed about why she was having so much trouble giving this guy a fair chance.

In an instant, she knew where her judgement of rich people had come from. Heath and Mitchell Mayfield had certainly contributed to her prejudice, as had her biological father, the one she had never met—the rich, married man who had abandoned her and her mother before she was born.

She thought she had forgiven them already.

What's wrong with me? Why can't I let this go?

It was a beautiful summer's day and the sun beat down on her face. A slight breeze blew and she could hear the gentle rustle of the mangrove leaves. The musty smell of the estuary filled her nostrils, and salt spray lay in a fine mist on her skin. In the distance, a sea eagle called out from its position high in the trees. She closed her eyes and tried to enjoy the slow rocking motion of the boat, but her insides felt like a ball of knots.

Fear.

The word rang out in her mind. Her eyes shot open.

Fear.

The word sounded again. That was it! *She was afraid.*

She sensed it now, deep inside her, eating away at her each day, stealing her happiness, holding her back. It was the driving force behind her judgement on those who didn't deserve it. It was turning her into a crazy person.

She realized forgiveness and fear were separate things. A journey of emotional and spiritual counselling had led her to forgive those who had wronged her, but she hadn't entirely dealt with the feelings. Or the fear it could happen again. Inside her heart, she was still afraid. And that fear was the driving force behind her judgement and misguided need for self-preservation.

"I don't want to be, God." She spoke the words aloud to Him in the sea and the air. "Take away my fear. I don't want it to eat me alive. I want to be free to love, to be happy, and to live the life you have for me. I want to live by faith, not fear. I know you love me and will always look after me, and Kye. You tell me that, and I trust you. Trauma has made me think

I need to fight to preserve my life, but I don't. Jesus, you do the fighting for me, just like you did when you died for me. Our lives are in your hands. They always has been, and they always will be. No matter what happens." Tears flooded her eyes and overflowed onto her cheeks. She sat and cried for what had to be the hundredth time that week. But this time it was different. They were tears of release, not of sorrow. She recalled some Bible verses. *I sought the Lord and He answered me, He delivered me from all my fears. Perfect love drives out fear.*

When the tears finally stopped, she knew this knowledge had somehow freed her. An invisible but overwhelming weight lifted from her shoulders.

This day was a new beginning. She made a choice to leave it all behind, to be free, and to discover joy, a decision to step out of her history and become who she was meant to be—free, happy and fulfilled.

She took a deep breath and began to feel calm wash over her. Aunty was right. God knew her so well. He loved her and Kye. No matter how bad it looked, He wouldn't let them down. He had a life and a plan and a purpose for her, and it was hard, very hard, but she trusted Him. She wouldn't let what happened to her in the past dictate her future.

Ani knew what she had to do. She had to speak to Nate Hollingsworth. To apologize, ask for forgiveness, ask for a second chance. *Help me to be humble. I'm not good at this. It's really hard to do.*

Seeking the forgiveness of a rich man went against every instinct.

She pulled up the anchor and started the

outboard.

As she entered the main waterway, she was blinded by a flash of light from the opposite bank. She reduced the power in the outboard in order to pinpoint the location of the light.

It looked as though it was flashing inland, from a small beach on the opposite side of the bank. To her knowledge there was nothing but thick mangrove through that part of the estuary.

She decided to go over and take a closer look. Perhaps it was something innocent. No doubt her heightened emotional state over the last few months was to blame for her overactive imagination. It was plausible the flash was nothing more sinister than a piece of glass in the sand.

She ran the front of the tinny up the narrow beach area and secured the pick in the sand. There was nothing but dense mangrove beyond. The low tide had made the raised area dry enough to walk on without sinking knee-deep in mud. She peered into the gaps between the trees.

It didn't look as though any people had been through there. All the low branches were intact. She picked her way deeper into the scrub, looking up occasionally to see if there was anything stuck above her.

The quiet hum of an outboard sounded back at the beach where she had come from, but she was too far into the trees to see who it was. It was most likely a fisherman on his way past.

She walked a few more meters in, stopping suddenly when a squeak sounded to her right. She looked through a gap in the branches to see the black wings of a flying fox. It hung upside down some distance away.

Ani smiled. The pointy ears and beady black eyes of the creature were trained directly on her. A squawk close by revealed several others. She was clearly on the edge of a colony. Ani made a mental note of their existence in that part of the estuary. The bats left the mangroves at night to feed on local flowers and fruit. They were a vital part of the ecosystem, distributing seeds and pollinating a variety of native species.

Whatever the flash of light was, she wasn't going to be able to pinpoint it without disturbing them, so she made her way back to the beach.

Oh no!

Where was her tinny? Had she lost her sense of direction and exited in the wrong place? No. The pick was still stuck in the sand. A neat cut had been made in the rope hanging off the anchor. Someone had cut her boat from its anchor and stolen it.

She ran to the edge of the water and looked both ways, finally spotting something grey a few hundred meters up the estuary. It was her tinny, snagged on a fallen tree.

Why on earth would someone cut the boat free only to push it out into the water? It made no sense … unless someone wanted to see her stranded. Anika looked back into the scrub, suddenly feeling vulnerable.

She weighed up her options. Her mobile phone was still in the tinny, so calling for help wasn't an option. She could be here for ages if she waited for someone to pass by, and the little beach she was stranded on would soon disappear under the rising tide. It wouldn't be long before she would have to climb a mangrove tree.

One look at her watch confirmed the tide had turned. If she wanted to get the tinny, she would have to swim for it.

This particular waterway was relatively safe. In all her time scanning the area she had never seen signs of any crocodiles. Not in this part of the creek. It would be a short, safe swim to the boat.

Without a second thought, she removed her shorts, polo shirt, cap, and sunglasses. Looking down she was thankful she hadn't done the pile of washing, and had been forced to wear an old bikini as underwear. It was faded and the elastic had deteriorated, but at least it was swimwear.

She adjusted the saggy material as best she could, and dived into the water.

Meters along the bank she found the current was much stronger than she had predicted. She had clearly underestimated the pull of the tide, so she increased the strength of her freestyle stroke.

She swam hard for a good few minutes, glancing up occasionally in order to stay on course. It didn't feel as though she was getting anywhere. When she stopped to catch her breath she realized she was in serious trouble. Not only was she being swept away from the tinny, she was a hundred meters into the middle of the waterway.

How could I have been so stupid? Panic set in for a moment before she turned around to find herself on a collision course with a floating beacon.

She grasped the edge as she went by.

Ani climbed up onto it as high as she could,

feeling the barnacles covering the surface of the waterline cut into her bare feet. *Ow, ow, ow!* She looked down to see blood staining the water. *Great. Now I'm croc bait.* Her heartbeat increased as she clung to the float. *This is bad.*

Her thoughts took her back to the incident with the crocodile. Neville's advice had been not to embark upon anything alone. It was advice she should have taken. After all, being stuck in a forest of mangrove was slightly better than being stuck on a floating beacon. She clung on, as remorse for her impulsive action set in.

She straddled the beacon for a good ten minutes, praying for a rescue. The hum of a tinny behind her brought a flash of hope. She did her best to crank her neck, finally managing to wave one arm back before discovering that if she didn't hold on she was going to fall off.

Ani could only hope to alert the driver to her predicament. Eventually, the outboard idled as the boat drew up. She cringed at the thought of the sight she must be. Faded multicolored bikini bottom with crinkling seams, knotted hair, and she could feel a clump of seaweed attached to the string of her bikini top. She rested her cheek on the slippery surface of the beacon and screwed her face up in embarrassment.

The front of the tinny passed her before the rest of the boat came into view. When she saw who was driving, her stomach did a rapid dive.

"What are you doing?" Nate grabbed hold onto a handle jutting off from the beacon.

Oh no. Why him? Why? She was sure she glowed

red from head to toe. Recovering her pride, she took a deep breath and tried to look nonchalant.

"I'm fishing. Obviously."

Nate ducked his head, but not before Ani saw the wide grin. "Well, good luck." He moved to leave.

"Wait." Pride wasn't going to get her out of trouble. "Someone cut my boat free. I had to swim for it, but the tide turned." She squirmed in an effort to stabilize herself.

Nate didn't move. His sunglasses and cap shaded his eyes from her view, but the grin widened before he pursed his lips and looked over to the bank. "I should keep going, you know."

Anika swallowed hard. "I wouldn't blame you if you did." Her voice was squeaky to her ears.

Nate's grin returned. "Come on. I'll help you in."

He held out one hand while holding the beacon with the other.

Ani took his hand and raised one leg to rest her foot on the side of the tinny. She inched her body away from the beacon. She thought she had her balance, and was about to make the jump when her hand slipped on the slimy surface. She barreled backwards into the water.

As she surfaced, Nate grabbed her hands and pulled her over the side in one swift movement. A thud sounded as her bottom slammed onto the floor of the boat.

A heavy chill hit her chest, and she looked down to find her bikini top was somewhat dislodged from its appropriate place. Mortification flashed through her before she threw her arms around her body, checking to see if the wardrobe malfunction had been noticed.

Nate's grin couldn't have spread any wider.

Her mouth dropped as horror engulfed her. "Please tell me you didn't see my boobs."

He didn't say a word.

She scrambled to right the material. Nate turned to take his seat at the back. His hand rested on the tiller. The grin remained.

Anika stared at him, beyond mortification, and well into complete humiliation. *This was not the humbling I meant.*

She frowned in appeal. "No, seriously, tell me you didn't."

A small chuckle sounded from between his lips.

She covered her face in her hands.

"Put it this way," he said.

She made a gap in her fingers to peek at him. He was still smiling.

"I didn't see anything …Pink" He paused for a second. "I can assure you that your modesty is intact, and in no danger from me."

Ani closed the gap back up to groan again, much louder. *I want a hole. A big black hole to form underneath me and swallow me up.*

She removed her hands as the tinny moved.

"Which way was your boat?"

She embraced his change of subject. "Straight ahead."

They made their way along the bank.

"There it is." She pointed to the tinny. It was still wedged among the branches of the fallen tree.

Nate pulled up alongside and wrapped a rope around a branch for stability. "It looks to be okay.

Where were you?"

"I pulled up on that beach." She indicated the shore. The tide had come in considerably and the little beach was now much smaller. Her clothing and sunglasses were long gone.

Ani explained the reflection, her investigation inland, and her discovery of the missing tinny.

"You're lucky it got caught up here. Not to mention the fact you could have drowned, or got washed out to sea."

She didn't answer him. Her knowledge of the area meant she should have known better.

"Why don't you take my boat back, and I'll drive yours? At least that way you'll have an anchor."

Anika nodded. She wasn't about to argue with him. She got to her feet and winced when the pressure against the cuts underneath shot pain up her legs.

"What's wrong?"

"The barnacles cut up my feet."

She sat back down and lifted one leg up to rest the ankle on her knee. The underside of her foot was a mess. It had stopped bleeding, but she had several painful cuts.

"Ouch." Nate examined her foot before straightening up and removing his sunglasses and cap. He pulled his t-shirt up over his head and ripped the bottom off, breaking it into two strips. "Here, wrap these around them."

She did as she was told and stood back up. It made a huge difference.

"You might want to put this on as well." He handed her what remained of the t-shirt.

She put it on. Even with the ripped bottom it still covered her to the top of her thigh. She was so relieved to regain some modesty that she breathed a huge sigh of relief.

"Thank you so much. I know I don't deserve your kindness." She sat back down and looked up at him.

"No, you don't." He took the seat opposite. "But considering that was a pretty heartfelt thank you, I'll overlook the manners you haven't shown before now."

He moved around the tinny, making an effort to prepare it for her. It was hard not to notice his physique as he moved. His muscular bare chest was tanned—he must often go without a shirt. She could see the ripples in the definition of his frame from the set of his wide shoulders to the noticeable six-pack.

Ani couldn't help herself, until he glanced back and caught her staring. She moved her head sideways in an effort to regain the appearance of aloof composure, and blinked several times to stop from thinking about the overwhelming effect of his presence.

He shut a tackle box with a thud. "That looks to be everything. You'll be okay to get back."

She avoided his body, focusing instead on his face. His tiger's eyes weren't nearly as fierce as they were earlier that day.

Now was her chance. She had to apologize. "I'm really sorry about what I said at the research station. I was wrong and ..." She searched for the right words. "I was hoping maybe we could start afresh."

The edges of his lips turned up. "Well, there

must be something decent about you. You do have a great kid. So I guess I'll have to make concession for that." His grin widened, letting her know he was teasing.

She smiled with relief and nodded her head. "Fair enough."

He held out his hand. "Nate Hollingsworth." His smile reached his eyes. Anika noticed how they glistened. Deep gold flecks flashed as the sun hit them.

She broadened her smile and reciprocated the gesture. "Anika Deumer. It's a pleasure to meet you."

His hand was warm, firm, and completely covered hers. An unexpected tingling ran up her arm.

The handshake should have been a short pleasantry, but neither one of them released their grip. Anika froze as seconds went by. There was something almost other-worldly about his eyes. They completely hypnotized her. It was only when the overwhelming urge to blink set in that the connection broke and they simultaneously dropped each other's hands.

She pulled nervously on the ripped edge of the shirt, feeling the need to cover herself further.

Nate ran a hand through his hair then retrieved his cap and sunglasses. "We, ah, we'd better get back."

He pulled the cable and the outboard came to life.

"Are you sure you'll be okay to take my boat?" He didn't look at her as he asked the question.

"Yeah, sure."

He nodded and stepped over into her tinny.

She took his seat at the back and placed her hand on the tiller. She waited while he settled and started the outboard.

"See you back on Resolution," he called above the combined noise of the outboards.

She nodded and gunned the engine.

Anika sat up with a start. She couldn't have had a worse nightmare if meat-eating dinosaurs had been devouring her.

She had always had vivid dreams. Thankfully, her childhood nightmare had ended long ago, but this new one was way too clear, even now she was wide awake. She didn't dare put her head back on the pillow for fear of a repeat.

Stretching out, she contemplated which was worse—the recurring dream where Kye had been taken away, or the romantic dream she just had involving a certain American.

A shudder ran through her body at the images burning in her mind. She had to admit the dream wasn't the first time Nate Hollingsworth had infiltrated her thoughts. The memory of his touch had popped up far too many times. She had treated the intrusive reflections by squashing them with a firm, "*Go away.*"

She repeated these words several times now, hoping the mental tactic worked on dreams as well as thoughts.

Her bedside clock read five-thirty. At least it wasn't too early for her to get up.

She heard Kye moving around in his bedroom before a loud rapping on the cabin door forced her feet to the floor.

Amos had said he would be there early to pick up Kye, but she hadn't known it would be before sunrise.

She plodded through the open plan lounge/kitchen/dinette and yawned as she unlocked the sliding glass door leading to the deck.

"Hey, Uncle. Kye's awake. I can hear him." She rubbed her eyes and pushed back the curtain for Amos to enter.

"Good morning."

The deep drawling accent made her jump.

"Sorry, I didn't mean to scare you. I seem to have a knack for doing that."

Nate stood in the doorway, a wide grin on his face. He was wearing a crisp white polo shirt and nicely tailored chinos. Ani caught a whiff of cologne. Her stomach did a strange flip-flop. *Go away.* The feelings didn't. But at least the firm reprimand helped her to recover from the shock of seeing him.

"I expected Uncle." She tried to collect herself.

"He had chores to do up at the restaurant, so I offered to come over and collect Kye. Is he ready?"

"He's up." She turned back to call out. "Kye!"

"I'm cleaning my teeth." The garbled reply came from the back of the cabin.

Ani turned back to him. "He won't be long."

Nate's eyes moved from her face down the length of her body to her bare feet and back again. "I hope I didn't wake you."

All of a sudden she became aware of her attire.

Singlet top and silky boxer shorts were definitely not the outfit she wanted to be seen in—certainly not by him.

"No. Come in and sit down. I'll go and put something else on." She headed towards her bedroom.

"Don't go to any trouble for me." His tone held a distinct teasing. It didn't help that he had already seen her in a lot less.

Anika shut her door and fought to quash her embarrassment. She flew around the room, looking for something decent to put on. Why was it every time she was in the presence of this man, she made a complete idiot of herself? She would never live down the bikini incident, and now he had seen her in her almost-there PJ's.

She checked her mirror. *Yep, hair looks like you stuck your finger in a light socket. Great.* She didn't bother with the brush. Instead she reached for a hair tie and smoothed it back into a ponytail.

She was on her way back out when she remembered something. She ran back in to grab the t-shirt.

Nate had taken a seat on the couch. She perched herself on the edge of a chair.

"I didn't know if you would want this back." She leant over the coffee table to offer him the t-shirt he had given her to wear.

The day they had returned to Resolution she had high-tailed it back to her cabin. It was only as she walked in the door that she realized she was still wearing his shirt.

"You shouldn't have bothered." He reached out

to accept the folded garment.

As he took hold of it their fingers touched sending an electric current down her arm. Ani quickly withdrew her hand, dropping the shirt in the process.

Nate retrieved it from the floor before looking up. "How are your feet?"

A good cleaning revealed the cuts weren't deep. She used some strong antiseptic for a few days and they had all but healed.

"Fine. No serious damage."

Silence fell between them. Ani looked anywhere but at him and racked her brain for something to say.

"Thanks again for the rescue." *Bad, bad choice.* She instantly regretted the mention of what would go down as the most embarrassing moment of her life.

Nate gave her a lopsided smile, almost as if he were trying not to laugh. "You're welcome. I hope you got rid of that bikini."

Ani rolled her eyes. "You had to mention it, didn't you?"

He laughed a deep rolling chuckle. "Hey, you were the one who brought it up."

"Something I am now sorry about." She closed her eyes as if blacking it out would make it go away.

Nate chuckled. "I'll change the subject. Did they ever find out who cut the line on the anchor?"

She brightened up at the fresh turn in their conversation. "No. I reported it to the police, but they couldn't do anything about it. Neville's convinced something's going on in the area."

Nate sat forward in his seat. "What sort of something?"

"Apparently there's been a group of fishermen camping on one of the islands. Neville says they have the proper permits, but he feels they may be up to no good. He's keeping a close eye on them."

Nate nodded.

Another long silence.

"Kye, are you ready?" she yelled out.

"Almost," he yelled back.

"Is he excited about today?" Nate glanced at his watch.

"He hasn't spoken about anything else for days." Ani was tired of hearing about Kye's planned trip out on Nate's yacht. He was so obsessed with the event she had used it as leverage to force him to do his school work. She supposed the constant chatter about Nate was one of the reasons he kept popping up in her mind and now, into her dreams. The other reason—that she found him incredibly attractive—wasn't something Ani was about to entertain, or explore.

Nate's eyes sparkled. "I'm excited as well. I can't wait to see his face when we get the Savannah out to sea. It's a beautiful day. Why don't you come?"

"I can't. I have work to do." She blurted out the excuse way too fast.

"I'm sure Yvette will let you take a day off."

The last thing she needed was a full day in his company. She shrugged her shoulders. "Sorry."

"You don't have to wear a swimsuit."

She covered her face with her hands and groaned. "I am never going to live that down."

Nate laughed. "If it's any consolation, I happen to think you look very good in a bikini, even when straddling a floating beacon."

She peeked through her fingers at him. An intense heat engulfed her cheeks as she saw the sparkle in his eyes intensify. She was reluctant to remove her hands from her face, certain she, yet again, radiated beetroot red.

"I'm ready." Kye threw his backpack on the floor and jumped into the spare seat next to Nate. The distraction gave her a chance to escape from Nate's stare.

"Hey, Nate." They greeted each other with some sort of secret handshake.

"All set, buddy?"

Kye nodded. "See you, Kiki." He came over for a hug and a kiss.

"Make sure you do everything Nate tells you."

He rolled his eyes. "I will." Kye grabbed the pack and skipped his way out the door. Nate didn't follow. He looked down at her from his towering position.

"You know," he said, "I think that's the first time you've actually said my name."

She could feel the heat returning, so she took countermeasures and got to her feet. Unfortunately, the action drew their bodies much closer.

"Well, I suppose I can't keep referring to you as 'that bloke', can I?"

He laughed a deep rolling chuckle. "It's good to hear you've upgraded my status."

He still didn't move towards the door. After averting her eyes to every wall in the room, she was finally forced to look at him.

The tiger colors stood out even brighter against

the white of his shirt.

Go away. She tried some telepathy, knowing her unspoken rebuke didn't come anywhere near meeting her eyes.

"Come on, Nate." The impatient voice sounded from outside.

He stepped away and moved to the door. "See you, Ani."

The door shut behind him.

Don't go. She shook her head. *No, no. Go away. Go away.* She fell into the lounge chair.

I am in trouble.

Big, big trouble.

CHAPTER II

Nate took a seat on the beach while he waited for Ani, Yvette and Dutch to join him. Despite the overcast sky, he didn't think it would rain. The forecast for the afternoon was high winds, so a decision had been made to test the tracking devices that morning.

He had been roped into the job by Yvette, who explained it was a difficult task to perform alone. She and Ani had attached tracking devices to dugong in the area, and now they needed to test their effectiveness.

Yvette and her husband, Dutch, would be in one boat, he and Ani in the other.

Nate wondered for a second if Yvette had told Ani about the arrangement. While she had maintained a pleasant demeanor, she was clearly still uneasy in his company.

He got out his cell phone and flicked through the photos. Almost every picture featured Kye. He stopped briefly to smile at one he had taken of the boy at the wheel of the Savannah.

Their trip four weeks ago had been a great adventure. It reminded Nate of the many times his uncle had thrown him aboard as a child and they had set sail. At first he had been surprised at how Kye had taken to the sea, but Amos explained how Anika and Kye's Pacific Islander heritage had provided them both with an affinity with the ocean.

Like any child, Kye needed guidance, and Nate felt a special connection with the boy. They were kindred spirits, alike in many ways. He could relate to Kye's clear desire for a father, as while he also had a devoted uncle, his father had been mostly absent during his childhood.

Nate had pegged the boy as an adventurer. Kye spoke many times of his mother's world map and the places they wanted to visit. He also loved stories, and Nate had marveled at the tales his imagination would conjure up as well as his elaborate descriptions.

He continued through the pictures until he found the one he was looking for. Last week, a group of them had taken the forty-five minute trip into Mackay to visit Bay, Flynn, and their newborn daughter in hospital.

Haven McKenna had come into the world with a bang, two weeks before her due date. The unexpected onset of labor had created a rush to the hospital in the early hours of the morning. Thankfully, all went well and the little strawberry-haired girl had been proclaimed healthy and strong.

Braden had asked Nate to send him a photo of the baby, so he had used his cell phone to get the best picture of the newborn.

He finally found the photo he was looking for. It showed Anika as she cradled the baby. Seconds before Nate had taken the shot, a dark blonde corkscrew curl had fallen over her face. She was so beautiful, a soft smile for the sleeping baby on her lips. Nate kept the photo on the screen so long the power-saver tripped out and he had to retrieve it.

He moved on to the next shot. It was taken seconds after she realized he had a camera pointed at her. Instead of focusing on the baby, her eyes beamed directly down the lens. Their bright blue color was every bit as vibrant in the picture as they were in reality.

That photo had forced Nate to finally admit the intensity of his attraction to her. He had often reminded himself about his resolution to stay away from women, but he couldn't deny that Ani had a potent effect on him.

At first he suspected the attraction was due to her initial hostility. He was unaccustomed to women hating him on sight. It had always been the opposite—they would throw themselves at him. It unnerved his masculinity to have Anika treat him like she had. But he also couldn't explain away the physical reaction she evoked in him, or the way she infiltrated his thoughts on a minute by minute basis.

He had it bad for this woman. It was a real problem because, despite his numerous invitations for her to join them, she always had an excuse to decline. She clearly didn't feel any desire to be in his company.

The morning they went to see the baby he had seriously considered moving on and getting away from Resolution before he did something stupid. But when Yvette had asked him to accompany her he didn't give his answer a second thought. He was between a rock and a hard place, wanting to avoid a relationship, but not being able to stay away.

I am in big, big trouble.

As Yvette, Dutch and Ani approached, he

flipped his phone closed and secured it in his pocket.

Anika gave him a polite, noncommittal, "Good morning."

It looked as though Yvette had told her about his inclusion in the day because she didn't seem particularly surprised or concerned about his presence. Nor did she appear ecstatically happy. The bland greeting irked him. *I can't even get the smallest flirt out of this girl.*

They all walked down to the tinnies tied to one of the floating pontoons.

She turned to him. "I think I'd better drive. I know where we're going."

He nodded.

They settled in and left the bay.

The trip to the site took a little over twenty minutes. Anika powered down the outboard and set up the monitoring equipment. A faint beep sounded from the black box.

"It's picked up a signal, which is good news. It's working, at least. I want to see if we can get a clearer pinpoint. We'll head over that way a bit." She pointed to a dense area of mangrove. "Can you drive?"

Nate made his way to the back of the boat while she moved forward. Their shoulders brushed as they passed. Anika almost jumped the final few feet to the front of the boat.

She really can't get away from me fast enough. He couldn't stem his disappointment.

He pointed the tinny in the direction she indicated and moved off. The beeping intensified as they closed in on the bank.

"Let's go in there." She pointed to a narrow opening in the mangrove.

The waterway snaked into the scrub. At one point it narrowed so drastically Nate wondered how they were going to get out. There was no room to turn the boat around.

He was relieved to see the area open up to reveal a wide circular clearing. One large mangrove tree sat in the middle of the expanse of water. Entrances to several other waterways jutted off at various angles.

Ani jumped to her feet. "Stop the outboard."

Nate did as directed. "What is it?"

"Over there." She pointed at the entrance to one of the larger waterways. "It's another illegal net."

Nate could now see floats marked with red crosses bobbing in the water as they held the net in place.

"The signal is in this area. Can you give Neville a call and tell him where we are? I'm going to stick my head under the water and see if the dugong's caught up in the net."

She had her shirt off before he could say anything, to display a distracting one-piece bathing suit. While it was more modest and better fitting than the bikini, it was still designed to show off her perfectly formed assets.

He swallowed hard and shook himself out of it. "I don't think it's a good idea to go jumping into the water."

Kye had relayed the story of the crocodile several times, with far too much enthusiasm.

She stopped to look around before removing her shorts. He had to swallow again.

"It's okay. I'll only be down there for a few seconds. I have to make sure the animal isn't caught, or it could drown."

"Then let me go. You stay here." She stopped to look at him as he removed his shirt.

"No ..." She didn't finish her protest because the blipping on the tracking device decreased, only to regain strength.

Ani sat back down to fiddle with the buttons on the monitor. "The dugong's moving." She looked up at him. "So at least it isn't caught in the net."

He picked up his cell phone to call Neville. He answered in two rings.

"Neville, it's Nate. We've discovered another illegal net." He gave their exact location before disconnecting the call.

"Neville's leaving Resolution now. I think we should sit up in that break to wait for him." He pointed to the small opening on the opposite side of the water. "Then, if whoever set this net comes back, they won't see us."

Anika nodded. "Good thinking."

The hole was a dead end. It was overgrown with mangrove and made the perfect hiding spot. Nate ensured they were out of sight and secured the tinny while Ani made some adjustments to the tracking equipment.

She took her time organizing the equipment, then reached over to retrieve her clothing off the floor of the tinny. Nate was relieved she was going to cover back up. The black fabric of the one-piece suit shone in the sun, casting distinct lights off every enticing curve.

He retrieved his t-shirt to do the same and was in the process of correcting the inside-out state of the garment, when the sound of a motor starting close by caused them both to freeze. Neither of them had managed to finish dressing.

"This can't be Neville," Ani whispered. She looked at her watch. "It's only been about fifteen minutes since we called him. No way he's gotten over here this quick."

Nate nodded and assessed their position. They were well camouflaged by the trees, but still had a relatively good view of the net and clearing. If they kept quiet, they could get away with spying on whoever came by.

They heard the burr of the outboard grow louder. It looked as though the boat was progressing up one of the larger paths, travelling at a fast pace.

Ani and Nate ducked behind foliage as the boat drew near. Whoever was driving the tinny drew back the engine to an idle. It still wasn't within sight.

All of a sudden several loud pops sounded from the same direction as the approaching tinny, followed by a whizzing noise directly above their heads. Nate recognized the sound. He threw himself at her, tackling her to the floor of the tinny. They hit the bottom with a heavy thud. A loud "oof," sounded from her, followed by a yelp of protest.

Ani looked in the air. "What was that?"

One more pop went off followed by the whizzing, lower than the first two.

"Shh. Be quiet," he whispered into her ear.

She forced her body to go still in his arms. "What is it?" Her voice was low and shaky.

"Gunfire."

"What?" She had forgotten to whisper.

"Shh. Keep quiet."

She did as she was told. The idling sound of the outboard continued for a few minutes, more than enough time for Nate to become aware of Anika's body pressed up against his.

The sudden heightening of engine revs pulled him out of his distraction. The tinny was heading their way. He could hear the quick increase and decrease of the outboard as the driver negotiated the twists and turns in the creek. The boat was travelling at full speed.

The tinny entered the clearing and stopped. Within seconds it was on the move again.

Nate pulled himself up.

"What are you doing?" Ani grabbed his arm as he rose.

He got up high enough to see over the edge of their tinny. The other boat had gone. He sat up further and tried to get a look at the driver as the boat disappeared into the mangroves. He made out a flash of white hair.

He looked back at Ani. She had let go of his arm and was curled up on the floor in a semi-fetal position. Her face was covered by her hands.

Nate sat back down next to her. "He's gone. I think it's safe to get up."

She didn't move. "Are you sure?" The words were muffled by her covered face.

He placed a hand on her shoulder and felt a tremor. "You're shaking."

She removed one hand from her face. One bright

blue eye stared at him. "Well, someone's shooting at me. Of course I'm shaking. I'm freaking out."

"The shots weren't going to hit us. If anything, it was only to scare us. I'm not even certain they were meant for us."

She removed the other hand and looked up at him. "How do you know?"

"The shots were fired well above our heads. If they wanted to hit us, the aim would have been much lower. Trust me. I've fired lots of guns."

"Really?" She sounded as though she didn't believe him.

"I grew up on a ranch. I've been shooting since I was younger than Kye."

Her face contorted in horror. "That's really dangerous, Nate."

He couldn't help but grin.

She didn't take his amusement well. Her chin jutted out with an indignant bump, but her eyes still held a haze of fear.

"Don't you dare laugh at me." The words were harsh but her tone was petrified.

"Oh, Ani, I'm sorry. Come here." He pulled her into his arms and held her tight. She rested her head against his chest.

"I won't let anything happen to you."

She was still, apart from a small nod. He bent his chin to feel her curls touch his lips. She made no move to pull free from his embrace, so he continued to hold her. Within seconds the noise of a boat forced them apart.

"Nate? Ani?" Neville's call came from the main channel.

"Through here." Nate turned and yelled in his direction.

"Righto."

He could hear the boat making its way through the same narrow opening they had entered through.

There was a pink tinge to the corners of Ani's eyes, but the fear had gone.

Nate gave her what he hoped was a reassuring smile. She managed to reciprocate.

"Okay?"

She closed her eyes and slowly nodded.

He acted without thinking, reaching out and pulling her back to him. She wrapped her arms around his waist and leant her head against his chest. Nothing but the shiny fabric of her swimsuit separated their skin.

Nate felt his body act in opposition to his resolve. He wanted more and, if circumstance had allowed, he wouldn't have hesitated taking their physical contact to a higher level. As it was, the loud burble of an outboard forced them apart. Neville was in the clearing.

CHAPTER 12

Ani took the first spare table she could see. The coffee shop was busy with lunchtime customers. Nate took the seat opposite, and set about sugaring his coffee.

"It's been over a week. I still can't believe the police haven't mounted a full search of the area where we were shot at," she said.

From the information Nate had given them, the police had concluded that the white-haired man was Bert. When they went to question the trawler owner, they discovered he had disappeared.

Nate frowned. "They think he was to blame for the gunshots and is on the run. They also suspect he was setting the nets. Apparently, Bert's professional netting license had expired, but it's possible he still has old nets on hand. The police told me the fish caught in the nets bring in a good deal of untraceable revenue, and Bert's wife has recently purchased several large items with cash. Their theory is that Bert let off some the warning shots to scare us out of the area." Nate stopped to sip his coffee.

"Of course it's all theory until they find him and bring him in for questioning. Bert's wife claims she has no idea where he is, and Coot hasn't seen him in days."

Ani looked around the coffee shop. "I guess there isn't anything more we can do but wait." She shook her head. "I can't help thinking there's more to it."

The clatter of coffee cups broke through their conversation.

She had been forced to bring Kye into town for a scheduled visit with Mayfield. It was the eighth visit since the court hearing, but the process hadn't become any easier for her.

It irked her no end that Mayfield and his personal assistant, Sarah Rhodes, were at that moment attempting to buy her son's love in the hobby shop across the street. She glanced out the window once more to see if they had finished.

"They can't be much longer." Nate had noticed her frustration.

Ani checked her watch for what seemed like the millionth time. She looked over at Neville, who sat in a dark corner with her solicitor. A schoolgirl giggle escaped Marlee's lips as Neville leaned in to whisper something to her.

After she had relayed Marlee's greeting to her cousin, he had insisted on accompanying her to appointments. It had been clear from the second they had seen each other that a spark of romance still flickered between them, and they had been out on several dates together. Now, Neville didn't miss a chance to tag along on any trip to town, in order to see Marlee.

Anika rolled her eyes at the sight of them.

"They're taken with each other." Nate grinned, as he too looked over at their loved-up exchange.

"He wants her to come out to Resolution for the kapmauri next month." She fiddled with her teaspoon.

"What exactly is a kapmauri? I heard it's a bit like

a Hawaiian luau."

"It's a traditional feast. All the food is cooked in the ground with hot coals. Apparently the resort puts on two a year." She put the teaspoon down and placed her hands firmly in her lap.

"Sounds like it's going to be a real experience." Nate picked the spoon up and used it to stir his coffee.

"So you'll be hanging around for a while?" She tried to make the question sound nonchalant, but wasn't sure she had succeeded. Thankfully, Nate didn't notice the quiver in her voice.

"I'll definitely be here. My uncle's paying me a visit." He looked at her over the rim of his cup before taking a sip. "So you're stuck with me for a bit longer."

Ani couldn't exactly pinpoint how she felt about that. The attraction aspect was fully satisfied, while her old self-preservation instincts screamed at him to go. She recognized the lie and told those old instincts they were no longer required.

"I'm sure you'll find plenty to do." She squirmed in her seat.

"Yvette's asked me if I can accompany you on the daily dugong tracking trips." His cautious look suggested he was sounding out her opinion.

This was the first she had heard of the plan. She twisted her napkin. It was bad enough that they had been thrown together once. Her sanity wouldn't survive a daily jaunt. Eventually he would leave. She couldn't see any real future for anything more than a casual friendship between them.

"I thought Neville was going to help me."

Nate put down his cup. "Apparently he's had to pull out. I think he may want to be free to head into town if the opportunity arises."

She glanced over at the couple and then reached up to rub the back of her neck. *That'll teach me for playing matchmaker.* She couldn't perform the tracking on her own. If she didn't come up with another option, she was stuck with Nate. How frustrating. *Thanks, Neville.*

"At least Marlee might distract Neville enough to stop him talking about the rest of us." She had discovered her cousin had filled Nate in on her entire life.

Nate picked up the last biscuit. "Don't be too hard on him. He's not malicious, and he has your best interests at heart."

"That's easy for you to say. You know everything about me. I don't know anything about you."

He wiped his mouth with a napkin. "What do you what to know?"

Everything. The thought pulled her up. She froze for a second to check she hadn't said it out loud.

"I'll reveal all, in the interests of fairness." A cheeky grin spread over his face.

"Okay." She considered the best way to take advantage of his offer. "I guess you'd need to start from the beginning, like where you were born."

"Wow, you really want my whole life story?"

"It's only fair, seeing as you know mine."

He shrugged in defeat and then launched into the facts of his life.

At the end of his story, Anika was surprised to learn that regardless of all the wealth, Nate had suffered hardships like the rest of them. Their discussion about faith had also been an amazing discovery. Although Nate had come from a very different background to hers, faith was something they shared.

"Your mother sounds as though she was a wonderful person." She had particularly enjoyed his description of her. She could see her death was still raw for him.

"She was." He looked away. His eyes emitted warmth as they reclaimed hers. "She would have loved you."

Ani could feel the heat in her cheeks. *Change the subject.*

"So you didn't mention any girlfriends?" *Oh, great subject change!* Was she ever going to not say the wrong thing to this guy?

He sat back in his seat. "Well, none worth mentioning."

She itched to ask why, but the fact she had brought it up was bad enough. She looked out the window. Kye was walking out of the shop.

"Here they come." She got to her feet and grabbed her handbag.

Nate signaled to Neville.

They exited the cafe as the others stepped onto the pavement. Mayfield was carrying a plastic bag.

"Hey, Nate, check out this." Kye pulled a die-cast model car out of the bag. "Isn't it cool? Grandad collects them. He's got hundreds in his place in Sydney."

Nate bent down to his level and examined the toy. "That's a real beauty."

Anika noticed that, although Mayfield was stone still, he had ventured closer to her than ever before. He usually stood well away, sending Sarah to fetch and deliver Kye.

Nate straightened up and extended his hand to Mayfield. "Nathanial Hollingsworth."

Mayfield hesitated before having the decency to step forward and extend his own. "Mitchell Mayfield." His voice was hash and to the point, as though he wanted to get the introduction over with.

As the two men separated, Nate squared his posture, pulled himself up to full height and looked the older man in the eye. He stood almost a head taller than Mayfield.

"We may share a mutual acquaintance." Nate took a small step forward.

"Oh, who might that be?" Mayfield's grin was snide and dismissive.

"Raymond Fry is a friend of my father's. I understand he is a well-known family court barrister here in Queensland."

A frown appeared on Mayfield's forehead. "Who's your father?"

"Nathanial Jackson-Hollingsworth the Fourth. We own the biggest family law firm in the state of Texas."

Mayfield's mouth opened slightly to join his dipping eyebrows. This was the first time she had seen the man show any significant emotion. The fact that he was visibly rattled gave Ani great satisfaction.

"Kye told me you were a yachtie."

Nate ruffled the boy's hair. "Not exactly. I've taken a year off from the family firm to do some touring up the coast."

Mayfield glanced back at Sarah, who looked equally stunned.

"So you're a lawyer?"

A slow, tight smile spread across Nate's face. "That's right. Mostly mergers and acquisitions. Amazing the people you come across, isn't it?"

Mayfield licked his lips. "Yes, it is."

Nate turned to Kye and bent down to put an arm around his shoulders. "Well, we'd better get going if we want to get back in time for some fishing."

Kye nodded enthusiastically.

Ani thought about those same arms holding her only days ago. She had felt so safe and protected that she hadn't wanted to leave them. It made her realize she had missed being held for a very long time. Now she yearned to feel his arms around her again.

"See you next time." Kye waved to Mayfield and Sarah, who looked at each other with baffled expressions.

As they walked away, the words Nate had spoken to her that day came back. *I won't let anything happen to you.*

It would be so easy to fall back on this man's strength, to rely on him to be her champion, as he had shown her he could be.

He'll be gone in a month. The thought pushed to the surface. He would be gone, and she would be left alone. Again. She would be forced to rediscover the strength to keep going. He couldn't be her rescuer, no matter how much she wanted him to be.

She had no choice but to find a way to keep Nate Hollingsworth at arm's length, both physically and emotionally. Which was hard, because apart from her desire to be close to him, she couldn't stop him from infiltrating her thoughts or her dreams.

"That's Jill done. Now to find Joe," Nate said as he pulled up the anchor rope and moved off in the direction of their next target. They made daily trips with the tide each morning to collect data on the movements of the dugong. To make the job easier they had named each one in order to distinguish between them. After several weeks' work, he had come to know the process by heart.

They had travelled a good distance when he powered down the outboard. They were in Joe's general stomping ground.

Anika adjusted the tracking device. "Why is this guy the hardest to find?" she groaned. "And he's always the last."

Nate revved the outboard. "Maybe we'll get lucky this time and he'll be in an easy part of the estuary."

She looked up from her clipboard. "I bet you anything you want that he isn't."

"Anything?" His interest piqued.

Anika tried to ignore him by fiddling with the clip on top of the board.

"Anything I want. Hmm. This could be interesting." He rubbed his chin and pretended to consider the bet.

She stopped to look up and give him a withering look. "Perhaps I need to redefine the anything. How about I give you a million dollars if we find him within thirty minutes?"

Yet again, she had successfully avoided a personal response.

Since they had been taking these trips, she had been careful not to engage in any romantic innuendo with Nate. Their time together consisted of business mixed with friendly banter, as well as the occasional heart-to-heart. After some gentle probing she had opened up about the challenges she had faced. To his surprise he had found himself doing the same.

She had also admitted to having read his online column. It pleased him when she praised his work. Knowing she had shown an interest in him was satisfying.

Nate shook his head. "I don't need the money." He had a better idea. "How about this? If we find Joe within thirty minutes, then you and Kye have to come and spend a night with me on the Savannah."

She raised her eyebrows. "I already told him he could go sometime with uncle."

Nate shook his head. "Not with Amos. With you."

She squinted at him. "Why me?"

For a million reasons. Nate decided he wouldn't list the personal ones. "Because you keep turning down my offers, and I want to show you my boat."

She picked up a pen and clicked the top button up and down. He'd noticed it was something she did when she was nervous.

There was no doubt he had come to know her much better, and he found Neville's description of her was entirely accurate. She was smart and funny, as well as strong-willed. The lack of physical contact in their relationship had done nothing to stem his desire for her. If anything, the developing friendship between them increased his compulsion to be with her.

"Okay, but what's in it for me? Odds are in my favor you know. We've never found Joe within thirty minutes." She stopped clicking to squint at him.

"I'll give you a million dollars if we don't." He lifted one corner of his mouth at his copycat reply.

She shrugged one shoulder and screwed up her face. "I don't need the money."

He laughed loudly, knowing her smart reply was also honest. She didn't need or want his money. In fact, money and all the things he could buy her weren't the least bit attractive to her. The size of his bank account, his prestigious birthright, and his power didn't appeal to her pursuit of happiness one iota. This knowledge threw him for a second.

"Well, what do you want?"

She placed her clipboard on the seat next to her. "If I win, you never ask me to go on your boat again." She uncrossed and recrossed her legs.

A wave of indignation rose within him. "Why do you hate my boat so much?"

"I don't hate your boat." She leaned back in her seat.

"Well, you must still hate me then." He focused on her face.

"No, I don't."

"Then why do you always turn me down?"

She opened her mouth but no sound came out.

Blip. Blip. Blip. The tracker sprung to life. It had picked up Joe.

She adjusted the settings. "No way."

Nate experienced an overwhelming sense of satisfaction.

Anika shaded her eyes and studied the bank. She peered at one particular spot. "I don't believe it. Over there." She pointed to a break in the trees. "Doesn't this guy ever run out of nets?"

Nate could see the net as it attached to each side of the gap. The middle floats holding the net in place were missing.

"It looks like it's been cut."

Anika sighed. "Or something's tangled in it and weighing it down. Can you get in a bit closer so we can check it out?"

"Are you sure you want to go in there? You don't want to head back and leave it to Neville?" He was reminded of the last time they had checked out an illegal net. Even though the previous incident had occurred a long way from their current position, he didn't want the gunfire that had sounded over their head last time to be aimed any closer this time.

She gave the question some thought before answering. "We'll check it out quickly, and then call Neville."

He nodded. "Promise me you won't jump in the water."

Ani rolled her eyes and lifted one hand. "I promise."

They moved into the net.

The blips on the tracker stopped.

"If something's caught up in there, it isn't Joe. He's left the area." She leaned over the side to pull on the net.

"Here. Hold us steady and I'll do it." Nate stood to swap places with her.

Ani sat at the back and took hold of a part of the net sitting above water while Nate reached over and grabbed the top. He pulled hard.

"Whatever it is, it's heavy." He had several feet of net out of the water when the top of a human head surfaced, along with the back and shoulders.

Nate dropped the net like it was on fire. It slowly receded into the water, along with the corpse.

"What was it?"

He swung around to her. She hadn't seen it.

"A body. Call the police."

Her face went as pale as a ghost, a color reflecting his own, he was sure.

She scrambled for her mobile phone.

Nate looked back down at the water, trying to clear the vision of the white hair and prominent tattoo adorning the man's back in elaborate lettering: Mary-Jane.

CHAPTER 13

"So Anika, have the police have found anything in the area where you found Bert?" Bay gently adjusted the baby to sit higher on her shoulder.

"Nothing, except the net he was trapped in. Not even a tinny." Anika pushed her hair back from her face as a gust of wind blew in from the ocean. "But they still haven't bothered conducting a full search of the area where we heard the shots. They're certain Bert was doing the netting. Apparently he also needed the money. One of the detectives told Nate the body showed no sign of injury. They've concluded Bert was the one who shot at us, and then he drowned when putting in his next net."

Bay patted Haven on the back. "Makes sense."

"But Nate's not convinced. He thinks whoever fired the gun was doing so from an elevated position. Bert was in a tinny on the water. Besides, makes no sense that a croc didn't take the body."

A war cry sounded from the beach a few meters away. The kapmauri had started earlier in the day with the construction of the ground oven that would cook the fresh catch. When the preparations were done, they had all decided to take a break from work.

Ani had formally met Nate's Uncle Braden. The Texan had arrived that morning to visit his nephew, as well as catch up with Bay, Flynn and the family.

Now Nate and Braden set about teaching everyone how to play American football.

She and Bay opted to sit the game out, preferring a comfortable chair at the top of the beach.

Haven let out a delicate burp. "That's my girl." Bay kissed her cheek.

"She's so good. You're so blessed." Ani reached over to run a finger along the baby's soft little hand.

"She's a real joy."

Shadows formed in front of them as Flynn approached from the beach. "How are my girls?"

"All ready for bed." Bay reached down to gather up a few things at the side of her chair.

"Here." He took the load from her and helped her to her feet. "I'll come up with you."

"Hey, Ani, we need you to come in for Flynn," Neville called from the makeshift field they had marked out in the sand.

She shook her head and tucked her legs up under her. "No, I'm way too delicate."

A chorus of laughter broke out from the field. "You are not, Kiki. You wrestle with me all the time. And Sam's playing." Kye pointed to Bay's sister-in-law on the opposite team.

Samara and her husband, Jed—Flynn's brother—had travelled down from their home on Thursday Island to meet their new niece. Anika had enjoyed getting to know Samara, and liked her and Jed very much.

"Come on, Ani. We need help." Samara waved her hand for her to join their team.

Samara, Jed, and Braden formed one team. Nate, Neville, Amos, and Dutch were the opposition. Kye had insisted upon being in Nate's team, but was pandered to rather than being an active member of the game. Nate's side currently held a huge lead.

A chorus of encouragement broke out from the group. Ani could see she had no choice but to comply. "Okay, but I can assure you I will be completely useless." She reluctantly made her way down the beach to join them.

Her team mates huddled up as Braden explained the game plan.

"I'll pass it to Ani. They won't expect that."

"No way. I don't know what to do."

"Catch it and run towards those." Braden pointed to the two sticks marking the goal line at the opposite end of the field.

She had liked Nate's uncle very much up until then.

"This is a really bad idea, guys." She glanced at each face in an effort to make one last plea for exclusion.

"I think it'll work." Jed nodded.

"Me, too." His wife backed him up.

Anika gave Samara an intense frown. "Traitor."

Samara smiled broadly at her.

They broke and took their positions.

It was all going to plan. She had the ball and was running for the line. She picked out a clear path when a large shape approached from her side and collided with her. It was as though she had hit a brick wall. Strong arms engulfed her, lifting her off her feet and stopping her in her tracks.

The tackling rules had been downgraded for Samara and Kye. Instead of bringing them to the ground, the men would grab and hold them. Ani had completely overlooked the fact that this technique could result in a close physical encounter with Nate.

She protested, but he held fast, and wasn't letting go. Ani took evasive measures, stamping down hard on his foot.

"Ow." He released his hold.

She jumped away and raced for the line to score a touchdown.

Loud cheers broke out from her team mates. Nate rubbed his foot while trying to maintain his balance.

Braden laughed long and loud. "I wonder what your old high school coach would make of that play, Nate, my boy."

"No fair." Kye crossed his arms and pouted.

"I agree, Kye." Nate limped down the field.

Anika walked over and handed him the ball. "Sorry, you took me by surprise."

Nate set his eyes on her as he juggled the ball from hand to hand in a threatening motion. "You are going down."

Anika couldn't help the smile spreading across her face.

She managed to avoid being a part of the next few plays.

"This will have to be the last one. We've got work to do." Dutch gestured towards the increasing activity around the kapmauri.

The team huddled up.

"I say we pass it to Ani again." Braden outlined his plan.

Jed grinned. "Great game plan. Win by taking the other team out." Sam smacked him playfully. He retaliated by tugging her long ponytail.

Ani shook her head in protest. "Do not give that thing to me again." The last thing she wanted was to be in the firing line of Nate's arms. A scene from the dream she had last night flashed into her mind. The slumber movies had become increasingly frequent, and she rarely went a night without Nate intruding upon her sleep. She flatly refused to give them additional ammunition by throwing herself in Nate's path. "I'm out."

It was agreed that Braden would pass it to Jed.

They broke and started the play. Right from the beginning it went wrong. Dutch tackled Jed, and everyone but Ani was covered. She found herself with the ball.

It was such a shock that she paused.

"Run!" Braden yelled to her.

She ran, but had only progressed a few meters when Nate appeared in front of her, grabbed her around the waist and pulled her down.

They landed with his body half covering hers, and the other half on the sand. His arms firmly held her to him, and their legs intertwined.

A huge grin filled his face. "Sorry. Are you okay?" The sparkle in his eyes suggested he was anything but.

Ani lifted a hand to wipe sand off her lips. "I guess I deserved that." The humor of the situation overcame her and she laughed.

Nate released his grip to brush some more sand from her cheek. Ani could feel his breath against her skin, his lips only centimeters away from her own. She tried not to look at him, sputtering at the sand in her mouth and focusing instead on the shoreline of the Island across the bay.

She expected him to let her go, but he did the opposite. The arm remaining underneath her tightened, pulling her body towards his. The conflicting action shocked her and she turned to frown at him.

There was no mistaking the desire in his eyes and, for a second, Anika knew hers mirrored the emotion.

"Are you okay, Kiki?" A small face above theirs commanded attention. Kye grinned when he saw she was fine. He let out a war cry and dived on them, straddling both their bodies.

Nate laughed, but Ani had the wind knocked out of her. "Kye, get off."

He threw his little arms around them. "Group hug!" There was no choice but to endure the affection. She eventually gained her freedom by tickling him.

She broke free and stumbled to her feet. Nate and Kye remained on the sand, wrestling each other. The sight of their rough-and-tumble brought a lump to her throat.

It was plain to see her son was completely devoted to Nate. Kye would be devastated when he eventually sailed away.

I will be, too.

The shock of her admission brought overwhelming emotion bubbling to the surface.

What am I going to do?

The kapmauri was a great success. The entire

resort had mobilized to produce an outstanding meal of seafood and quality meats. Several guests had commented to Anika about the wonderful time they'd had, as had many of the locals who attended.

The weather had been perfect. There was a cool change in the air that cut through the humidity. The full moon shone brightly, casting flecks of light on peaks of water, and forming a golden highway that trailed all the way to the shore. The moderate waves rolling in didn't overwhelm the sound of the traditional Island music.

Amos's brother had travelled from the mainland to play the guitar, and his wife and daughters danced and sang. Anika joined them in between assisting with the logistics of the event.

As the night drew to a close, only a small group was left, mostly those who lived on the island, along with Nate and Braden, and a few of the locals who had come over by boat. Anika could see Kye fast asleep on a blanket next to Nate. They all formed a cozy circle around the fire.

Anika watched three men who had arrived late. They sat to one side under some coconut trees, drinking cheap beer and getting louder and louder. They were all dressed tidily enough in t-shirts and shorts, but their unshaven faces and greasy hair gave them each an unkempt look.

She jumped as one of them fell to the ground. The other two laughed at his antics.

"Who are those clowns?" Flynn and Dutch stood to glare at them. Neville stood and joined them. "Those three fishermen who were camping over on Tanner Island. They took off a few weeks ago, but I saw they were back yesterday."

Dutch frowned. "Bit of a strange place to camp. There are no facilities, and it's a long way from the mainland. Besides, it's an awful spot when a south-easterly blows. Why set up there?"

Neville shuffled his feet. "Don't know. It's a bit shady. I've been watching them."

One of the men threw a bottle against a coconut tree.

"Oy, settle down!" Flynn yelled over to them.

They stopped their revelry to glance over. "No worries. Sorry, mate," one yelled back.

The most inebriated of the group pointed to Ani. His hand swayed as he tried to focus on her. "Hey, there's my little blonde chick. Why don't you come over here and talk to us?"

Ani ignored him.

He turned back to his friends. "She doesn't wanna talk to us. She's probably with that Yank. She must be a right proper ..." A flow of curse words exited his mouth.

"Shut up, will ya." One of the men didn't appreciate his friend's antics.

Ani had heard much worse from drunks, especially when living with her mother, but she was irritated by this fool and his insults.

She wasn't the only one. All the men in the group got to their feet. Nate took several steps towards the group before Flynn reached out and placed an open hand on his chest. "We'll get rid of them. Can you take Ani and Kye back to their cabin?"

Nate eyeballed the men for a moment before nodding.

Ani collected her things in preparation to go, even though she wasn't thrilled with the plan. Nate picked up the sleeping Kye, and indicated they should leave.

Flynn and Dutch approached the group.

"Time to go. Who's sober enough to drive?"

One put up his hand. "I've only had a couple of beers. Come on boys, let's head off." He started off to the pontoon where their tinny was tied.

The voice of the drunken buffoon was faint, but Ani could still hear his comment. "I could've jumped her heaps of times when she was cruisin' around."

His statement made her uneasy. She couldn't recall ever having seen any of those men.

They reached the cabin and she opened the door for Nate. He went through and placed Kye in his bed, pulling the sheet over him and tucking him in. He hadn't stirred.

Anika made an abrupt turn, taking a direct line to the front door. "Thanks. He would have been a heavy load to carry over that distance."

Nate didn't follow her. He stopped at the couch and put a hand on the back of it. "I hope those idiots didn't upset you."

She lifted one corner of her mouth. "I've heard far worse, trust me."

Nate frowned. "I'm sorry to hear that."

She had caught him staring at her several times through the night and noted how the dark green color of his shirt highlighted his eyes. The effect was still present, even in the soft light of the cabin.

He rubbed the top of the couch and smiled. "You have a beautiful voice."

She rolled her eyes. "I'm a bit rusty. When I was on Thursday Island we would sing all day and night. We had a song for every job. We didn't live there for long, but it was one of the things I loved about being there. One of the rare good childhood memories."

She knew she was babbling. She placed a hand on the door, and made a dramatic show of faking a yawn. "I'm really tired. It's been a long day."

Nate patted the top of the couch and looked at his feet before moving to her. "I suppose that's my cue to leave."

She leaned away from him as he passed. He turned around at the door, one foot still inside the cabin.

He was so close she could smell his aftershave, a heady mixture of spice and salt. She struggled to regulate her shallow breathing, not knowing what course of action to take in order to put some distance between their bodies.

His focus went from her eyes to her lips and back to lock on her. His eyebrows slanted down in a slight frown. "Why do you always push me away?"

She turned to stare at her finger as it rapidly tapped the top of the door handle. *Don't look at him.*

She fought to conjure up a witty response. Time slipped by as his gaze remained fixed on her. She searched her mind for an answer that would satisfy him, as well as get him out of the cabin.

She could feel her breathing deepen, and her heart rate thumping in her ears. *I won't look at him.* She had no clue what to do next.

One finger touched the tip of her chin forcing her to respond. She tilted her head towards him in response to the pressure.

Ani knew her eyes would give her away, and her need for him would be obvious. He consulted them for a bare second before grabbing her waist and pulling her close.

His lips lingered millimeters away from her own before, with a mere whisper, they gently touched hers. His body warmth enveloped her as he pressed in. Her hands reached up to encircle his neck. She had no inclination to resist, no desire to pull away.

Lips met hers once more, this time with a promise of forever. The kiss sent tingles down her spine as she responded with every bit of her own longing for him. It seemed to last seconds, minutes, hours. As they moved to part Ani couldn't bear to have it end. This was what her entire being had yearned for—to have him touch her, kiss her, hold her. She reached down to touch his chest. Her hand splayed over the contours of his body.

He pulled her to him again and kissed her hard. She reached up to run her fingers through the hair on the back of his head. It was almost as though some unknown remote control button on her body had been activated. Her desire for him, and what it meant to be in his arms, completely overrode any sense of reason.

Suddenly he lifted her up so her feet didn't touch the ground. He moved into the cabin and slid the door closed with his foot, all without taking his mouth off hers.

Anika pulled back to regain her breath, then closed her eyes as his lips made their way down her neck. Her hips involuntarily thrust into his as he lifted the hem of her polo shirt. His hands were warm on her skin, probing the flesh of her waist. She copied his movements, lifting his shirt and caressing the curve of his lower back.

The soft flow of his mouth and hands increased in unison, becoming more and more demanding. She couldn't help but follow his lead. It was only when he paused to remove his shirt that the realization of what they were about to do hit home.

What am I doing?

Nate grabbed her to him again, his bare chest hard against her palms. His lips explored the soft skin behind her ear, and he pushed her shirt up further. She fought the desire to give in.

"Nate." Her voice was unnatural to her ears.

She balled her fists in an attempt to stiffen her body against him. "Nate, stop." It was so hard to say the words.

He paused.

"Stop. Please."

He pulled back without releasing her from his arms. His tiger eyes pleaded with her to withdraw her protest.

She closed her eyes so she didn't have to see him. Her balled fists pushed at his chest so hard he had no choice but to let her go.

When she opened her eyes he was reaching to the floor to retrieve his shirt. He pulled it back over his head.

He ran a hand through his hair in a disjointed motion. "Ani, I'm so sorry. I just ..." He sighed. "I got carried away." His chest heaved through the material of his shirt. "I want you."

His statement pulled her up. *He wants me? He wants me? Not, he loves me, he cares for me, or he can't live without me? Just, he wants me?*

Anger swept over her. Heath had wanted her, and look what happened the second he had her.

She tried to swallow the lump in her throat. "So that's it?" Rage stirred a melting pot of bile in her stomach. "You just want me?"

His eyes widened as if he had been caught out in a misdemeanor. "Hey, I didn't mean it like that."

She stepped back, placing some much-needed distance between them.

"How did you mean it? A few cuddles and kisses and she'll fall into bed with me? That goes completely against my faith."

"No. That's not what I want. It's not what I meant." Nate looked affronted.

Ani crossed her arms. "You wanted to know why I always push you away. It's because you don't have the right to take what you want from me, and then leave without a second thought. You're going to have your fun and sail away. I have a child, Nate." She waved a hand in the direction of Kye's bedroom. "A child, whose entire happiness rests on my ability to make good decisions. How do you think it's going to be for him when you leave?"

"I don't have any plans to leave, Ani."

He reached for her but she pulled further away. "Maybe not today, but what about tomorrow? In a week, a month? Eventually you will leave, and you'll leave us behind. That's not something I need in my life."

She knew she wouldn't cope. She had to put an

end to this attraction before it got out of hand, and out of her control. For Kye's sake, if not for her own.

Nate opened his mouth but then closed it again.

He took a step towards her then stopped. "Ani, I ... It's not what you think. It's not like that."

A sharp, short huff sounded from her lips. "Then tell me, Nate. How is it?"

He shuffled his feet and shook his head. When he looked back at her his eyes showed confusion. "To be honest, I don't know exactly."

His words hurt. *What did you expect? A confession of undying love?* It was ridiculous. What did she want from him? Ani had to admit, like Nate, she didn't know.

She grabbed hold of the edge of the sofa beside her and rubbed her eyes with her palm. The lump in her throat was returning.

Nate ignored the distance she had placed between them, and moved towards her. He grabbed hands and held them in both of his.

"I don't know where this is heading, but I do know I have never in my life felt this way about anyone." His voice was soft, and his words did nothing to strengthen her resolve.

She had managed to avoid his eyes by focusing on a spot on the floor, but when he released her hands to tilt up her chin she had no choice but to look directly at him.

The dull light of the cabin cast soft shadows over his face. "We'll take the time to work this out." His grip on her jaw tightened. "Okay?"

She nodded as best she could under the forced constraint. "I think I need some time to think."

He pulled her to him and placed a soft kiss on her forehead before releasing her and stepping away.

"Ok. I promise I'll give you some time."

He was out the door before she could respond.

She sank into the cushions of the sofa. *What am I going to do?*

CHAPTER 14

Nate sat on the back of the Savannah, a hot cup of coffee in his hand. Tinges of blue sky crept through the dawn grey, suggesting the day would be fine. A flurry on the surface of the water sounded to his right as a predator chased bait fish, no doubt seeking a tasty breakfast. Loud cackles of a kookaburra broke over the water from the island. The shore was peaceful, and the beach vacant in the early morning. The occasional wisp of smoke rose in the air, emitting a streak of grey from last night's fire.

Nate lifted his legs to settle on an adjacent chair. If only he could rewind last night and do it all over again. There was so much he would have done differently. There was no doubt he had lost control. He had allowed the pull of his physical attraction for Anika to take priority over his reasoning.

But no matter how many alternative scenarios existed, there was always the same problem.

He thought he knew his mind. Clearly, he was drawn to Anika, and wanted to be with her, but he could now see he hadn't had the wisdom to think beyond that. Ani was right about his intentions going against their shared faith. He had allowed himself to lose sight of God's expectations and as a result he had completely blown it.

You're an idiot. He ran a hand through his hair and cringed at his foolishness. Raw desire was one thing. A considered relationship was another, and this one came as a package deal.

A child was involved. Any relationship he and Ani had involved Kye simply by his very existence.

Nate closed his eyes and breathed in the morning air. He hadn't slept a wink. The problems he sought to make sense of battled all night with the memory of her lips, her body, the way she had held him.

Then his thoughts progressed past the physical. He contemplated his life moving on from Resolution. How would it feel to wake up every morning knowing he wouldn't see her that day? Or Kye? To experience a whole day without conversation with her, or a chance to run an idea for a column by her, as he had become accustomed to doing lately.

All at once the situation overwhelmed him. *What do I do, God? Where should I go from here?*

This was unchartered territory for him. Never before had a woman so infiltrated his life. Sure, plenty had come and gone. He had even been semi-serious about a few, but the emotions raging in his soul were all new, and more than a bit scary. None of his previous relationships had come with a ready-made family.

Before Kye, he had limited experience with children. He had always thought fatherhood was something he would eventually get around to in life, but he didn't have a set time frame. He had always enjoyed his single status, free to go and do as he pleased without encumbrance or responsibility. Yet here he was, not prepared to pull up anchor and move on because of the way he felt about a child and his mother.

Nate downed the last of his coffee. He could see

Amos getting into one of the tinnies tied to the floating pontoon and head out in Nate's direction. It was a short drive to the back of the Savannah.

"Morning." He got to his feet to secure the rope.

"Hey, Nate." Amos stepped aboard.

"Feel like a coffee? Uncle Brae's still asleep." His uncle was staying with him on the yacht. Thankfully, he had retired before Nate had returned from the island last night.

"No, thanks. I wanted to talk to you."

His curiosity sparked. Amos wasn't one for formalities.

"Take a seat." Nate indicated the spare chair.

Amos settled before proceeding. "What I'm going say is none of my business, but I got to say it." He rubbed the stubble on his chin. "You're a good bloke, Nate. I like you lots. But Ani, well, she's sort of like a daughter to me."

Nate sat up a bit straighter in his chair.

"I've seen the way you two are with each other and it makes me nervous." Amos paused to rub one hand along the armrest. "She's not your regular girl. Our Ani's a bit different. There's nothing you can buy her that'll make her happy."

Nate took a deep breath. "I worked that out a while ago."

He nodded. "Yeah, well, like I said, you're a good bloke, Nate. Thing is, if you're not prepared to give her everything you are, don't take nothing from her. Cause she and Kye don't deserve anything less than all of you."

Nate knew that despite his simple life Amos was one of the most valuable and wisest friends he had ever known, and he was right. If he was going to pursue a relationship with Ani it would require an ultimate commitment.

Nate owed the man nothing. Amos had already conceded that it was none of his business. But he wanted to be completely forthcoming. "I think I'm in love with her, Amos. It's a strange place for me to be."

The steely depths of the man's brown eyes chilled Nate to the core. "Well, you best get sure before you go any further, because Ani's got a lot to deal with right now. She don't need no more heartbreak, and Kye's real attached to you. You've got to sort it out, Nate."

He looked out to sea. "I know." Then he fixed back on Amos. "I will. I give you my word."

A slow grin surfaced. "Then that's good enough for me." He got to his feet. "I got some cleaning up to do. I'll catch you later."

Nate moved to unhook the rope of the tinny. "I'll be over soon to give you a hand."

Amos waved as the boat pulled away from the Savannah.

Looking over to the shore, Nate could see Kye sitting on the pontoon, waiting for his uncle to get back. The boy waved both arms in a vibrant greeting.

Nate lifted one high in return.

Ani stopped short the second she rounded the corner of the island. She hadn't had the strength to get out of bed that morning, and now it was well past midday.

Not to mention the aggravation she had endured earlier from Kye.

"What is wrong with you, Kiki?" Her son had complained at the unholy hour of five o'clock. "I want to go and see what Uncle's doing. I'm bored here. There's nothing on TV, and the water's calm. We could go fishing."

His whining was doing her head in. She wanted to be left alone.

"Uncle will be busy cleaning up after the kapmauri." She had buried her face in a pillow and willed him to quit disturbing her.

"Can't I go help?" The whine in his voice was incredibly grating.

"I am not getting out of bed to take you there, so go find something to do."

"Harrumph." He had stamped his feet all the way through the cabin and out onto the patio only to yell out minutes later. "Hey, Kiki, Flynn's walking along the beach. He says can I go with him to see Uncle."

She pounced on the opportunity for a chaperone. "Go then." She stuck her earphones in her ears and closed her eyes. Peace at last.

Except peace continued to elude her, just as it had all night. Not only had her conscience waged war on her, her subconscious had as well. While every waking thought was aimed at removing Nate from her life, every moment she spent asleep produced a vibrant dream in which he played the leading role. She was starting to think she needed serious help.

God, I need you to help me overcome this. I don't have

the strength.

Hours later, she had eventually pulled herself out of bed and steeled herself to face him.

Ani stood and scanned Resolution Bay. There was a vacant spot in the water where the Savannah had been moored.

She peered up and down the beach and then turned and scanned out to sea. There was no sign of the distinctive white hull. A heavy force hit her chest. He had gone.

"Kiki, can't we go skip some rocks or something? This is boring." Kye kicked at the water as he spoke, sending another gush of spray flying into air. They were sitting on the edge of the floating pontoon. Anika had spent the best part of the afternoon trying to teach her son a mathematics unit from his correspondence work. She had finally given up after having to battle his poor behavior, as well as her lack of concentration. Now she could see the change of environment had done nothing for his disagreeable temper.

"Kye, if you don't stop stressing me out, I'm going to send you back to your room and you can spend the rest of the day in bed." Ani put a hand over his knee in an effort to stop his annoying action. The hem of her sundress was wet though.

Kye stopped, but dropped his head and stuck out his lips in a firm pout. "If Nate was here, he'd take me."

Ani took a deep breath in an attempt to control her irritation. Nate had been gone two days, and in that time Kye had said his name a thousand times. His blatant admiration for the American was not something she wanted to deal with right now. Not when Nate's leaving was all she could think about.

"Well, he's not here is he? And besides, I am your mother, and I say what goes." She flung the words at him with a good deal of authority.

Kye looked sideways at her. "Sorry." His bent head indicating he'd reached her boundary. "Nate said I could go on the Savannah again when he gets back. I really want to go, Kiki. Can I go? Please say I can."

Ani rubbed a hand over her forehead. She could feel the headache that had been threatening all day starting to take hold.

"Kye, we don't know anything about Nate's plans. We don't know when, or even if, he's coming back." The statement triggered a see-saw of emotions. Saying his name gave her a warm tingly feeling, and the thought of his absence being permanent sent her stomach into free fall.

"He will be back. He said so. He told me to make sure you knew that." Kye's voice escalated to the point of squealing.

Ani threw her hands in the air. "Kye, will you please stop. You are driving me crazy." The boy had continuously repeated his assertion that Nate would return. Ani had convinced herself Nate was gone for good. After all, he didn't find her to explain his plans. No call. No text. She said she needed time to think but what had happened between them had clearly spooked him so badly he'd left.

The sway of the pontoon put a halt to their

quarrel. They turned to see Jed and Samara approaching. Ani groaned. No doubt they would have heard the bickering.

Jed bent down to them. "Hey there, Kye. Do you feel like going on a bush walk with me?"

The boy's face lit up at the suggestion. He looked over to Ani. "Can I, Kiki?"

She sighed with relief. "With pleasure." She looked up at Jed and mouthed "thank you."

Jed smiled and led the boy back to the footpath.

"Feel like some company?" Samara asked.

Ani patted the vacated spot beside her and smiled. "Sure."

Samara settled onto the pontoon before speaking. "How's things?"

Ani wondered for a second what would happen if she honestly answered the question. She decided that as much as she liked Samara, it was a little early in their friendship to be offloading her troubles.

"Apart from my son wearing me down, I'm fine." She only half lied. Kye was wearing her down, even if she didn't feel in the least bit 'fine.'

Samara paddled her feet in the clear water and looked out to the bay at an approaching tinny. "I love this island. It always reminds me of who I am." She stopped to glance over at her. "Did I tell you Jed and I fell in love here?"

Anika smiled. "Neville's storytelling has beaten you to it." She shrugged, "And Bay shared some things with me. I hope you don't mind." It was one of the most awesome tales of forgiveness she had ever heard.

Samara laughed. "Not at all."

"Sometimes I wish I had a knight in shining armor story to tell." Ani picked at a bit of stick stuck on the end of the pontoon as she spoke.

"Hey, I wouldn't go that far. Jed does not own a suit of armor. And I don't know how many real relationships resemble fairy tales."

Ani frowned. "What do you mean?"

"Well ..." Samara paused briefly. "Life is full of choices, and love is a choice. I don't know if it ever simply happens to us. I think it's more likely we choose to love in spite of differences and pitfalls."

Ani recognized the truth in the statement, but didn't get a chance to ponder it further. A tinny ran up to the pontoon, and she recognized the driver as the drunken buffoon from the night of the kapmauri. He leered at her from underneath the brim of his dirty cap.

Samara gently touched her shoulder and spoke quietly at her side. "Every relationship comes with challenges, Ani. Just don't let fear dictate your choice." Ani smiled at her new friend.

"Afternoon, ladies." The buffoon interrupted them as he boarded the pontoon.

They both gave him a polite acknowledgement.

"You haven't seen my wallet by any chance? I think I lost it the other night."

Ani pointed in the direction of the reception building. "The lost property is kept up there. You'll have to go and ask at the desk."

She could see the man's eyes through the lens of his sunglasses. His gaze fell directly on her cleavage. She straightened up and pulled on the straps of her dress.

The man's leer intensified. "Cool. See you later?" His tone made it obvious it was a question.

Ani frowned and gave him a withering look. "I doubt it. I've got work to do."

The man clearly wasn't fazed by her rejection. He gave a slight chuckle. "No, I'm sure I'll see you." He turned and ambled down the pontoon.

Samara got to her feet. "The world is full of creeps."

Ani laughed. "You are not wrong there." She moved to follow her when something in the man's tinny caught her eye. There were three floats stashed in the front of the tinny, each marked with a red cross on either side of the white ball. The same markings as the floats attached to the illegal nets where they had found Bert.

Ani pulled out her phone to take a photo and looked over to Sam. "I have to find Neville."

"I don't remember the last time I had a barbeque on the back deck." Braden flipped the steaks sizzling on the grill.

"Not much beats it." Nate bit into a sausage.

"Except maybe a kapmauri. That was some delicious seafood." Braden licked his lips. He was clearly recalling the feast five nights ago.

Nate didn't reply. He had avoided talking about that evening.

When Braden had suggested they take the Savannah for a sail up north, Nate had jumped at the idea. After his talk with Amos, having some time away from the island to think sounded like a great plan.

Unfortunately, the distance had done the opposite. In the four days they had been away, Nate had missed Anika and Kye more than he'd thought possible, to the point that they were only two days into the trip before he had suggested they double back. Braden had managed to talk him into continuing through to the Whitsunday Islands, and then to Bowen. They were now docked in Bowen marina.

"Here we go." Braden slapped the two steaks onto plates. "I hope you're hungry. These look mighty tasty."

"Not particularly. I might leave mine for later." Nate had found his appetite had dwindled along with his happiness.

"Right, that's it." Braden dropped the tongs on the table. "I've never seen you off your food. You need to snap out of this, Nate. If you can't live without her, then get back there and tell her so."

Nate sat back in his chair. He should have known his uncle was discerning enough to see through him. He sighed and dropped what remained of his sausage. "It's not that simple."

"Well, get to simplifying it. You can't let this go on."

Nate snorted. "Sure, but what do I do?"

"What do you want to do?"

"I don't know. It's a ready-made family and that scares me senseless."

His uncle wiped his brow. "You're right there. That little boy clearly wants a daddy, and I'd say he's got his eye on you for the job. He was mighty unhappy to hear you'd be gone for a few days."

The memory of Kye's downcast face as he explained his departure flashed into his head. He couldn't get over the feeling he was letting the child down. It hurt.

"The thing is. I don't know if I'd be any good at it."

"Well, you asked God to show you the life He had for you, and I know from experience the answers He gives aren't always the ones you expect. I suppose you thought you were asking Him to define your career. Perhaps He had something else in mind."

Nate frowned. "What do you mean?"

"When you ask for something with all your heart, God tends to go all the way. Sometimes it takes a while to get there. Often there are things we need to learn along the way, but eventually we see His purpose."

He understood what his uncle was getting at. He had been praying for direction, and then his Bible reading that very morning had given him the chills. He recalled the passage;

Sons are a heritage from the Lord; children are a reward from him.

His mother had highlighted the passage, and in the margin was written. *"I know Nate's son will be like him. He will bring Nate great joy."*

"I can't help feeling as though I'm meant to be Kye's father."

Braden raised his eyebrows. "Well, God's certainly given you a great love for both the boy and his mother. There's no denying that."

"I do love her. In a very different way to anyone

I've ever loved before." Nate considered the ups and downs of their relationship. The physical desire was one thing. The friendship and shared purpose they had were the things he didn't want to live without. She forced him to think, held him accountable, and challenged him to be a better person.

Nate thought back to the night of the kapmauri. He had wanted to discuss what had happened between them before he left, but hadn't been able to find her, and she had asked for time to think. He had to respect that. "I think I've made a big mistake," he said as he turned to Braden. "I've messed up."

"What do you mean?"

Nate took a moment to formulate an appropriate explanation. "Let's just say the last time I saw Ani, I let my physical desires override both my brain and my faith. Ani didn't appreciate it."

Braden let out a hearty laugh.

Nate shook his head. "I know. You don't have to tell me. I'm an idiot."

"You're no idiot, son, just human." Braden laughed again. "So she gave it to you?"

Nate gave him a reluctant nod.

Braden responded with firm pat on his shoulder. "Well, that sure is the sign of a good woman. True love is never an easy road, Nate, but by gosh, it's the best ride you'll ever have."

Nate knew what he had to do. *Don't make the same mistake twice.* He had to rein in his physical attraction to Ani in order to prove to her who he was and how he felt about her.

Anika sat on the park bench and watched her child play. The scheduled visit had lifted Kye's spirits.

She had also decided to embrace the distraction, even though it required her to be in close proximity to Mitchell Mayfield.

When they had arrived, he and Sarah had come over to greet them. A wide smile appeared on his face as he bent down to say hello to Kye.

Mayfield was not looking well. His face was drawn, his eyes sagged with heavy grey circles and his complexion had a strange yellow hue. But he was clearly ecstatic to see Kye, who wasted no time in charging to the play equipment.

Anika closed her eyes and listened to the childish banter around her. It was over a week since Nate had left, and each day had brought a flood of emotions.

After her conversation with Samara, she had finally admitted to herself that she was in love with Nate. Not in the way love was so often portrayed in the movies, but in the day to day fulfilment of love. The anticipation of seeing him, the conversations they had, the friendship they shared, and the way he cared for Kye. At some point she had chosen to love him. Now his leaving gave her no choice but to move on.

The new awareness of her feelings also forced her to acknowledge his leaving was for the best. At the very least, he had gone before these realizations had set in. If he was still a part of their lives, she didn't know what she would do. He didn't feel the same way for her. Sure, he had admitted he had a strong attraction to her. He wanted her. But he didn't love her.

She promised herself not to speak about him, or mention his name. Each time someone spoke of him she made an excuse to leave the conversation. She didn't want to hear every person reiterate Kye's message that Nate would be back. Avoiding the future was the only technique aiding her sanity.

Ani knew she couldn't settle for a casual romance that would ultimately come to an end and leave her devastated. At least now, with his exit from their lives, she could trust herself not to give in to her need for him.

She closed her eyes and repeated the Bible verse she had memorized days ago. *When you are broken hearted, I am close to you.* She drew on the strength of those words.

The discovery of the floats in the buffoon's tinny had also been a welcome distraction. Neville was excited by the new development, even though the man had claimed he had found the floats in the estuary. Everyone on Resolution had been unsettled by the thought that Bert had masterminded the entire operation. The police were now considering the prospect that Bert wasn't acting alone, or that he was a victim, and so they had further cause to keep a close eye on the group of campers. Another officer had been assigned to patrol the region, which was welcome news.

Ani watched a toddler squeal in delight as he ran by the bench where she was sitting. The park was spread over a large area. Today it was packed with children and parents. Several people blocked her view of Kye. When the way cleared she picked him out of the throng. Mayfield was crouching down and speaking to him. Her son's posture stiffened. She wondered what Mayfield was saying that had caused him to bristle.

Kye screwed up his face and yelled at Mayfield, then at Sarah, who was standing next to them. He turned and ran at full tilt towards her. His legs were going so fast he stumbled before reaching her. Ani perched on the edge of the bench, anticipating an upset child.

Kye stood in front of her, tears were falling down his cheeks, and his lips puckered in an angry rage. "Grandad says I might go to live with him. Why is he saying that?"

Ani pulled him to her, trying to soften the blow he had endured. "He had no right to say anything like that to you." A wave of anger rose within her.

"I don't want to live with him. I don't want to. I want to be with you." A loud wail resonated on her shoulder.

Red heat rose to her face. She felt torn between keeping calm enough to comfort her son, and giving in to the rage whirling inside.

"It's going to be all right. No one is going to take you away from me. You're my boy." She cradled the top of his head and kissed his blonde curls. No matter how bad it looked, God had them both in His plan. The worst was here, but her trust in Him had given her a peace she couldn't explain. She knew He wouldn't let them go.

Mayfield had followed Kye back. He now stood some distance away. The shuffling of his feet suggested he didn't quite know what to do. Sarah placed a hand on his arm and said something Ani couldn't hear.

She ignored their presence and comforted her child until he had settled, then she pulled him away to wipe the tears from his eyes.

"Go now and wait in the car for me." She kissed his moist cheek.

He nodded and ran off without looking back at his grandfather.

Anika sat for a second and stared at them. She took deep breaths in order to compose herself before approaching them.

Mayfield met her halfway. "I'm so sorry. How is Kye?"

To her surprise she could see he was indeed sorry. It was a surprise to see raw emotion coming from Mitchell Mayfield. Regardless of the genuine apology, Ani had no intention of holding back.

"Are you such a fool as to think you will succeed in taking my child from me?" She moved closer to him, invading his personal space.

Mayfield opened his mouth then closed it again. He blinked rapidly and looked back at Sarah for support.

"Your pursuit of everything will end with nothing. You failed at having a relationship with your son, and now you will fail at having a relationship with your grandson, and all because you're only capable of pursuing what you want, what you think is best. Wake up." Ani turned to Sarah. "If you care for him at all, you will stop him now before it's too late."

She turned and strode away.

Nate adjusted the binoculars in order to get a better look at the boat anchored inside the creek. There was no doubt from the distinct lettering on the side - it was the Mary-Jane.

"It's definitely her." He looked back at his uncle, who was keeping the Savannah on course.

They hadn't been far outside of Bowen when they had come across an unusual sight. A prawn trawler anchored in the mouth of a creek with a mass of tinnies hanging off the end of it. It was a secluded location. To the best of Nate's knowledge, the mouth of that particular creek was only accessible from the ocean.

The unusual number of tinnies piqued their curiosity. They had sat and watched for over twenty minutes, noticing the high level of activity stemming from the boat. There was a lot of coming and going for a vessel designed for a somewhat solitary existence.

"What are all those guys doing?" Braden accepted the binoculars from Nate.

"I have no idea." Nate had watched three tinnies leave the vessel in the last few minutes.

"I was told the Mary-Jane was docked permanently since Bert's death. I wonder who's skippering her." Nate couldn't help a spark of interest from igniting. He had never believed Bert was the one who had shot at him and Anika.

"I'm going over to take a closer look. We can anchor there." He pointed to a safe place along the shoreline, out of sight of the Mary-Jane.

"Do you think that's wise? They could be up to no good." Braden frowned.

"I'll never know if I don't check it out." Nate had a burning desire to investigate further, but he conceded his uncle's point. "Radio the police if I don't return in thirty minutes. That should give me enough time to get over, have a look, and get back."

Having worked on the boat, there was no reason why he wouldn't go over to pay his respects. He decided this would be his excuse if asked why he was there.

His uncle nodded before helping him to launch the yacht's tender. "Be careful."

Nate pulled the engine to life.

The trip over was difficult in the choppy water forming the mouth of the creek. Nate finally pulled up at the back of the Mary-Jane as one man left and another prepared to go.

The man who was leaving turned to wave goodbye to the one on the back of the boat. "See ya, Jim." He nodded in Nate's direction before gunning the outboard.

Jim looked up from his task of knotting a huge black garbage bag. The other man reached out to stabilize his tinny.

"Don't bother coming aboard mate. This is the last lot." Jim indicated the bag.

Nate could see it splayed the deck, and contained a heavy mass.

The investigative nature of his legal training kicked in, and he decided to play along.

"That's a shame. I was hoping there was some left."

Jim straightened up and leaned against the side of the boat. "You a Yank, eh?"

"Yep."

Jim placed a hand up to block the sun from his vision. He was a scruffy looking character, unshaven, and dirty. Nate looked down at his own attire and was thankful he most likely looked in a similar state. He hadn't bothered shaving the last few days, and the lack of clean clothing had forced him to wear a few pieces that really needed to be thrown away.

He looked over to Jim's tinny. From the equipment strewn in and around the boat it was clear he was in the fishing business. "What do you want with this stuff?" The man squinted at him.

Nate had a choice. He could own up to being out of his element, or continue to play along until he was found out. He decided the latter would produce the best results.

"I've been working as a deckhand for a fisherman down south. I thought I'd come over and check this out." He took the chance that whatever was in the bag had something to do with the man's profession. Thankfully, Jim seemed to accept his explanation.

"Well, this stuff's not much use to him unless he's got a professional license." Jim pointed to the three bags already stowed in his tinny. "There's enough bait in this lot to last me months."

Nate ran with it. "They say it's the best you can get." He reached out to help Jim load the final bag into his tinny. It was exceptionally heavy.

"That's right." Jim stopped to catch his breath. "Dugong meat's prime bait for crabbing. Mind you,

I paid a hefty price for this lot. It won't be worth buying if Coot puts the price up again."

Nate took a moment to consider what Jim had said. Coot was clearly involved in the illegal netting if he was now selling dugong meat as bait. Nate recalled how Bert had said his wife's expensive tastes had kept him working hard.

Perhaps the police have it wrong. Maybe Coot's been the one setting the nets, or at least helping.

"I hear he's a bit greedy." Nate sought to test out Jim's willingness to gossip.

"Yeah, too right." The fisherman adjusted the cap on his head. "He's in the cabin with his mate drinking his profits right now. The little ..."

A string of uncomplimentary descriptions for Coot followed. The colorful language riled Jim further. "Not to mention his scheming sister. She's the one behind this price rise. Old Bert never had bait as good as dugong, but he's been selling his by-catch for years, and always asked a fair price. Now his missus has taken over, she's got dollar signs before her eyes. If bait wasn't in such short supply, I'd tell Coot where to go."

Nate finally twigged as some of the pieces fell into place. All prawn trawlers were required by law to throw back the crabs, stingrays, and unwanted fish that became trapped in prawn nets, but Bert had been keeping the by-catch and selling it to local fisherman for cash. Now Coot had continued the lucrative sideline, except he was also killing and selling the dugong that got caught in his illegal nets. There was one thing Nate still needed to know.

"I hear Coot's been the one behind the illegal

netting down around Resolution. Is that right?"

Jim looked behind him into the boat. He leaned to the side to peer around the huge freezer taking up a good part of the back deck before moving in closer to Nate.

"Yeah, of course. How do you think he's getting the dugong meat? They reckon Bert was behind it, but there's no way he would have been setting those nets." Sam stopped to check his back again. "Bert told me he caught Coot netting a few years back. He told him he'd give him a hiding if he ever did it again. Bert wasn't stupid. He knew the game would be up if he got caught. Selling by-catch is a lot easier than offloading dugong. Now that Bert's gone, it's plain stupid to keep doing it." Jim stopped to spit into the water.

"Bert's missus will be spurring Coot on. She's running around in a new car and all. Besides, I hear there's a few fish and chip shops around buying the fish Coot catches in the nets as well. Wouldn't put it past that woman to do away with Bert to keep the cash flowing, if you know what I mean?"

Nate nodded. Foul play would certainly explain the suspicious way Bert's body was found.

Jim leaned over to untie the rope of his tinny. "Come to think of it, this better be the last lot I get from Coot. If he keeps setting nets, the Fisheries are going to catch him sooner rather than later." He nodded towards his tinny. "Gotta get going. If I don't get outta this creek soon there won't be enough water left."

Nate nodded to Jim.

They moved off in opposite directions before

Coot decided to make an appearance. Nate gave a lazy wave over his shoulder at Jim's retreating back. It had certainly been a profitable expedition to the Mary-Jane. He revved the little outboard, determined to get back to the Savannah as soon as possible.

CHAPTER 15

Anika did a double take and blinked hard. There was no mistaking the white hull sitting in the prime anchorage of Resolution Bay. It was definitely the Savannah.

Nate was back.

The sun broke the dawn as she stood and watched the vessel pitching in the swell. A flood of emotions surged at the sight of the boat. At first, there was foreboding because she had to face him after what had happened between them, then anger that he had dared to run away in the first place, and then excitement over seeing him again soon. It was the last emotion she tried to squash. She searched her reactions and made a conscious decision–anger would serve her well.

Nine days. Nine days he's left me in the lurch. Taken off without a goodbye. Left me to deal with what happened. Nine days. Try as she might, the indignation wouldn't ignite sufficiently to turn into anger. The truth was it had been horrible without him.

The murmur of voices pulled her out of her daydream. She looked down the path to see Nate talking to Flynn some distance away. He must have been heading her way because he was facing her, and Flynn had his back to her. Ani's heart skipped a beat at the sight of him. He was every bit as handsome as her dreams wouldn't allow her to forget. A drop in her stomach prompted a sick feeling that produced a burp. The taste of the breakfast she had consumed ten minutes ago flavored her mouth. Vegemite was not appetizing the second time around.

Thankfully, the aftertaste pulled her out of her numbness. If she continued down the path she was going to run into them. *No way.*

She had settled on a strategy of avoidance when Nate glanced down the path and caught her staring at him. She held her breath as they made eye contact.

Oh no. She didn't think. Her legs swept into motion and she turned around to run back down the path.

"Ani, wait up."

The voice sounded behind her as she rounded the bend and sprinted as fast as she could into the sanctuary of her cabin. She locked the door and drew the curtains closed. She inched away from the door as Nate's shadow grew larger as he climbed the steps to the patio.

"Ani, I was on my way to see you." A heavy rapping sounded on the glass.

Anika sunk into one of the chairs and stared at the door. *Okay, now what?*

She would have been far better off continuing down the path. Now she was stuck there, alone, and back at the scene of the last encounter with this man.

Great. She put her head in her hands. *Stupid. Stupid. Stupid.*

"Ani, I saw you go in there. What's the problem? I just want to talk to you." She could see from the shadow that he had both hands on the door. "Please."

She rolled her eyes. As if pleading was going to

sway her into letting him in. But what choice did she have. She was stuck. Literally.

"Ani, I won't touch you. I promise. Just open the door." One hand moved to his side.

Anika froze. The fact was, it was her inability to keep him at arm's length that she didn't trust. How could she have any contact with Nate and not show him how much she loved him? As painful as it was, she had talked herself into believing he wasn't coming back even though Kye—and every other person she met—insisted he would return. It was easier to believe her own lie than to trust the word of others. At least the lie held some form of self-preservation.

Ugh. Self-preservation again. Now look at where your delusions have led you, right back into fear.

She couldn't lie to herself any more than she could lie to him. She was sure one look at her would reveal her feelings for him.

There was no way she was opening the door.

She maintained her silence while his shadow moved from side to side, back and forth.

"Ani, please open the door. What I have to say, well ... I need to see you." The grey mass became increasingly agitated as it mirrored his body. "It'll only take a minute. I promise. Anika?"

The shadow moved to one of the deck chairs. "Fine. I'll stay out here as long as it takes. You'll have to come out sometime."

Ani cushioned her head against the headrest. She sighed as the clock on the wall showed she was now fifteen minutes late for work. *How am I going to get out?*

She scanned the room for an exit point and then remembered. The security screen on her bedroom window was loose, something she had been meaning to ask Amos to fix.

Tiptoeing to the room she jiggled the screen. It popped open without much fuss. With as much stealth as she could manage she crawled out the window and carefully shut it behind her.

Freedom. For now at least. Cowardly freedom.

As she made her way along the overgrown bush path to the resort she acknowledged the reprieve would be short-lived. She was still stuck on the island, and she would have to face him eventually.

Ani wondered what would happen if she gave in, simply gave up the fight and handed the entire situation over to God. She wasn't doing a good job of handling it herself. Hiding in her cabin and stealing out the back window like a criminal wasn't the epitome of wise decision-making. And even if she could avoid Nate, there was no way she could avoid her feelings for him. Even her subconscious wouldn't give her a break from that.

She stopped short on the track to look skyward. Huge eucalyptus trees rustled in the wind. Their raw scent filled her nostrils.

Okay, God, I admit I'm in trouble. I love this man. I can't fight it, I can't ignore it, and it's obvious I can't deal with it because I'm back to choosing fear. So I'm going to stop. My way is not working. I want to do this your way. Show me what that is, because I'm really making a mess of it.

Nate paused before opening the door to the research station. A distinct frustration with Ani caused his jaw to pop. They had arrived back in Resolution Bay late the night before.

He couldn't sleep after anchoring, unable to quiet his thoughts long enough to achieve the peace of mind necessary for rest. All he could think about was the next step in his relationship with Anika.

Finally he had come to the conclusion that he had to find her and convince her he was here for the long run.

Unfortunately, he had spent most of the morning sitting outside her cabin, waiting for her to emerge from her self-inflicted imprisonment. He had finally been set straight by Amos and Kye who told him Anika was at the Research Station.

She must have left the cabin through a window. Thankfully, he didn't have the chance to feel sorry for himself. Kye was overjoyed to see him, and the boy's reception almost made up for his mother's avoidance tactics.

He spent some time fishing with Amos and Kye before deciding he would track Anika down and say what he had to before he completely lost his nerve.

He pushed on the door. The bell on top sounded, signaling his entry. Yvette looked up from her desk.

"Nate, it's so good to have you back." She raced to give him a heartfelt hug.

He looked over his shoulder at Anika, who was seated at another desk across the room. She stared up at him from under her eyebrows while tapping her pen frantically on the desk.

"It's nice to receive such a warm welcome." He

made a point of sounding slightly sarcastic while looking at Ani.

Yvette pulled away. "Well, why wouldn't it be warm? We all missed you." She looked over her shoulder. "Didn't we, Ani?"

Her blue eyes grew wide. "Yeah, sure." She tilted the corners of her mouth in an attempt to smile. It failed to impress. She then dropped her head and tried as best as she could to swing corkscrew curls onto her face.

Yvette looked back at him and shrugged.

"Yvette, is there any chance I can have a word with Anika?"

The older woman raised her eyebrows. "Of course." She gestured towards a spare chair.

"Alone?" Nate smiled to cushion the blunt request.

Yvette wasn't fazed. She gave him a knowing look. "Certainly. I'll go and grab a coffee at the restaurant. Take your time." She took a brief look between them before slipping out the door.

Anika jumped to her feet. "Wait."

Her protest was in vain. Yvette had gone. Nate moved to block the exit.

She stared at him, hands on hips and pursed lips. "That was rude."

Nate lifted one eyebrow and smirked. "Ruder than leaving someone waiting for hours on your veranda because you climbed out a window?"

She stared at her feet.

"Why are you avoiding me?"

She looked back up at him. "Avoiding you? Correct me if I'm wrong, but wasn't it you who took off a week ago?"

Nate moved a few steps into the room. Anika swiftly pulled her chair in front of her so that both the desk and her chair created a barrier between them.

The strange behavior stopped Nate in his tracks. "What are you doing?" He looked from the furniture to her startled face. "You're acting like I'm some psycho stalker. I just want to talk to you."

She remained behind her barrier. "Well, you've got me cornered, so talk."

"Okay." He stood for a second in order to collect his thoughts. This was not going to plan. He did not envisage having to hold her captive for this conversation. He determined to forge ahead.

"After what happened ..."

No, bad start.

"Last time I saw you ..."

Worse. Don't go there.

"What happened between us was ..."

Was what?

He raised his eyes to the ceiling. *Good grief.* He rubbed his hand over his forehead in frustration. *Spit it out.*

He looked back at her. The fall of one of her curls onto her forehead made his heart skip a beat. She was so incredibly beautiful. He wanted to grab her and never let her go. Not like it would happen any time soon, not with the way she'd rearranged the furniture.

He wet his lips and closed the gap between him and the table. She stiffened as he placed both hands on its surface and leant into her as far as the table would allow.

Her eyes were so vibrant against the green color of her polo shirt, Nate almost lost his nerve. Instead, he collected himself and stared her down.

"Ani, I want you to know I'm in."

He didn't get to explain further because she raised her eyebrows and threw a hand in the air. "In for what, Nate? You left, remember?"

"I left because after what happened, I thought we both needed some time to think. You told me you needed that. I wanted to give you that space, but I made a point of telling everyone I would be back. I tried to see you. I just about beat your door down. When I couldn't find you, I told Kye to let you know. Didn't he tell you?"

She drummed her fingers on the back of the chair. "Yes."

"Didn't you believe him?"

She bit her lip.

"You didn't want to believe him."

She dropped her head. He had hit a nerve.

"Ani ..." He walked around the desk towards her. She took countermeasures, swinging the chair so it was repositioned strategically between them. The barrier stopped him short.

He took a deep breath. "I promise I will stay at Resolution as long as it takes to show you how I feel. I'm not going anywhere."

She closed her eyes. "Nate, you are making this so hard." She opened them again to look at him. "What do you want from me?"

He acted without thinking, pulling the chair from her gasp, setting it to the side and closing the gap between them. She stiffened so dramatically that he stopped short of reaching for her. Instead he grabbed one of her hands and held on tight.

He paused to read her eyes: uncertainty, fear but also as clear, was the longing. He held onto that. "I want you. Every bit of you."

He saw her swallow hard and blink. Her mouth opened slightly but no words came out. Nate fought the impulse to kiss her.

The sudden intrusion of the bell above the door forced them apart.

"Nate, here you are." Kye ran into the office, followed by Amos.

The older man was quick to assess the tension in the air. He held back. A slow smile spread across his face.

Kye didn't possess the same discernment. He skipped around the desk to Nate's side.

"What you doing? Helping my Mum?"

The boy's presence sparked an idea. Nate turned to bend down to his level. "I need your help, Kye."

Kye's face lit up and he puffed his chest out with manly acceptance of the calling.

"Kiki lost a bet with me a few weeks ago. She promised to come to a slumber party on the Savannah with you and me." He glanced up at Anika. She had turned pale.

He almost abandoned the idea. *No.* There was no way he was going to allow her to avoid him further.

Nate admitted the plan was a little sneaky, but continued regardless. "I need your help to convince her to go."

Kye pursed his lips and placed his hands on his

hips. He looked up at his mother. "Promise is a promise."

She gave them a frustrated frown. "I didn't technically lose that bet, you know. We only had a fix on that dugong for a few minutes. We didn't actually find him."

"You going back on your word, Ani?" This time it was Amos who spoke. Nate exchanged a knowing look with the man. Amos grinned.

"Why is everyone ganging up on me?" Anika pouted.

They stared at her in an unspoken effort to wear her down.

She looked from one to the other, then threw up her hands and let out an exasperated breath. "All right, I'll go."

Nate couldn't help but match Kye's smile.

He pulled himself back up to full height. "Good, that's settled. Uncle Brae leaves tomorrow morning, so we can have our slumber party on the Savannah tomorrow night. You're welcome to join us, Amos."

Amos shook his head. "Sorry, Nate. Tide's good tomorrow night. Gotta go catch some mud crabs." Amos stifled a grin as he gave his excuse.

Nate looked at Kye and Ani. "Looks like it's just us."

Kye jumped up and down on the spot. "Cool. Can I bring my fishing rod?"

Nate nodded. "Sure thing."

He noticed the deep crease on Ani's forehead as she fidgeted with a loose thread on the back of the chair.

If only he could succeed in extracting a fraction

of enthusiasm from her.

The Savannah was the most beautiful boat Anika had ever seen. Even with its clean lines and modern furnishings, the yacht possessed an other-worldly charm. The natural wood and leather combined to create an opulent yet homely feel to the interior of the vessel.

Anika lay back on the huge semicircular couch and rested her arms on the table fixed in front of her. She closed her eyes to feel the sway of the boat. It was almost as if the yacht and the water were one, so smooth was the rise and fall beneath her. The feeling was a huge contrast to a tinny slapping and jolting in the swell.

No sooner had she relaxed than her other senses sought to invade her calm. Nate's aftershave wafted occasionally on the breeze entering, then swirling around the cabin. Then his voice, deep and clear, pricked her ears as he and Kye fished off the back deck.

Anika gave up trying to relax and opened her eyes again. She looked around the cabin. It was incredibly spacious. The galley and dining areas were well appointed. Below the waterline were three cabins. The main at the front of the yacht, was a king-sized room equipped with a television and ensuite. There was also a queen-sized room and a room of bunk beds, both of which shared a bathroom. All were well designed, and quite spectacular.

She looked over to see a workstation set up on one side of the cabin. This was where Nate did his writing. There was also a television and what looked like a computer game center hooked up. It was all neat and organized.

It had been love at first sight for her and the Savannah. The second she stepped aboard the yacht it was as though the vessel had cast a spell on her. She had been a self-proclaimed nutcase over this visit to Nate's yacht. The anticipation of having to spend time with him, and on his turf, had wrapped her up in so many knots she had almost lost it. But now a sense of calm she couldn't explain enveloped her. Perhaps it was being on the water. Or maybe it was the security the Savannah evoked. Whatever it was, Ani was feeling dangerously like she was at home.

Her eyes scanned the cabin once more before settling on a photo high on a shelf. She reached up and retrieved it. A woman held the reins of a horse while a young man, definitely Nate, sat astride. They both had wide smiles. Ani examined the woman. The physical similarities between the two were obvious. She had to be Nate's mother.

Movement at the entry to the cabin made her jump, and she looked up to see Kye run in. Nate entered behind him.

"Gotta go to the loo," her son proclaimed in a loud voice before bolting down the steps to the cabin bathroom.

Nate took a seat next to her, shuffling around the semicircular couch so his body almost touched hers.

Her entire left side tingled at his closeness. He didn't seem to notice her reaction as he smiled at the photo in her hand.

"That's Ginny." He pointed to the horse. "She

was one terrific horse. I haven't ridden nearly as much since she died a few years ago."

Anika smiled at his revelation. It was nice to know something so intimate about him. She pointed to the woman. "That's your mum?"

He gave a short nod.

"She's beautiful." Ani looked at the woman with the simple attire and sleek ponytail. There was something organic about her, a presence shining through, despite the age of the photo.

She sensed Nate looking at her and made the mistake of turning to face him. His smile reached his eyes. She quickly diverted her attention back to the photo in her hands.

"You remind me of her sometimes." His voice was soft.

"How so?" Ani didn't think she looked anything like the woman in the picture.

"She wasn't wrapped up in her wealth," Nate said. "She didn't care what people thought of her. And she was a natural beauty. She knew exactly who she was."

Anika smiled down at the photo. That was certainly a compliment she was happy to accept.

Nate leaned in closer and lifted a hand to wrap a finger around one of her curls. Her stomach went into a flutter and a mass of tingles ran up and down her spine. She didn't dare look at him again. After all, she still wasn't fully convinced he would stick around. What could the possessor of all this affluence possibly see in her?

"Just like you, she was incredibly beautiful inside as well as out." He leaned in closer to place his lips on her cheek. Ani closed her eyes.

She expected nothing more than an affectionate peck. But as Nate's lips lingered on her skin she couldn't help but feel the pull of his desire for her. She betrayed her reason, leaning into him. Nate's lips left her skin to gently repeat the kiss a little further down her cheek. He continued with another, and another, until he reached the corner of her mouth.

Anika couldn't have kept her self-control intact, even if she had wanted to. She turned towards him as his arms encircled her waist and pulled her close. His lips were warm and gentle. She wrapped her arms around his neck as her body melted into his. All resolve to resist him was discarded with one kiss.

"Ew. Do you two have to do that here?" The boy's voice intruded upon their passion. Ani pulled away from Nate. Kye stood in front of them with one hand covering his eyes. But the massive smile on his face suggested he was anything but disgusted.

The burden of parental responsibility returned in a great rush. Kye had never seen her in the arms of a man before. She'd dropped the ball.

"Did you flush the toilet? Or wash your hands?" She attempted to divert attention from the situation. *Oh well, nothing like a bathroom reference to kill a passionate moment.*

Kye dipped his head. "Sorry." He turned and trod back down the steps. A flush was heard, followed by the running water of the tap.

Ani took the opportunity to scoot around the couch and jump out the other side. Nate didn't move.

She stared at him from her now safe position a meter away. He had a huge smile on his face.

"What?"

He shook his head and picked up the photo, carefully replacing it back on the shelf. The grin never left his face.

When he looked back at her he was still wearing the same silly expression.

Ani found his amusement completely exasperating. She tapped her foot in frustration. "If you have something to say, then say it. Don't sit there mocking me."

Nate leaned back and rested his arms on either side of the recess at the top of the couch. His eyes met hers. "I am so in love with you."

It was as much the tone of his voice as the words he said that melted her. Ani could feel her mouth drop open and her eyes widen.

"I finished the job." Kye proclaimed as he ambled past her. "Nate, can we go back to fishing?"

He broke eye contact to address the boy. "Sure," then maneuvered himself out of the couch.

"If you've finished kissing my mum, that is." Kye's cheeky grin was directed solely at Nate.

Ani felt a red flame creep up her neck and burn her cheeks. Even the tips of each individual hair follicle was on fire.

Nate playfully rustled Kye's hair and grinned. "Hey, she kissed me."

Ani's mouth dropped even further. "That's a lie. I did not," she called to their retreating backs. Their giggles proved she didn't have a scrap of dignity left.

Despite the embarrassment she rolled her eyes and couldn't help but smile. He was in love with her.

A flash of sunshine spilling into the cabin beamed directly into Nate's eyes. He knew if he ignored it for long enough the sun would move beyond the slit in the curtain. Finally, he decided to move himself rather than wait for nature to oblige.

The effort it took to get comfortable again only served to wake him further. He opened his eyes and recalled the events of last night.

After a barbeque dinner, he had set up a computer game for Kye while he and Ani played Scrabble.

He couldn't recall the last time he'd had so much fun playing board games. They had laughed hard at some of the wacky attempts each of them had made to pass off gibberish as words. It was so easy to be in her company that at times it was almost as though she and Kye had always been a part of his life.

At ten o'clock, Anika had insisted upon bed for Kye. The little boy had embarked upon a campaign to prolong the night's entertainment, insisting on the movie he'd been promised earlier. Finally, after being worn down, Ani allowed them all to move to Nate's cabin, because it was the only television with a DVD player.

Nate now discovered they had all fallen asleep, as the television was still on. It looked as though the movie had turned itself off, and Anika was curled up on the bed next to him.

He could hear Kye on the computer game upstairs trying to beat his score from last night.

Nate yawned and contemplated getting up to

supervise the boy. He rubbed his face in his hands in an attempt to relieve the fuzziness of their late night.

Ani stirred next to him. He reached over to tuck the sheet around her. He didn't expect for her to grab his arm and pull at him. She managed to position herself in the crook of his armpit, her body lying partly on top of him and her arm reaching around his waist in a tight cuddle.

Nate didn't know what to do. He certainly didn't want to reject the embrace, and decided he would be a fool not to enjoy her affection while it lasted. No doubt the moment she awoke she would pull away in horror.

He buried his face in her curls. They were soft and smelt like a pleasant mixture of flowers and salt. He gently squeezed her to him. Ani responded by wriggling closer and throwing her leg over his. Their bodies were now as close as two could be.

Nate found himself in a horrible predicament. He had thought it was madness not to make the most of the situation. Now he had a dilemma. He was male, it was morning, and the woman he loved and desired more than anything was draped all over him. There was a child in the next room, and it was all a horrible test for his self-control.

He squeezed his eyes shut and tried to think pure, benign thoughts.

The technique didn't work.

He had to get out of there. Maybe it was a bad idea to have Ani stay overnight. But he'd thought Kye would be a sufficient chaperone. *Goes to show how wrong you can be!*

He slowly lifted her arm from around his waist

and pulled his body sideways in order to escape her.

She moaned and simultaneously ran a hand over his chest while tilting her head to place her lips on his neck.

"Hm." She groaned, then sighed. "I love you, Nate." The words were slow and sleepy as they escaped her lips.

He froze. He could see her eyes were still closed. She was still asleep.

Nate couldn't stifle his amusement. Ani may have her conscious mind under control, but her subconscious was happy to give her up.

A loud and triumphant cry from the top of the stairs made them both jump. Kye had scored big.

Nate felt Ani stiffen next to him. He looked down to see her eyes wide open.

She whipped up to sitting position and stared back at him.

"What did I just say?"

The satisfied grin was impossible to wipe off his face.

She bit her bottom lip. "Seriously, Nate. I know I said something. What was it?"

He moved to elevate his torso, propping his elbows behind him. The action drew him closer to her.

"You said you loved me."

She slapped a palm on her forehead and closed her eyes.

He couldn't let the opportunity pass without clarification. "So do you?"

"Do I what?" She dropped her palm.

He shook his head, partly in amusement and

partly in frustration. "Do you love me?"

Her eyes shot from one end of the cabin to the other. "Do I have to answer that?"

"If you ever want to get off this boat you do, because I'm not letting you leave without a straight answer."

She squirmed. "Man, why do I have to be cursed with sleep talking? I swear I haven't had a decent night's sleep for months. No wonder I'm a walking zombie most of the time. Not to mention being the crankiest mother on the planet. And it's all because of you." She stopped ranting to give him an icy glare.

"What have I done?" Nate suspected she was avoiding his question.

"You have been giving me nightmares." The accusatory tone flew up an octave.

Nate sat back a fraction. "How do you work that out? What have I ever done to give you nightmares?"

"You made me fall in love with you. Now I can't get you out of my head. It's driving me crazy. You are driving me crazy!" Her blonde curls bounced along with her rant.

The whole conversation was so hilarious that Nate couldn't help but burst out laughing.

She frowned and gave him a shove. "It's not funny. You are responsible for my rapidly decreasing state of mind. I feel like a raving loon. I'm worse than when we met."

He felt a fresh wave of laughter bubble up to the surface. He grabbed her around the waist and pulled her back down on the bed.

She retaliated with a pillow to his face.

They both laughed and pounded each other with

whatever soft object was within their grasp.

"Pillow fight!" Kye threw himself on the bed to join in the action.

After a decent pummeling they all called a truce.

Each of them sat in their respected corners to catch their breath.

Kye sat opposite and looked at them both. "It's great that we're finally a family, hey." His grin spread from one ear to the other.

Nate turned to gauge Anika's reaction. Her face registered complete shock.

He decided Kye's statement needed his endorsement. "It sure is, Kye."

The little boy grabbed his stomach. "Can we get some breakfast? I'm really hungry."

"How long have you been up?" Anika skirted off the bed and gave him a gentle push towards the door.

"Ages." Kye stopped to roll his eyes. "You woke me up, Kiki. You were talking so loud I couldn't sleep."

She turned to give Nate a stunned glance before following Kye up the stairs.

"What did I say?"

"I dunno. What you're always going on about. Nate this. Nate that. Blah blah blah. Whatever. We all know you like him."

A sharp breath sounded from Anika.

Nate paused on the edge of the bed to collect himself. He was in serious danger of exploding. Not just from laughter, but also from joy.

CHAPTER 16

Anika searched the pages of the legal document once more. The jargon was confusing, but the general purpose was clear. Mitchell Mayfield was proceeding with his custody suit.

She placed the document back down on the kitchen bench and took a few deep breaths. Nate and Kye were wrestling on the floor of the cabin lounge. Kye had the television remote control and Nate was determined to reclaim it.

It was only yesterday they were together on the Savannah. Despite initially having to be duped into setting foot on the yacht, Anika had done everything she could to delay returning. It had been a wonderful escape from everyday life on Resolution.

The feeling of being with Nate, being a part of his life, was an experience she wanted to go on forever. It had crossed her mind late in the afternoon, minutes before they were about to leave the Savannah, that if Nate suggested they pull up anchor and sail away, she would have agreed. The comfort, love and support he offered were hard to resist. The fact they were unmarried was a hurdle she found herself pushing aside in her mind. After all, her mother had embarked on plenty of relationships and had never been married. It was the thought of her mother that pulled her up.

What was she thinking?

She remembered the responsibilities she would

leave behind, and the people who would be hurt by such a drastic course of action. But most importantly, there was the impact such a decision would have on her faith. God had spent years working on her, showing and teaching her ways to trust Him. He was her father, her strength, and her supply. He was there before Nate and He would be there after he was gone, even if that was when they were old and grey. Her strength didn't come from another person or from within herself. The strength that had changed her life came from God. It was the most important relationship she had. If she ran away, or allowed herself to rely on the strength of another, she was bound for disaster. She had to trust in God's plan.

Ani looked down at the document on the bench. *Even for this.* She closed her eyes and prayed for the solution to this new hardship.

Right when she thought she had seen some resolution in her life, another battle emerged. She had spent months fighting the attraction to Nate, convinced it would result in her undoing. Now, when she cast aside her forced control and placed the situation in God's hands, another call to battle sounded.

"Ani, what is it?"

She opened her eyes and forced a smile.

But Nate was already on his feet and by her side within seconds.

Leaning her head against his chest, she saw him pick up the document.

"Kiki, are you okay?" Kye called from the lounge.

She pulled herself away from Nate to nod at her

son. "Sure. I'm a bit emotional, mate. Can you go and unpack for me please? I need your dirty clothes for the wash." She didn't want to discuss the situation with Kye until she got her head around it.

He slumped and dragged himself to his feet. "If I have to."

"You have to."

Ani waited until he had walked through his bedroom door before speaking to Nate. He was flipping through the pages of the document.

"I think Mayfield's going ahead with the custody suit," she said.

Nate flipped back a few pages. "Judging by this, he hasn't taken your advice to drop it."

Nate threw the document back on the counter and squeezed her upper arms. "I don't want you to worry about this. I've got a few tricks up my sleeve that will sort this out once and for all. You and Kye are my priority. One day soon I'm going to make that official. But, for now, I have to go and make a few phone calls. He won't succeed." The flecks in his eyes sparkled as he stared at her.

He pulled her in for a long hug.

"But what if he does, Nate? Kye will have to go and live with his grandfather, basically a stranger." She could hear the panic in her voice.

"I don't want to live with Grandad."

Anika spun around to find Kye in his bedroom doorway, a pile of crumpled clothes in his arms. He threw them on the floor and screwed up his face in defiance.

"You told me I didn't have to."

"Kye, this is not something I can explain easily."

She could see he was agitated, but needed time to plan the best age-appropriate explanation.

Kye clearly wasn't interested in giving her any time. "I don't care. I'm not living with him. I'm staying here. We're a family now. Nate said so." With that he ran out the cabin door.

Ani put her face in her hands. "Great. Just great."

Nate rubbed slow circles on her back. "I'll go talk to him." He kissed her head.

She didn't look up until she heard the door shut.

Nate's patience waned at the recorded message. It, yet again, told him his connection had failed. He had only succeeded once in reaching the States, before the phone cut off.

He recalled Kye's tear-stained face. The memory prompted him to redial the numbers.

Leaning back on the leather chair, Nate glanced around Bay's office. She had been happy to oblige when he asked if he could use the space and her telephone—he didn't trust the reliability of his cell phone for such an important call.

He finally heard the telltale beeps of a connection, followed by a pause, and then the ringing of the phone.

"What do you want?" The sleepy timbre of his father's voice sounded on the other end. It was surprisingly clear considering it spanned the Pacific Ocean.

When he couldn't get his father on his private office line, he had called his home without giving a thought to the time difference.

"Sorry, I didn't look at the time. Did I wake you?"

"Nate." His voice brightened considerably. "Doesn't matter what time it is. It's good to hear from you."

The muffled murmur of a woman's voice sounded in the background. "Hang on."

Nate smiled at the rustle of fabric and the heavy thud of feet. It didn't surprise him that his father wasn't alone, especially now he realized it was the middle of the night in Texas.

His voice sounded again. "It's been too long. If I didn't read those articles each week, I'd be worried about you."

A pang of guilt pricked his insides. He hadn't called his father for over three months.

"Sorry. I guess you could say I've been busy."

"Well, we're talking now. So have you rung to tell me you're on your way home?" There was a hopeful inflection in his voice.

"Not yet." Nate knew the news would disappoint him. Since the required twelve months on the Savannah had finished three weeks ago, Nate had been bombarded with a full-scale e-mail campaign to entice him home to the States.

"Well, what are you waiting for? Fun's over. Time to start your life."

Nate smiled at the abrupt rebuke. If only his father knew how seriously he was taking that exact concept. He forged on with the purpose of his call. "I need your help. It's a very important favor."

"Go ahead."

Nate explained the situation with Mitchell

Mayfield, the attempt to gain custody of Kye and even his own feelings towards the boy and his mother.

"So would it be fair to say you are planning a future with this woman?" Jack interrupted him for direct clarification.

Nate smiled. It was in his father's nature to interrogate him.

"Yes. I'm afraid you're going to become a father-in-law and a grandfather at the same time."

There was complete silence on the other end.

Eventually Jack said, "Well, you're not a boy any more. I have to respect you know what you're doing."

"Actually, it was your advice that helped to convince me this is the right thing for my life."

Nate heard his father scoff. "What would that have been?"

"Don't take the love of a good woman for granted."

"Did I say that?" He sounded horrified.

Nate laughed. "Yes, you did. And I do believe it's the best advice you've ever given me."

"Had I been drinking?"

Nate laughed again. "Yes."

His father chuckled. "Well, drink or not, it's great advice. Consider the custody suit fixed. I don't have any muscle in the Australian justice system, but I know a few people who do, and they owe me. It won't last long. It sounds to me as though it should never have reached this point in the first place."

"Thanks, Jack. I owe you."

Another scoff sounded down the line. "You owe

me nothing. I owe you. You were there for me when I needed you. It's a pleasure to return the favor." There was a brief pause before he continued. "But there is one request I will make."

Oh no, here it comes. Nate didn't expect the favor to come without a catch.

"Come home for a visit. Even for a few days. I want to see you."

The raw emotion in his voice was a surprise. Jack Hollingsworth wasn't comfortable with affectionate verbal expression. But Nate missed his father. They had spent so much time together during the years he worked at the firm. Nate also conceded that a visit to the ranch would do him good.

"I'll stay here until I can sort everything out, then I promise I'll come home for a visit."

"Fair enough."

The woman's voice sounded in the background again. "I've got to go, Nate. Don't leave it so long to call again. And don't think I won't hold you to that promise of a visit."

Nate said goodbye and disconnected the call, then pressed the button to get a dial tone. There was one more call he had to make.

Nate awoke with a jolt from his semi-slumber. He had retreated to his cabin on the Savannah three hours ago, but his overactive mind wouldn't allow him to rest. Listening carefully, he tried to determine the source of the thud that had awoken him. All was quiet, with a faint splash of water against the hull the only sound.

Nate moved to check the clock. One thirty in the morning. *Why can't I sleep?* He knew the answer. He had left several messages for Mitchell Mayfield to return his call but, despite his persistence, the man hadn't obliged. The entire day had passed without his cell phone ringing.

Nate's frustration began to brew again. He wouldn't be happy about the custody situation until he had spoken to Mayfield. He had to know he had done everything he could to stop the proceedings. Then it was up to Mayfield if he continued down an unwinnable path.

A faint whiff of smoke caught his attention. The smell intensified as he sat up and turned on a light. He jumped to his feet and raced out of the cabin.

Strange red and orange light flickered outside the main door. A plume of smoke seeped in through the cracks and collected on the ceiling in a grey stream.

The Savannah was on fire!

Nate raced up the stairs and into the galley, grabbed the fire extinguisher and headed for the door.

He stopped to revise his plan, racing back down the steps to the main bathroom. There were two large windows in the ceiling that lifted out onto the deck. Their purpose was to provide ventilation for the wet area, but they were also a vital escape route from the cabins.

Nate threw the extinguisher up ahead of him and lifted his body up to squeeze out the opening and onto the deck. He ran to the source of the pluming smoke.

It was a relief to see the fire hadn't spread past the cockpit. The last flame disappeared as the extinguisher fizzled and died, empty.

A frenzied rustling and a string of expletives sounded from the back of the boat. He caught sight of a figure. It was Coot, and he was on the duckboard. A tinny floated a short distance away.

It looked as though he had somehow managed to lose the rope of his tinny. He was swishing his hand around in the black water, feeling for the end, which was difficult to pinpoint due to the darkness of the night.

"Hey!" Nate yelled.

Coot stood up and turned to face him. His eyes were wide and his mouth fell open in shock.

Nate reacted without thought, throwing the extinguisher at him. Coot managed to get his hands on it, but the force sent him tumbling backwards into the ocean.

Sprays of water flew into the air one after the other as Coot surfaced and thrashed violently.

"Help me. I can't swim." He managed to get the words out through mouthfuls of water.

Nate reached down to hold out a hand. Coot grabbed at the lifeline, and Nate hauled him back into the yacht, then forced him down onto the deck.

"Why did you set fire to my boat?" He could feel the anger rising up to consume him.

"I ... I wanted to get back at you for dobbing me into the cops." Coot blinked hard to dislodge the water dripping off his shaggy hair and into his eyes.

Nate didn't think. He grabbed the man's shoulder and pulled back his fist, not taking his eyes off the pathetic face. It was only when Coot cringed, halving his already tiny stature that Nate paused.

He examined the frail, shaking mass curled up on the deck. Coot was a cowardly fool.

Nate took several deep breaths, forcing himself to relax and loosen his fists. Without a word he made his way back into the cabin to retrieve his cell phone.

Neville kept them in suspense as he settled into one of the restaurant chairs. Anika couldn't help her own impatient wriggling as she and Nate waited for him to speak.

The fire on Nate's boat had been the night before last. Nate had made his statement to the police, and an investigator had been aboard the Savannah. Neville was about to give them an update on the results of the incident.

"Coot's behind bars. Doesn't look as though he'll be out anytime soon. They've charged him with arson and attempted murder." Neville paused to take a swig from his bottle of water.

Nate sat forward. "What about the netting?"

"Yeah, they got him for that too. He owned up to setting them all. Said Bert had nothing to do with it. He says Bert caught him just as he set up a net. They started yelling at each other, and then Bert suddenly grabs his arm and falls overboard. Coot took off. Makes sense, because the coroner reckons Bert died of a massive heart attack, not drowning, so Coot's off the hook for that one. But he'll get in strife over leaving Bert there to get stuck in the net."

Anika frowned. "What about the gunfire?"

"They found a revolver in Coot's stuff. No ammo though. He reckons he's never shot it. He says it's for show."

Nate moved back from the table to cross his arms. "Those shots didn't come from a revolver. It was a rifle."

"The cops still don't know what happened. They think maybe Coot's lying, and he owns other guns he's not telling them about." Neville took another sip of his drink.

"They also got Coot's sister. She was selling the fish he caught in the nets to a few takeaway joints. Coot wanted to get you, Nate, because he saw you that day you went over to the Mary-Jane. But the Fisheries were on to him long before that. They've been gathering evidence for a while now. He's been selling stuff to their undercover guys. They would've had him anyway."

Nate shook his head. "Great. So the Savannah's damaged for nothing."

Ani reached out to rub a hand down his arm. The damage to the yacht was a shame. The cockpit was a mess, and most of the instruments would need to be replaced. But Nate hadn't been hurt, and for that Anika would be eternally grateful.

The interior had suffered minor smoke damage. Nate had been bunking in Amos's spare room, since he could no longer live aboard. Neville had taken up permanent residence on the mainland. It was no secret he had stepped up his wooing of her solicitor.

"How are things with Marlee?" Ani watched with interest as a red tinge engulfed her cousin's face.

"Pretty good. I'm thinking of asking her to marry

me soon." A shy smile formed to accompany the blush.

Ani had spoken to Marlee when the latest document concerning the custody suit had arrived. It had been a complete surprise to the solicitor, as her office hadn't received a scrap of paperwork to back up the document sent to Anika. Marlee had asked her to fax it immediately so she could look into its origin. They had ended their conversation with a few comments about Marlee's love life. Neville was assured of a positive response to his proposal.

"That's great news." She got up to give him a hug.

Nate reached over to give him an affectionate slap on the arm.

The revving engine of the island's transfer boat sounded in the bay. They all looked out to see it dock on the floating pontoon.

Amos and Kye had gone over with Dutch to pick up guests from the mainland. Kye had pleaded with her for permission to go several times, and Anika had finally given in. She had previously been reluctant to allow Kye to make the trip, considering he would most likely be a hindrance to the men. Coordinating guests and their luggage onto a boat would be difficult enough without a child underfoot. But this day they all had relented and allowed him to go. Kye had been so down since the news of the custody suit, and then the fire on the Savannah, it was a small concession to lift his spirits.

Anika collected her bag in order to walk down and meet the boat.

Nate shook Neville's hand and followed her.

"Thanks for the update, Neville. Keep us posted on the investigation, as well as any reason to celebrate."

"No problem, Nate. Sorry about the Savannah."

Nate took Ani's hand. "Nothing that can't be fixed."

She smiled at him, knowing he had already organized the repairs. They turned to go.

"Oh, hey, Ani," Neville called after them.

She turned back to him.

"I know that after finding Bert, you and Yvette stopped monitoring the dugong in the area, but can you stay away from that patch a bit longer?"

"Isn't it safe now they've caught Coot?"

Neville got to his feet. "Should be, but I've still been keeping an eye on those blokes who were camping on Tenner. The cops don't know where that fella you found with the floats fits in to the illegal netting. They think maybe he was telling the truth and he did find the floats he had in the creek. We did another search of their camp. They don't have much to show for a long fishing and camping trip. I noticed they're packing up to leave. Be good if you keep out of there till they've gone."

Anika nodded. "Will do."

She and Nate reached the pontoon as Dutch began offloading the passengers. She felt Nate stiffen next to her as they approached the boat.

He drew a sharp breath. "What is she doing here?"

Ani noticed his confused expression and followed his gaze.

He was watching a skinny woman with shoulder-length white blonde hair, the kind of style from an exclusive hair salon. She was dressed in a skintight blouse that sat off her shoulders, and an expensive-looking pencil skirt. It was frightening to see how skinny she was, with protruding collarbones and limbs jutting out at sharp angles. Her face was severe, with tight skin stretching over cheekbones, and her head looked enormous on her tiny frame. She reminded Anika of a model in a fashion magazine. As she waited her turn to disembark she fixed a steely look on Nate, and a slow, tight smile spread across her Botoxed lips.

Ani looked up at Nate. His jaw clenched hard as his eyes remained on the woman. He kept a firm hold of her hand.

They watched Dutch help another female passenger out of the boat. Dutch then turned to offer help to the blonde woman. She held out a dainty, manicured hand in the fashion of royalty and stepped down onto the pontoon. As she walked towards them, her ridiculous heels clunked on the surface and she fought to maintain her balance.

Kye and Dutch followed her, while Amos saw to the last of the luggage.

"Nate. How are you?" Her voice was smooth and controlled, and her Texan drawl matched Nate's. She pulled her shoulders back. The action accentuated her perfectly formed assets.

"What are you doing here?" Nate's response was outright hostile.

The woman forced a pout. "That's no way to greet an old friend, especially considering how close we once were. I know your daddy taught you better manners than that."

Who was this woman?

Nate didn't respond. Anika could see the redness creep up his neck. His grip on her hand tightened as he stared at the woman.

The woman turned to her. "You must be Nate's new girlfriend. I'm Caroline. I'm the old girlfriend." She gave a half smile and raised one eyebrow as she spoke.

Ani didn't know what to do. This woman was clearly someone Nate didn't like. She wished he had filled her in on this past relationship, then she would at least be aware of who Caroline was.

Kye came to give her a hug. "Hey, Kiki. I was good. You can ask Dutch."

Ani pulled her hand away from Nate's to return her son's cuddle.

Dutch appeared beside them with Caroline's luggage in his hands. Two expensive suitcases were unceremoniously dumped at their feet.

Amos had gone ahead to show the other couple to the reception area.

"If you follow me, I'll see you to the reception." Dutch looked at her with thinly veiled disdain.

"Oh, I thought I'd stay on the yacht with Nate. After all, it wouldn't be the first time we've shared the same space." The eyebrow rose again.

She was clearly baiting him. The tilt of her chin gave her away.

Ani could see Nate's jaw twitch.

"Our days of sharing space ended a long time ago, Caroline. Didn't I make it clear where we stood last time I saw you? It was over twelve months ago." He took a step towards her. "I don't know what you're doing here, but it would be best for you to get back on the boat and go back to where you came from."

"Well, unfortunately you're stuck with me for two days. Dutch told me the boat doesn't return until then. He was good enough to arrange a cabin for me."

Dutch leaned into Anika and whispered. "Yeah, that was before I had to put up with her on the ride over."

Ani couldn't help but smile.

Caroline readjusted her handbag to sit firm on her shoulder. "In any case, I'm here because your father sent me with a message."

Nate frowned. "Why didn't he call, or come himself?"

"Well, this is important. You know how busy he is. It would be impossible for him to get away."

Nate rolled his eyes. "So give me the message."

"I'm way too tired now. We'll have to meet up over dinner." She moved away, taking cautious steps on the floating pontoon.

Nate called to her retreating back. "I'll meet you in the lounge at five. We won't be having dinner."

"If you say so."

Dutch picked up the bags. "This way, Caroline. It'd be my pleasure to tell you where to go."

She threw him a withering look. "It's Car–o–line. Not Car–o–lynne. I have already told you that." She made her way along the path, not waiting for his reply.

Dutch looked very close to exploding.

"I don't know what is wrong with you people.

It's a simple matter of inflection," she called back, without turning.

Dutch gritted his teeth and made a face. "More like infliction." He didn't bother to keep his voice down.

The comment was heard by Caroline because she turned and gave them all a death stare before continuing on her way.

Dutch rolled his eyes. "You had a lucky escape from that one, Nate." He smiled at Anika. "I can see your taste has dramatically improved." He ambled down the path.

"I hate that lady." Kye made a face.

"Hate is a very strong word, Kye. You shouldn't hate anyone." Ani tweaked her son's screwed up nose.

"She reminds me of an ugly troll. She complains all the time and she's mean." Kye furthered his point by making a troll-like expression.

Nate broke out in a huge grin and put a hand on his shoulder. "Your mother's right, Kye, you shouldn't hate anyone. But I'd understand if you disliked her, because to be honest, I feel that way too."

The boy nodded. "Well, I dislike her an awful lot."

Nate ran to answer the cell phone.

"Nate?" His father's voice rang out over the line.

"Jack, I'm pleased to hear from you." Although it wasn't the call he'd expected, his father was certainly someone he wanted to talk to.

"I, ah, think we may have a problem." Jack sounded sheepish.

"Would this problem come in an emaciated blonde form?"

For a moment, there was silence at the end of the line and then Jack said, "I assume she's arrived."

Nate sighed. "What's this all about? Why did you send her here?"

"I didn't send her. I only found out a minute ago where she was."

"So she isn't here to relay an urgent message from you?"

"Is that what she said?"

Nate was fast becoming frustrated. His father was not being forthcoming about Caroline's sudden arrival on Resolution. "What is this all about?"

Another long pause. "Let's just say my indiscretions are catching up with me."

Nate could just imagine what sort of indiscretion his father had conducted with Caroline, and at this point he didn't care. They could both do whatever they wanted as long as she was kept out of his life. It irked him that she would intrude upon his happiness.

"I don't care what you've been up to, Jack, just tell me why she's here."

"She thinks you jilted her."

Nate scoffed. "Are you serious? Come on, you know what she's about."

"Of course I know. She's been playing games with me for months."

Nate had to smile. Caroline had certainly met her match with Jack Hollingsworth. If she thought she could snag herself a rich husband from that relationship, she was in for a huge shock. Jack wasn't the marrying type.

His father continued. "She told me she needed a few days break, but I found out from one of the partners that she's gone to Australia with the sole purpose of causing trouble for you."

"How did she know where I was?"

Jack cleared his throat. "She was with me when you rang the other night."

He shook his head. "Thanks a lot."

"I had no idea she harbored a grudge, but apparently you shattered all her aspirations when you broke it off."

Nate was well aware of Caroline's aspirations, and they had nothing to do with loving him.

"Looks like I'm stuck with her then. I'll have to deal with it as best I can."

"On a separate issue, my contacts in Australia have assured me Mayfield won't succeed in the custody case. Should it get as far as court, they'll bury him."

Nate brightened at the news. "Thanks."

They spoke for a few minutes longer before saying goodbye.

Nate sat for a long time on the veranda of Amos's cabin and contemplated these new developments.

Explaining his relationship with Caroline to Anika had been one of the most embarrassing experiences of his life. Not only did the retelling put him in a very bad light, but by the end of the conversation, he felt like a complete fool.

There wasn't a single attribute the two women

shared. It didn't help that Ani looked blindsided by that fact.

In the end he had tried to convince her he wasn't the same person he used to be. He found himself repeating this line of reasoning over and over again, until finally he told her she was going to have to trust him. He had shown her who he was and now, in the face of this past mistake, she was going to have to decide whether to believe him or not.

Nate had to let the situation go. He knew Caroline was diabolical, but short of storming her cabin and forcing her back to the mainland, there was nothing he could do to stop her.

He sighed and made a choice. *God, you know her plans. Please thwart them.*

CHAPTER 17

Kye powered into the cabin at top speed. The force with which he slammed the sliding glass door produced a shudder that reverberated around the cabin.

Anika looked up from her lunch preparations to chastise him. "Kye, that is no way to treat our home."

The little boy was breathing hard. "I'm sorry but this is an emergency. That lady's coming. You know — the troll."

Ani put down the butter knife down. "What do you mean, she's coming? And don't call her names. It doesn't matter how much you dislike someone, it's never right to call names."

Kye's eyes were wide. "I saw her, and she's coming this way."

"She's probably going to see Nate at Amos's cabin." Ani resumed her task of buttering bread. Nate had told her about his father's phone call. He hadn't met Caroline yesterday afternoon, sending a note instead. It was short and to the point, relaying his disinterest in her presence and wishing her a safe trip home. They had both successfully avoided any area she might be present.

"Yeah, probably." Kye nodded in agreement, but peered out the glass to see if she was right.

She sent up a silent prayer. *Please God, don't let the presence of this woman ruin anything.*

Anika had been on tenterhooks since Caroline

had arrived yesterday afternoon. Nate had done his best to explain the dynamics of their past relationship, but Ani had been confused. How could the same person who fell in love with her have had a relationship with someone like Caroline? They were like chalk and cheese.

But she knew Nate and she trusted who he was—a man who wanted to be in their lives, a man who shared her faith; and a man who would never seek to hurt her.

"Kiki." Kye's high pitched voice made her look up. "She's here. She's walking up the stairs. I told you she was coming."

A soft knock sounded. Ani looked toward the door as Caroline peered through the reflective glass.

"Don't let her in, Kiki. She's worse than a wicked witch."

Anika turned back to him. "That's enough, Kye. I do not want to hear you insult her again. Do you hear me?"

Her son pursed his lips and narrowed his eyes in a display of defiance.

Anika walked to the door and slid it open.

"Afternoon." Caroline's greeting was dismissive. She was wearing skintight shorts that made her lily-white legs look like twigs, and a peasant top that would have been beautiful had her shoulders not resembled a coat hanger. High-heeled wedges completed the outfit, and provided her with inches of unnecessary height. "Mind if I come in?"

Anika looked back at her son. He shook his head in a violent show of displeasure.

"Now is a bad time. I'm in the middle of

preparing lunch." She offered the woman an insincere smile.

"Well, this won't take long." Caroline pushed past and entered the room.

Anika had little choice other than to follow her.

Kye was mirroring her mood, except he lacked the ability to disguise his feelings. His eyes squinted and his jaw gutted out at the intruder.

"Kye, you can go and watch a movie in your room until I call you. Put on your earphones." She had to get him out of the lounge. The best way to shelter Kye from anything this woman had to say was to run interference. The noise of the DVD player should muffle the adult conversation.

He backed into his room.

Ani looked back at Caroline. "Can you make it quick?" As far as she was concerned, this woman forfeited any requirement for manners when she barged uninvited into her cabin. "We're about to eat." As if to further her point she left Caroline standing in the lounge while she moved back to her task of making sandwiches in the kitchen.

Caroline stood her ground, placing her hands in the pockets of her shorts and scanning the room.

"This is real cozy. Incredibly insignificant, but then I guess it's to be expected in Hicksville."

Ani looked up from the activity to stare at her. "If you've come to insult me or my living conditions, you're wasting your time. I'm not interested in your assessment of either."

A rapid snort sounded in response. "You should be thanking me. I came halfway around the world to warn you. Nate isn't who you think he is."

Ani paused her ferocious buttering of bread. "You have no idea who Nate is. You haven't had anything to do with him for over a year. You have no right to come here and make trouble for him."

Caroline extracted one hand from her pocket to run through the length of her hair.

"I may not have seen him for a while but I knew him intimately, for over two years. And I can certainly tell you who he's not." The other hand flew from her pocket to rest upon her hip. "He's not a man to fall for a small-town nobody with no class and no breeding. Have a look at yourself. Don't you own a hair brush?"

Anika couldn't believe the audacity of the woman. Shock stopped her from responding. Caroline took advantage of Ani's numbed state.

"You don't have one iota of class. Nate is a pedigree Texan, with a reputation to uphold. Can't you see he's playing with you? Trust me. I'm doing you a favor by filling you in. He's only interested in the chase, nothing more. When he tires of you he'll take off, just like he did to me." She took a few slow paces forward.

"Besides, they tell me you have island blood. Getting serious with a native is virtually sacrilege. Besides, do you seriously think his family is going to allow him to marry someone with that kind of tarnished heritage?"

A new flood of emotions hit her. Caroline's words were like weapons piercing her soul. It hurt. A lot. Dry heat coursed through her body and a sinking feeling sent her stomach plummeting to the floor.

She closed her eyes tight. The darkness served as a backdrop to a sea of faces. Heath, as he thrust money at her, the privileged girls at the airport, the superior looks Mitchell Mayfield gave her each time she saw him.

The old feelings of insecurity and worthlessness surfaced. Throughout her childhood she had been told she wasn't good enough. All her life she had told herself the same thing. Perhaps Caroline was right. Perhaps she wasn't good enough for Nate. After all, they had grown up worlds apart, exactly like she and Heath. He was from a rich society family, while she didn't even know who her father was.

Classless and fatherless.

In her past the thoughts would have prompted a surge of self-preservation. She would have reared up and responded in kind to Caroline. But the familiar destructive words bouncing around her mind rang out as a mass of lies. There was an overwhelming sense of untruth, not only to the words in her head, but to Caroline's attack.

A new voice overcame the old.

You are not a mistake, for all your days are written in my book. I knew you before you were conceived. My thoughts towards you are as countless as the sand on the seashore. For I am your Father and I love you even as I love my son, Jesus.

The running list of Bible verses replayed one after another in her head. Each one memorized, to remind her who she really was. She was the child of a heavenly father. She was the delight of the creator of heaven and earth. She was loved. She was cherished. And she was worthy of all He had for her, and all He had given her, including Nate.

She opened her eyes to find Caroline's smirking face watching her. A heavy weight tugged at her heart. This woman wasn't the evil witch Kye thought she was. Ani recognized the symptoms in the tilt of her chin and the set of her eyes. She may have money and world-appointed status, but she was every bit as damaged in her soul as Anika used to be.

Caroline was weighed down with bitterness.

It was the same struggle Ani had overcome, the burden stopping her from being free to love, the burden her faith had extinguished, and a burden that she no longer carried.

A rush of sympathy for the woman engulfed her. "I'm so sorry to see you hurting so much, Caroline." Ani stepped out from behind the kitchen bench and walked several steps to face her.

Now it was Caroline's turn to freeze from shock. She recovered far more quickly than Ani had. "I don't know what you mean. I'm not hurt."

Anika took a deep breath. "I think you are. I think that in the depths of your soul, you are a deeply hurt person."

Caroline dropped her hands to her side. She licked her lips and broke eye contact to stare at her feet.

By the time Caroline looked back, Ani could see she had regrouped. Her eyes narrowed and her tiny frame thickened under the unmistakable weight of renewed hostility.

"Nate's going to get very bored with a spineless tramp like you. And even if he doesn't, your kid will eventually drive him away. Nate is not the fatherly type."

Anika despaired for the woman. She wasn't merely drowning in bitterness, she was happy to stay there. But a slamming door interrupted her.

Kye stood at his bedroom door. His face was red with anger, and his little arms were stiff by his side. Fists formed hard on both hands.

Ani swung around to face him. "Kye, I told you to put on a movie." A flash of fear surfaced for her son. Kye had dealt with so much during the last few weeks. He didn't need to be a party to this.

He raced towards Caroline.

"Don't you talk to my Mum like that. You don't know anything. You're nothing but an ugly troll. You've got a huge head and evil eyes." He stood his ground, fists clenched at his side.

Rather than being affronted the woman stared the child down. "You little creep."

Kye didn't hesitate. He jumped forward and flung a foot directly at Caroline's shin. She buckled under the attack, reaching down to rub the affected area.

Fury flamed on her face. "You dirty little ..." A flow of curse words that should never be heard by a child followed.

That's it. It was one thing for Caroline to spew hatred at her but her child was a completely different matter. A wild protectiveness overcame Ani as she threw herself forward, placing a barrier between the two.

"Get out." She pointed to the door. "Now."

Caroline paused for a bare second, then turned on her heels and left the cabin. Anika locked the door after her.

Kye had deflated on the sofa. Tears stained his little cheeks.

Ani took the seat beside him. "You know she's wrong, don't you? Nate says he loves us both and I believe him." She wrapped an arm around his shoulders.

He nodded while wiping his nose on his forearm.

"She's just a sad and unhappy lady, Kye, but she doesn't have to make us unhappy. Her words can only hurt us if we let them. If we know she's lying, then we shouldn't believe what she says."

He threw his arms around her body. "I know, but I still don't like her. I don't like her a whole lot."

Anika couldn't help but smile. She kissed his head. "I love you."

"Love you too." The muffled voice sounded from underneath her embrace.

She pulled him away to look into his blue eyes, so like her own.

"Kye, it's still not right to call her names, especially when I told you not to, and kicking her was very wrong."

His face changed in an instant from lapping up the maternal attention to outright defiance. "She called you bad names."

"Yes, she did, but that doesn't make what you did right. You don't have to like someone, but you do have to treat them how you would want to be treated. You owe her an apology."

Ani thought back to her own tirade of name-calling the first time she had met Nate and the humiliation she had to endure after the attack. The embarrassing lesson had done her the world of good.

She knew it was unlikely that Caroline would accept Kye's apology, but, as his parent, she required him to offer one.

"No way. I'm not going to. She deserved it." He crossed his arms.

"It's not your job to make her pay, Kye. I want you to apologize. It would be the right thing to do, even if she did the wrong thing first."

Tears welled in his eyes once more. He got to his feet. "I'm going to see Nate." He stamped his way out the cabin.

Anika closed her eyes and took a few deep breaths before reaching for the phone. She had to talk to Nate before Kye covered the few meters to Amos's cabin.

The number was busy.

She threw the phone on the coffee table. It would have been good to give Nate a heads up on the situation, but he would know how to handle Kye.

Best give them some time alone.

Nate picked up his cell phone on the second ring. "Hello?"

"I have a call for Nate Hollingsworth from Mitchell Mayfield." The secretary's voice was short and to the point.

"This is he."

"Putting you through."

As the hold button was activated, Nate took a few deep breaths. Finally the call he had been waiting for.

He moved from his position on the lounge to stand at the glass door and look out at the water. He could see the top of Amos's head as he fished alone on the rocks.

A small figure appeared on the sand. Kye. The call was put through before Nate could open the door and call out to him. Kye would no doubt walk down to see Amos.

"Nate, this is Mitch Mayfield. I have a message to call you. Is it Kye? Is he all right?" There was overwhelming concern in the man's voice.

"Kye's fine. He's a bit unsettled. He's lucky to have such a good mother." He couldn't resist the dig.

"Yes, he is."

Mayfield's response set Nate back. *That was unexpected.*

His silence prompted Mayfield to speak. "I apologize for the time it's taken to return your call. I've been on leave. I told my staff they were not to disturb me while I was away. I walked back in the door minutes ago."

Nate was taken aback further. He didn't expect Mitchell Mayfield to provide any explanations on his tardiness.

"This is simply a courtesy call, Mayfield. I have a vested interest in the result of the custody suit you've brought against Anika, and I wanted to give you a chance to halt the advancement of the suit. My involvement assures it will be unwinnable, and I suspect there may be a part of you that would be negatively affected by an immediate loss of contact with your grandson."

There was silence at the end of the line for a good

fifteen seconds. Finally Mayfield spoke. "I don't understand the purpose of your call considering the most recent correspondence sent to Anika and Kye."

What? This conversation was getting stranger by the second.

"I would have thought the correspondence you sent Anika gave a clear indication as to the purpose of my call. The document clearly outlines your intention to proceed with the custody suit."

Nate took a seat on one of the chairs while he waited for Mayfield's response.

"Excuse me a moment." Nate heard muffled voices, as though Mayfield had put his hand over the mouthpiece of the telephone. Nate could still make out the words he spoke. "Which document did they send Anika Deumer? Get me Smyth. I want an explanation."

"I'm sorry." The voice was clear again. "I suspect my office has forwarded the wrong correspondence. After the last contact I had with Anika and Kye, I made the decision to withdraw from the custody suit. I outlined this intention in two letters that my office were directed to send to Anika. I'm guessing they sent the wrong ones. The document Anika has received was drawn up some time ago. It was shelved and should have been shredded, considering it's now obsolete."

Nate took a breath and considered the man's explanation.

"So you're not proceeding with the suit? There will be no further attempt to gain custody of Kye?"

"That is correct. I have no intention of proceeding with any legal avenue of custody."

Mayfield stopped to sigh. "Nate, can I talk to you honestly?"

"Go ahead." The request was unusual, given his impression of the man, but he didn't see any harm in it. It may even help him to understand Mayfield's motivation.

"I'm dying."

Nate sat up. He hadn't expected him to be so honest. Nate remained silent while Mayfield continued.

"I was diagnosed with cancer ten months ago. I've been on leave for the last few weeks undergoing treatment aimed at extending my life. The specialists think it may give me a few more years, if I'm lucky."

"I'm sorry." Nate wasn't sure what else to say. He hadn't expected Mayfield to share something so personal with him.

"Thank you." Mayfield continued. "When I found out, I was angry. It was a blemish on my ambition. I sought numerous second opinions looking for one that would tell me what I wanted to hear. That was, until I attended a funeral. The man was my driver and he had died of the same disease they now told me I was going to die from. This was not a rich man. He and his family survived on minimum wages. I only attended the funeral because he was my longest-serving employee." Mayfield paused for a moment.

Nate could hear him swallow hard several times. The clink of a glass confirmed Mayfield had paused for a drink.

"Nate, I have spent my entire life acquiring wealth, and seeking status. I was groomed to be the heir to a legacy of legal masterminds. I have surpassed every expectation my father had for me. But attending that funeral made me realize everything I had spent my life working so hard for amounts to nothing. Not one comment was made about this man's work. All the eulogies talked about his respect for others, his generosity of spirit, his commitment to his wife and the love he had for his children."

Mayfield paused to swallow once more.

"Then they spoke of his faith and his belief that the end of his life was only the beginning. It was the one glimmer of hope I'd received since they told me I was going to die. I began to question, not only my life's purpose, but my life's end. So I sought to find a purpose for my life before it was too late. I missed the chance with my own son but I thought I had another chance with Kye. I set about to provide the life for him I assumed he didn't have."

Nate frowned at his reasoning. "Kye has a wonderful life. Anika has provided a stable and loving home for him."

"I agree — now. But I'd allowed myself to believe the stories my son told me. Heath knew I was disappointed in his behavior. It was partly my fault. I wasn't there for my son as he grew up. His mother, my ex-wife, spoilt him rotten. He was her golden child, incapable of wrong doing or error. I was more realistic. I wanted him to make something of himself. Unfortunately, I wasn't allowed to have any significant influence on him. This was partly due to my own ambition."

Nate couldn't help but think of the similarities in

his own upbringing, except his mother was the opposite. She was a strong, capable woman. She never allowed him to abuse the privilege he was born into.

"Heath became very good at manipulating me. He told me whatever story would put him in the best light. I believed him when he told me Anika was a gold digger and the child wasn't his. I assumed that was the end of the situation. I found out later his mother had furnished him with the funds to either buy her off or provide her with an abortion."

"Anika wouldn't have been interested in either option." A defensiveness wall mounted inside him.

"I understand that now. But when I became aware of Kye's existence I decided to find out whether the boy was my grandson. It was apparent as soon as I saw a picture of Kye that he was Heath's son. Then I did some research into Anika's past. It was a recipe for dysfunction. It was easy to judge her. I saw an opportunity to rescue Kye from this repeated pattern of abuse. I also thought I could bestow my life's successes upon him, to leave something behind."

Nate couldn't help the blunt scoff.

"Yes," Mitchell said. "It was foolish."

Nate hadn't expected that confession either. This man was full of surprises.

"At each meeting with Kye it became increasingly apparent I had misjudged his mother. She was not the person Heath had portrayed. Kye is a terrific child. He's bright, generous, and likeable. No child is that way without the positive influence of a good parent. It was clear I would lose a custody suit. There was no substance to my claim. It sent me into a spiral. What would be my legacy now? I no longer had a cause to pursue. I panicked."

"Is that when you told Kye he could go to live with you?"

"I thought I could persuade the boy into wanting my legacy, but he wasn't interested in the things I could give him. He knew the value of the home he had. I walked away from that disaster and stumbled upon a new perspective. My assistant, Sarah, has a strong faith. She's driven home the fact that Anika is an excellent parent. She also told me legacy didn't start with what we leave each other. It began with what God provided for us. It's made me think further about my mortality."

Nate smiled a huge grin full of delight. "We must set aside a time to talk further, Mitch."

The man chuckled at his response. "I'd like that. I do have one more thing to say. I would understand if Anika and Kye didn't want a relationship with me. I've given them no reason to trust me. But I have a lot to give. I want to give it to them. I want my grandson to have the part of me my son never did. Could you tell them about our conversation? I can see you have their best interests at heart. I want you to know, regardless of my past misjudgment, I now feel the same."

Continued contact with Mayfield would have to be Anika's decision. But there was some hope Nate could offer.

"Anika is an exception to her past because her faith has lifted her out of it. You can be assured she will take your request into serious consideration."

"I can't ask for any more than that. Please tell Anika I will oversee the posting of the correct correspondence today. Thank you for your time, Nate."

Nate made the appropriate response, hung up the telephone, and sat thinking about the conversation.

The sudden entry of Anika, followed by Amos, broke his contemplation.

She stopped to scan the room. "Where's Kye?" Her smile was forced.

"I saw him go down the beach a while ago. I assumed he was going to see Amos." Nate stood.

"He's not with me." Amos looked between them in wide-eyed confusion.

Anika looked back out the door. "Oh, no."

"What's wrong?"

"Caroline came over. Kye overheard what she was saying and got upset. He misbehaved and I asked him to apologize. He didn't want to. He must have taken off."

"We'll find him." Nate took her hand and led her back out the door.

"I'll check the beach here. He could be hiding round the back of the cabins." Amos set off in the opposite direction.

Nate and Ani hurried towards the main resort building. "You'd better fill me in on this visit from Caroline."

CHAPTER 18

Anika stopped to look at her watch. They had spent over half an hour searching the resort for Kye, but the little boy remained a few steps ahead of them. Bay had seen him in the kitchen storeroom. Flynn had spotted him running around the corner of the reception area. Dutch had caught a glimpse of him jumping off one of the cabin verandas. Neville had also arrived, and had seen him down on the pontoon.

All six of them now gathered at the top of the beach to find he had moved on from there as well.

"He's up to something. I'm sure of it." Ani couldn't shake the feeling her son was on a mission.

"It's not like him to go running off, is it?" Bay repositioned baby Haven on her shoulder.

"No. He's usually a pouter when he gets upset. All this activity is making me nervous." Anika could see Amos approaching them. He was alone.

"If he's around our cabins, he's hiding real good."

Nate turned around to scan the resort. "I guess we break up and cover the area again. One of us is bound to run into him eventually."

Amos took a few steps closer to the beach. He placed a hand above his eyes to shield his vision from the afternoon sun. "My tinny's missing."

A blood-curdling scream rang out from a cabin behind them. Amos's discovery was momentarily forgotten as they all hurried in the direction of the commotion.

Caroline exited her cabin at high speed. Another shriek sounded from her as she barreled down the veranda steps.

The reason for her distress was all too obvious. Apart from the telltale stains on the white sundress she was wearing, she was also sporting a head full of bright blue hair sticking out from her scalp in stringy clumps.

She spotted them and stomped their way. Tight fisted hands swung as she approached.

Bay gasped. "I wondered why Kye was hiding a big bottle of blue food coloring behind his back."

A tsunami size wave of dread washed over her. Her son had been responsible for Caroline's new look.

Caroline stopped at the rim of their gathering. Her face was bright red and her tiny body looked even more skeletal under the heightened hair. It looked as though Kye had doused it with coloring, and it had dried at all angles. The white blonde color of Caroline's hair had provided the perfect base for the bright blue dye.

"I fell asleep on my outdoor sun lounger, and woke up like this!" Caroline's last few words were delivered in a high-pitched squeal. She fingered the ends of her hair and stamped her foot. "Your devil son is responsible." Her bony finger pointed directly at Ani.

Ani didn't know what to say. She was horrified. There was an embarrassed silence from the group behind her as the blue-haired fiend stared her down.

A slow series of snickers broke out around the

group. First Dutch let out an explosive splutter. He covered the outburst with a heavy cough. Then Flynn let go what could only be described as a squeak. His face looked decidedly pained as he desperately tried to hold in the emotion.

Amos and Neville had the widest grins Anika had ever seen.

Bay was the only sober face. She bit her lip in nervous reaction. When Haven let out a delighted squeal, Nate exploded in an eruption of outright laughter. The group imploded in a chorus of hilarity. Even Bay abandoned her discomfort and giggled along with the men.

Anika couldn't help but contribute.

Caroline shot death stares at each individual, her face as red as a beetroot.

Her anger did nothing to squash the amusement of the crowd. After a prolonged period of non-stop noise, it became clear none of them were going to settle down anytime soon.

With a snort of disgust, she turned on her heels and stomped a few paces before turning back. "Go ahead and laugh. You'll soon stop when I sue you, for the hair, and for assault. I have a bruise on my shin."

Unfortunately, the statement, combined with the sight of her screwed-up features, only served to provoke a fresh wave of laughter.

She turned to stomp the rest of the way to her cabin, blue hair bouncing along as if it had a life of its own. Her cabin door slammed behind her.

The laughter died down in ebbs and flows. There was much wiping of eyes and holding of stomachs.

Nate let out a sigh and looked around the circle of friends. "She really did look like a troll, didn't she?"

That was it. A collective uproar broke out among them again. But this time it subsided more quickly.

Anika forced herself to be serious. "I do need to find my son."

The fact that Kye was still missing had a sobering effect. They all settled down.

Flynn leaned over to accept Haven from his wife. "Do you think he would have taken off in your tinny, Amos?"

"Not normally, but Kye would've known he'd be in big trouble. He could've got it in his head to take off for a bit. I don't know anyone else who would've taken my tinny."

Amos was right. Considering his actions, it was quite possible Kye had left in order to escape the consequences.

Nate took her hand. "We'd better get out and have a look for him. He's probably gone north. He's been talking about a lookout on Miller Island. He might have gone there."

She nodded. Kye had been persistent in his desire to explore the area.

"I'll scout the south islands with Amos." Neville looked over at Amos. "We went fishing on a reef up there a few weeks ago. He could've gone back that way." Amos and Neville paired up and headed for the pontoon.

"I'll go and check out around the mainland." Flynn bounced his daughter up and down as he spoke. "Dutch, can you get some staff together and coordinate a better search of the resort?"

"No problem." Dutch turned to walk towards the reception.

Bay gave her a quick hug. "He won't have gone too far." She retrieved her daughter from Flynn.

A sense of paralyzing fear for her son froze her. *Please God, please. Keep him safe.*

Nate pulled her to his side for a reassuring hug as they walked to the pontoon. He kissed her temple. "Don't worry. We'll find him."

Ani watched the dark grey clouds roll in as the tinny bumped through the choppy water. The weather had worsened considerably since they had left the pontoon at Resolution.

Miller Island was the second last northern island in the group. Tanner was the last, then beyond Tanner was the open sea.

The approaching storm hindered their progress. Ani and Nate were both wet through.

The salt spray flew in plumes at each rise and fall of the tinny. A head-on sea wrestled against the outboard.

"I sure hope Kye didn't go out in this," Nate yelled. Anika could barely hear him above the noise of the boat and the waves. She turned to see him fight to steady the boat against the pull of the waves.

With a sigh, she wiped her eyes and faced forward once more, praying her faith would conquer the disastrous scenarios of her imagination. *I fear no evil, for thou art with me.* One of the most famous verses pushed through her impending fear. She held onto that promise for mile after mile of nothing but white water, as they inched closer to the storm.

"Over there!" Ani pointed to the grey shape high on the beach.

Miller Island wasn't nearly as large as the other islands in the group, being less than half the size of Resolution. It hadn't taken long to circumnavigate.

They entered the sheltered side of the island to find a semicircular bay finished in a perfectly formed beach less than one hundred meters long. It was sheltered from the storm by a rocky outcrop.

Nate cut the outboard to idle. "That looks like Amos's tinny."

Anika nodded. "It is. See the scrape along the side? That's where Neville pulled alongside a barge last year."

The storm had gone around them for the most part. Ani cringed as a flash of lightning struck the distant mainland. A rolling groan of thunder followed shortly after. The black sky above them proved they were still on the fringe of the monster. As they made their way to the beach, the sky opened. If they hadn't been soaked before, they certainly were now.

They got onto the beach without being swamped by the waves, and secured the boat.

Anika checked the sand around Amos's tinny, eager to spot any sign of Kye's footprints. If she could only work out the direction he had gone, perhaps it would give them some idea of where he had entered the scrub.

Unfortunately, any footprints had been washed away by the heavy downpour.

"How did Kye get the boat that far up the beach?" Nate yelled over the noise of the rain.

He had a good point. It looked like an impossible task for a child to pull the weight of a boat that distance.

"The tide's still going out. Maybe that's why it's up so far." Anika could only assume the falling tide had more to do with the placement of the boat than Kye's muscles. Still, even with the receding water, it was inconsistent with a child's strength.

Nate found some shelter under a tarpaulin in the tinny, and called Resolution to update Bay on their position. There was no news on Kye.

He hung up the phone and replaced it the waterproof bag. They each grabbed a torch from the tinny and prepared to trek into the scrub. They would need the torches as the dull light faded.

The overgrown nature of the island helped to pinpoint a well-worn track jutting off from the beach.

"That way."

They made their way down the first few meters of track. Flashes of lightning broke over the mainland, followed in time by the accompanying roll of thunder.

Several meters in, the track widened and a progressing incline forced the scrub to fall away to rocky patches.

Anika breathed heavily as she followed Nate up the path. She paid more attention to the placement of her feet than she did to Nate. His sudden stop tripped her up. She fought to regain her balance after almost colliding with him.

"Big problem." Nate stepped aside to reveal the cause of his stop.

There was a fork in the path. The rain had turned each fork into a small stream, making it impossible to judge which one Kye had taken. The rain blurred Anika's vision as she peered up the incline of each pathway. There was no indication where either path led. Uphill was the only distinguishing feature.

Anika wished they had thought to bring one of the other men with them. They all had extensive knowledge of the area, and would have had a better idea where each of the paths led. Not that the result would have been any different. They would still have been faced with the same dilemma — not knowing which route Kye took.

Nate leaned over to be heard above the noise of the wind and rain. "What do you want to do? Should we split up? Or pick one to go down together?"

Anika did a three-sixty scan of the conditions. There was a good chance the weather would get worse before it got better.

She thought about her son, scared and alone, out in the ferocious conditions. There was no choice.

"We have to split up. It's not going to be long before it's dark, and it'll be much harder to find him then."

Nate nodded. "This way looks slightly better." He pointed to a marginally straighter path. "You take that one. Have you got your cell phone?"

Ani pulled out her phone and checked the screen. "There's still service, so we're not out of range."

"Keep in touch with me."

She looked up at him through the grey tinge of rain. Water ran in heavy streams down his face and dropped off his chin. He pulled her into an embrace. Their wet, pants and t-shirts sandwiched together to form a soaking mass of fabric. His body was warm under the coolness of the material.

"Be careful." His breath was hot against her ear.

He pulled her away to give her a weak smile and pulled her close again.

The heightened wetness of his lips against hers did nothing to lessen the impact of his kiss.

They broke away simultaneously.

Ani walked several steps along her chosen path before turning to see Nate watching her. She smiled again and gave him a wave.

They both moved off up the hill.

Thirty minutes of walking, and the twisting, turning path had amounted to nothing. Following the path to its end, Anika found herself back on the same beach she and Nate had started on. The two tinnies sat just as they had left them.

The rain ceased as the cusp of the storm moved over the mainland. Ani could still see the faint glow of lightning in the distance. Stars shone in the north.

She walked the length of the beach, straining in the light of the torch for signs of her son. There were no new tracks in the sand.

Sitting at the edge of the bush track, she wrapped the tarpaulin around her, pulling her legs up to her chest. A rush of tears threatened to smother her chilled cheeks.

What if we don't find him? What if he's hurt? What if he's lost?

Each scenario brought a new sense of helplessness.

She took out her mobile phone and checked to see if she had missed calls. She and Nate had remained in close contact since they parted. The last call had been five minutes ago. Nate had reported that he had reached the lookout but Kye wasn't there, and Nate was making his way back to the beach.

Anika didn't know how long the return trip would take him. Her torch was dying, and she turned it off to conserve the little battery she had left.

She heard a rustle in the scrub behind her. Two voices sounded through the darkness.

"It's this way."

"How would you know? You've only been here once."

"I'm telling you, this is it."

"You idiot."

Neither voice was Kye or Nate. Before she could size up the situation, a beam of light and two figures emerged from the track. She jumped to her feet, leaving the tarpaulin behind on the sand.

The man in front stopped short at the sight of her. He dropped a huge object he had been carrying in one hand but continued to hold a powerful torch in the other.

The man behind him came to stand next to him. He dropped what she could now see were garbage bags.

"Who are you?"

A torch light shone in her face.

"I'm looking for my son. We think he's lost here. Have you seen a seven-year-old boy?"

It was impossible to see their faces behind the beam of light aimed at her. She reached up a hand and blocked it from blinding her.

The figure with the torch stepped forward. "What makes you think he's here?"

She pointed to Amos's tinny. "We think he took my uncle's tinny from Resolution."

The other man broke out in a snicker, then stepped up beside his mate. "Hey, I know her."

The torch light shone down her body to her feet, then back up to her face.

A rush of fear swept through her. *Who are these guys? And what are they doing here?* She retrieved the tarpaulin and used it as a wrap.

The man with the torch turned to his friend. "She's the little blonde chick you liked so much."

"Yeah." The second man said to his friend, then addressed Ani directly. "I told you I'd see you again."

Recognition set in. This was the buffoon from the kapmauri, and one of his friends, the ones who had been camping on Tanner Island. But Amos had said they had packed up and gone.

"What are you doing here? Where's my son?" She had to know if these men had any connection to her missing child.

"Hey, we don't know where your kid is. We haven't seen him." The man with the torch waved it as he spoke.

"Then, what are you doing here?" She pulled the

tarpaulin tighter.

"None of your business." The man with the torch turned to his friend. "Get those bags in the boat, Gary. The sooner we get out of here the better."

"Can't we stay for a bit now we got some company?" Gary didn't move.

The torch shone in his face. "No, you idiot. Ray'll be wondering where we are."

Gary remained still. "Mate, I haven't been near a woman for three months now. I'm starved. And I've had to watch her running around in her tinny for most of that time."

Anika took several steps back. This was way too much information. A chill ran up her spine.

"I don't give a toss how hung up you are." The man holding the torch scoffed. "You might have a rape conviction, but you're not gonna force one on me." He stepped towards Gary. "Get this stuff into the boat so we can take off."

Ani remembered the way Gary had blatantly ogled her, and felt a slight relief. At least the man in charge appeared to possess some level of decency.

Gary bent to pick up the garbage bags. "You're a mongrel, Dave. When we get back, I'm gonna take out your sister."

Dave spanned the short distance between them, swung, and thwacked Gary on the head with his torch.

The injured man let out a pained cry and crouched down, holding his head. "Oh, you ..." A string of swear words followed.

Anika looked up and down the beach. She considered her chances at making a run for it, but she didn't have time to move. Dave aimed the beam of the torch toward her again.

"Get over there, out of the way." He signaled to the edge of her and Nate's tinny. "Now!" He took several steps towards her with the torch held in strike position.

Anika looked over at the injured Gary. Dave might not be the kind of man to force himself on a woman, but he was clearly capable of assault. She did as she was told.

Dave moved to Amos's boat and reached into the cavity in the front. The shape of the object he pulled out was undeniably a rifle. He shone the torch back on Gary, who was still rubbing his head. "Now get this stuff in there." He indicated the bags and Amos's boat with the torch.

Gary straightened up. "Let's take the other one. It'll be easier to get back down to the water. That boat weighs a ton."

Anika put two and two together. It wasn't Kye who had stolen Amos's tinny. It was these men. So what were they doing here? *And where is my son?*

Dave lit a path while Gary struggled towards her with the two bags. He then threw one bag into the boat and picked up the other one. Anika looked up from her place in the sand.

Gary expelled a hefty breath as he lifted the bag high enough to clear the side of the tinny.

All of a sudden, a rip sounded, and the bag burst open. In the light of the torch Anika could make out a flow of green leafy matter gushing from the open seam. The accompanying stench identified the contents — marijuana. The two men chorused a flow of curse words.

Dave balanced the gun on his bag at the top of the beach and ran down to them. "You'd have to be the biggest idiot I've ever known. Man, I hate you. I don't care how much this stuff's gonna net us. Three months with you wasn't worth it."

"It was your idea to use these bags. I said we needed something tougher but, oh no, you're the penny-pincher."

"If you don't shut up, I'm gonna knock your block off, you ..."

The men sparred back and forth.

"We don't have any more bags, so you'll have to throw it all in the boat and sort it out when we get back." Dave held the torch while Gary scrambled to pick up the marijuana and scoop it into the tinny.

"What are we gonna do with her?" Gary threw the comment over his shoulder while he continued his task.

A loud groan sounded from Dave. "I suppose we're stuck with her, thanks to you."

A deep chuckle sounded from Gary. "You mean I get to keep her."

"Well, we can't leave her here to dob us in, can we?"

Anika couldn't believe it. They were going to take her with them.

Gary pointed a finger at her. "You owe me, baby, especially after I saved one of your precious dugong from that net."

Dave thwacked hard him on the arm. "You're full of crap. You saved nothing. I was the one who kept the area clear. You just sat up in the lookout and smoked pot all day."

Ani took a deep breath. That explained how they had the floats, and most likely explained the gunfire. They were keeping out any activity in their growing area. She looked over in frantic desperation at the distance between her and Gary's bag at the top of the beach. She could see the shape of the rifle sitting on the top of it. If she made a run for it, she could reach it before he grabbed her.

The shrill ring of her mobile phone made her jump. The caller identification showed Reception, indicating the caller was Bay.

"Answer it." Gary shone the torch in her eyes. "If you don't, they'll send someone to look for you. But, one wrong move, and I'll thump ya."

Ani reached into her pocket and pulled the phone out of the plastic bag. Without thinking through the consequences she jumped to her feet and hit the connect button. "Bay, send help," she yelled through the mouthpiece. "Now they will come looking." She threw a defiant stare towards the beam of light.

It wavered from her face, then a heavy blow struck the side of her head, sending her hurtling to the sand.

"You dumb cow." Dave's voice was muffled by a high-pitched ringing.

Ani sat up in the sand and blinked hard, trying to clear the piercing noise. She prodded the area of impact. Her fingers were covered with a sticky substance, and she could smell blood.

The ringing subsided as she looked up at the men. The force of the blow had hurled her a few meters away from them.

Dave shone the light back on Gary, who had finished shoveling the drugs into the boat.

"Get her in, will ya." He turned to walk back up the beach. He had only advanced a few steps when an ominous click halted his progress.

He shone his torch towards the sound, only to be met by a matching beam aimed at him.

In Dave's torchlight, Ani could see Nate standing next to the bag of drugs, his rifle aimed directly at Dave.

"Get that light off me." Nate held both his torch and the rifle.

Dave dropped the light from Nate's face to his chest. "Okay, man. Don't do anything stupid. That gun's loaded."

"I know it's loaded."

Through the muted ringing Ani could hear the control in Nate's voice.

"You, over there." Nate briefly flashed at Gary. "Get on the sand, face down, and spread your hands and legs."

Gary hesitated. Nate let off a shot over his head.

"Okay, okay. Don't shoot me." He fell to the sand as instructed.

"Now, throw your torch to Ani." He trained the rifle sights back on Dave.

The man didn't move. The torch remained in his hand and he swayed in a taunting manner.

"What you gonna do if I don't?"

A succession of pops echoed from the rifle. It was followed by a collection of plinks as the bullets hit the sand, centimeters away from Dave's feet. The man did an unsteady jig as he dodged the spitting sand.

"Don't test me. I'm a crack shot, even in this light." Nate trained the torch on a wide-eyed Dave, who didn't hesitate to throw the torch to her. She retrieved it and aimed the light at Gary.

"Now get over there and join your friend." Nate indicated that Dave should also spread-eagle himself some distance from Gary.

When he was down, Nate moved closer to them.

"Ani, get the rope from the tinny."

It took her no time to retrieve the coil and pause for further instruction.

Nate still had his light on the men.

"She's going to tie your wrists and then your ankles. I suggest you stay very still because, if you move, I'm going to shoot you both, first in one leg, and then in the other. And, trust me, I will not miss. Put your hands out in front of you."

The men did as they were told. Anika tied their wrists, and then their ankles.

Nate moved closer when the job was done. He kept the rifle trained on the men but glanced her way. She could see his frown in the torch light.

"How long have you been here with them? Did they hurt you, other than the knock with the torch? I saw that."

She pulled up the bottom of her wet shirt and held it against her ear. It was still bleeding.

"No, that was it. There's a bit of blood, but it'll be okay."

"What sort of low life hits a woman?" His voice was loud and aimed at Dave. "Perhaps I should even the score."

Dave's shoulders shivered. It didn't look as though they had any more to fear from either of them.

"I got a call from Bay. They found Kye," Nate said.

A short breath escaped her and she closed her eyes. "Thank you, God. Where was he?"

"In your cabin. He knew he'd be in serious trouble after turning Caroline into a troll, so he hid for a while and then decided to go back home and accept his punishment."

Ani shook her head. "It was the only place we didn't look."

Nate chuckled. "My cell phone's in my pocket. You'll have to come and get it to call them back. Tell them to get the cops here before I do something to these two that I might regret."

Anika moved over and retrieved the phone. She couldn't resist placing her arm around his waist and giving him a short hug.

Nate turned to kiss the top of her head, keeping his eyes on the men at all times.

It felt like an age went by while they waited for the police to arrive. The storm had long passed over, and a distinct calm enveloped the island. A helicopter was the first to arrive. It hovered over them, beaming a floodlight on the scene to assist the police in pinpointing their location.

Neville and Amos weren't far behind. Neville took over guard duty and freed Nate to take Ani in his arms. It was a huge relief to be comforted.

Bay had the forethought to send clean clothing with the men. It was wonderful to get into dry clothes. A first aid kit in one of the tinnies made short work of the cut on her ear.

Moonlight flickered through the clouds as the police arrived.

It was well past one in the morning before the men were safely in custody and the detective turned his attention to her and Nate. "I wish I could let you go and get a few hours' sleep, but it will be much better if you can come with us now." He looked hopeful.

Nate had barely left her side since Neville had arrived. "I don't know about you, but I couldn't sleep even if I wanted to."

She nodded. "Let's get it over with."

"Great." The detective led the way to the patrol boat.

<h1 style="text-align:center">CHAPTER 19</h1>

Ani looked around the group gathered at the restaurant for dinner. They had all come together to celebrate the capture of the third man involved in the gang. After a three day search of the islands, the man called Ray had been found and arrested that morning.

"Where was he?" Dutch asked. He had been away from the island all day and was yet to hear the story of the capture.

"Hiding out on Tanner. He couldn't get off because their tinny was stuffed. So they stole Amos's to get the crop out of the area quick." Neville had been privy to the details, having helped in the search. "He knew the cops would be looking for him because he saw the helicopter the night the other men got caught."

"Did they have any more dope hidden?" Dutch reached for a sauce bottle.

"Heaps." Neville pushed it towards him. "The three of them had dope stashed all over the north islands. They grew most of it by tying plants to the top of the mangrove trees. Dope plants are hard to see against the green of the mangroves. I've seen it done before. It's real hard to spot. They had a great look out built in there, and everything."

"Well, it's good to know they won't be around for a fair while. That sort of operation is bound to net them some serious jail time." Flynn patted a sleeping

Haven on his shoulder as he spoke.

"Not for one of them." Neville looked over at Ani. "The bloke that gave you a hard time—Gary—he spilled about the whole setup. Looks like he'll get less time than the other two."

Ani shook her head. "You're kidding? What did he say?"

"Just that Bert had come along, probably looking for Coot. One of the other blokes shot at him to warn him out of the area. Musta been that time when you and Nate were down there. They reckon they never saw Coot though."

"I knew Bert didn't have a hand in it." Nate gave her shoulder a reassuring squeeze.

"They also cut the anchor on your tinny, Ani. They wanted to give you a scare—keep you out of the area."

"How did they grow the dope in the trees, Neville?" Kye screwed up his nose in confusion.

Nate smiled and ruffled his hair. "If I were you, I'd stay away from mischief-making endeavors."

The comment aroused a round of laughter from the group. Kye bowed his head.

Kye had been the embodiment of remorse, not just for his attack on Caroline, but also for the trouble he had caused with his disappearance.

"Have you heard any more from the lovely Caroline?" Bay raised one eyebrow as she looked at Nate.

"Not a peep. I spoke to my father today. He told me he had managed to contact her while she was still here, and had ordered her home. He told her she would be sorry if she didn't leave immediately."

Nate smiled as he turned to Ani. "That's also why she kept quiet when Kye was apologizing."

Ani nodded, finally understanding Caroline's unexpected reaction to her son. She had been so sure that Caroline would make it hard for the boy, and was shocked when all they received from her was a sour look and a short, "Fine."

"Well, it's nice to have some peace on the island again." Yvette raised a glass as she spoke.

There was a chorus of agreement around the table and they all resumed their meal.

Nate leaned into her, close enough to whisper. "Did you get to talk to Mayfield?"

Anika had received the letter from Mitchell Mayfield that morning. She had read it to Nate, and said she would phone him.

It was an amazing story and one in which she couldn't help but rejoice, which was a very strange reaction. The thought of it made her smile. To be so moved by a man who had caused her so much heartache was a bizarre feeling.

"I did," she answered Nate just as quietly. "He apologized again and asked me what he could do to right the wrong. I couldn't believe it."

Ani had been taken aback by the intensity of his turn-around.

"I think he's had a real change of heart." Nate smiled and turned back to his food.

Nate was right. Mayfield was a man on his own spiritual journey. Ani knew the burden of all he had brought upon her had lifted.

It was a wonder to Ani how God could somehow turn this all around and put His order to right, not only in her and Kye's lives, but in Mitchell Mayfield's as well. She found it ironic that Mayfield had judged her based on her past. Yet she had shown him who she was and he had believed her, just as she had believed Nate.

Ani also understood that her faith had revealed to her who she was. Caroline's attack could have had very different consequences. She could have allowed it to destroy everything. But, instead of believing what Caroline or the world said she was, she chose to believe what her heavenly father told her He had made her to be. It was the final truth that had set her free from doubt.

Looking around the table full of friends and family, a sense of unbridled excitement enveloped her. What would the future bring?

Anika sat on the warm sand, looking out at the ocean. The late afternoon light threw bands of red in the sky, and the waves lapped the shore in rhythmic motion. She closed her eyes to hear the sounds of the water as it collided with the shoreline and the rocks.

A heavy hand rested on her shoulder as Nate took a seat beside her. "Here you are. I've been looking everywhere for you." He put his arm around her waist. "I was thinking you had disappeared like Kye."

Anika rested her head on his shoulder, pleased that the last week's events were now behind them. "No way, I'm more than happy to stay put. Yvette told me to go home. We've put the finishing touches on her research. She presents it to the department next week."

"So, it's all over. No more chasing dugong."

Ani sighed. "Not for a while. But Yvette's certain the findings will lead to further research. She wants me to stay on, but I'll have to forgo pay for a while until she gets another grant. Bay told me I can take any job I want at the resort, so I guess I'll have to think about what I want to do."

Ani was happy to take a job at the resort to fill in time, but she had to admit that the scope of work wasn't where her happiness lay in the long term. She had the need to get out and explore. Being stuck behind a desk, in a restaurant, or cleaning rooms wasn't going to satisfy her for long.

"I have something to run by you." Nate shuffled slightly to one side, making her lift her head and turn towards him.

He removed his arm from around her and rubbed his hands on his cargo pants.

"The Savannah goes in for repairs in a few days. Which means I'm essentially homeless for at least three months. My submissions to the magazine have come to an end, and I'm waiting to hear what they want me to do next. Then, there's my father who's been pressuring me to come home for a visit. Uncle Brae also called last night and asked me the same thing."

Anika could feel the tension between them. He was going to leave Resolution. She was convinced. It felt as though a fist had smacked her on the top of her head.

"You're leaving, aren't you?"

He leaned further away. "Not without you and

Kye." He stopped to pick up her hand. "Ani, I want you to come with me. I want the first stamp in your passport to be to my home. I want to show you where I grew up and introduce you to my family."

Her heart skipped a beat. A trip to America. An adventure to Nate's world, his country, his people.

The weight lifted and a cloud appeared below her. Its invisible lift sent her spirit flying.

"Nate, I would love that. I know Kye would too. We both have our passports. When can we go? Tomorrow?" She jumped to her feet and looked down at him, still holding his hand and pulling at it. "Do we leave tomorrow?"

He smiled up at her. "I was thinking more like next week. That is, if you can wait until then."

She let go of his hand and did a spin in the sand. "I can't wait."

He laughed as he got to his feet and grabbed her mid spin. "So I take it you're happy about the plan?"

"Ecstatic." As she looked into his eyes she knew her happiness stemmed more from the fact that she would be with him, than from the long-awaited stamp in her passport.

"Well, seeing as the first plan went so well, I hope you're as enthusiastic about my next one." An uncertainty flickered in his eyes as his hands held her waist firm.

"Ani, I told you not long ago that I wanted you. At the time I didn't know what that meant. I only knew I wanted to be with you. Not just in a physical sense, but all the time. Every day. Every hour. Every minute." His wide smile reached the corners of his mouth. He was so handsome, Ani wanted to reach up and place her lips on his.

"That hasn't changed. Except now I want you more than ever. I want you next to me when I wake up each morning. I want you by my side in everything I do. I want to be a father to your son, and for him to know he has a father who loves him more than anything." He pulled her away from him to fumble in his pocket and retrieve a small box.

One hand flew to her face as he opened it and sank to one knee. He held her hand and looked up at her. "Ani, I want you to be my wife, and I want to be your husband. Will you marry me?"

She stared in mesmerized silence at the sparkling diamond ring sitting in the box. It was the most beautiful piece of jewelry she had ever seen. Three brilliant-cut diamonds sat in a row with the band also inlayed with tiny diamonds. The simple elegance of the ring was perfect for her.

She shifted focus from the ring to Nate's expectant face.

He pointed to the three diamonds. "One for each of us."

He smiled and waited for an answer. Her chest pounded, and a light-headedness washed over her as shallow breaths robbed her brain of oxygen.

"Nate, are you serious?" The second it was out of her mouth she knew how ridiculous the statement was. It seemed so incredulous that he wanted her, wanted them.

A huge smile developed, replacing the anxiety. He glanced up the beach, then down to his kneeling position, and finally back at her. "It doesn't get any more serious than this, Ani."

She couldn't help but return his smile. "Yes. Yes, I will marry you."

He stood to take the ring from the box and place it on her shaking finger.

A happy tear slid from the corners of her eyes as he dropped the box on the sand and lifted her off her feet into a bone-crushing embrace.

His lips were on hers within seconds. The kiss continued as he gently placed her feet back on the ground.

"Oh, man. Are you kissing my mum again?" a little voice yelled from the top of the beach. They moved apart to see Amos and Kye ambling down to them.

"Yes, and you'd better get used to it, kid, because there's going to be a lot more of it. Your mum just gave me permission to kiss her for the rest of her life." Nate called back.

Kye skipped the last few meters towards them. "What, like all the time?" He curled his lips in horror.

Ani and Nate both laughed. He bent down to Kye's level. "Your mum is going to be my wife. Do you know what that means?"

"You're going to be my dad? For real?" The little boy's face broke out in an expression of sheer joy.

Nate nodded to him. "That's right."

"Is it true, Kiki?" Kye looked to her for confirmation.

She bent down to join Nate. "Is that okay with you?"

"Is it ever!" He threw himself towards them, unbalancing their squatting positions and sending them all toppling backward into the sand.

They all laughed as Kye straddled them for a group hug.

Amos stood above them. A huge grin adorned his face.

CHAPTER 20

Anika checked the provisions aboard the Savannah one last time and pushed down a sudden panic over the amount of food stocked. Was it enough for the three of them?

She turned to find Nate grinning at her from the cabin door. "We can always stop on the way. There are a number of ports between Resolution and Cairns, you know."

She shut the cupboard door. "I know, but I don't want to run short. It's our maiden voyage."

Nate laughed. "Don't worry. If we run out of food, there's an ocean of fish to catch. You can bet it won't be long before Kye insists on wetting his line. He's been complaining about not having enough fishing time since we got back."

Anika rolled her eyes. She had noticed her son's burning desire to get back on the water. Three months in America followed by several weeks back on Resolution had Kye complaining that he had endured enough 'landlubbering.'

Ani knew how he felt. As much as they had both loved Nate's country, the ranch with its wide open spaces and loving family atmosphere, even she was itching to feel some salt against her skin.

Nate entered the cabin and stole a kiss, then playfully thwacked her bottom. "I can't tell you how good it is to be able to do that."

Ani laughed and recalled the way they had

fought to control themselves during the three months they were away.

Nate grinned. "I'll check upstairs one last time. Can you do the same down here?"

She nodded and lifted her head for a repeat kiss.

Nate turned around at the door. "Ready for your honeymoon, Mrs Jackson-Hollingsworth?"

A soft blush warmed her cheeks. "As ready as I'll ever be with a seven-year-old along for the ride."

As if on cue, Kye stuck his head under Nate's arm. "Are we going yet?" A pained look crossed his face.

Nate tucked Kye's head playfully under his armpit and rubbed the top of his head. Kye squealed in protest.

"We've got a few more things to check. Are you going to help me and stop complaining?"

Kye tried to nod under the forced confinement.

"Come on then." Nate freed him, and they both went to check that the yacht was set to sail.

Ani leaned back on the bench. The last three and a half months had gone by so quickly.

They had left Resolution the week after Nate had proposed. The only stopover they made on their way to America was a few days in Sydney to see Mitchell Mayfield.

After a series of conversations with the man, Ani was convinced that allowing Kye to continue to see him was for the best. Not just for Mayfield, but also for her son. Now the custody threat was over, Kye was thrilled to see his grandfather. Mayfield had done his utmost to assure Kye he was never again going to suggest he live with anyone other than his mother and Nate. He had also gone above and beyond to assure her he was sorry for the hardship he had caused.

In some ways, Ani could understand his motivation. She had been removed from her home because her mother had failed to protect and love her. There were cases of abuse and neglect in her family lineage. Why wouldn't Mayfield jump to those conclusions? Now he knew better, and he had acted on that knowledge. It was enough for her to know he trusted her, so she could also trust him.

Anika had left Sydney determined she would allow him to use whatever time he had left to develop a solid relationship with his grandson.

Then they had flown to America.

Ani was every bit as excited as her son on the plane ride over. She had finally realized her dream to travel, and was so proud of the stamps in her passport.

The time they had spent at Running Brook Ranch would go down in her memory as some of the best days of her life.

Nate had taught both her and Kye to ride horses. That was a hilarious undertaking, but an experience they had enjoyed immensely.

She loved the freedom at the ranch, the wide open spaces, and the wide valley stretching as far as her eye could see.

Then there was Nate's extended family. All were exceptionally welcoming to both her and Kye. His Aunt Lane had even shed a tear when it was time for them to leave, exclaiming how wonderful it was to have a child in the house again.

Ani could see Nate was thrilled with their easy adaptation to his home.

But, like all her people before her, the sea eventually pulled them back. Even Nate revealed he missed life on the rolling waves. His love affair with the ocean wasn't anywhere near over.

A call telling them the Savannah had finished repairs, and was ready to set sail, brought them flying back to Resolution. There was also the added event of their wedding on the island. They had used the three months they spent at the ranch to organize the event. It turned out to be no small undertaking. Anika's adopted extended family alone filled the resort and much of the mainland accommodation. Not one of Amos and Aunty's clan had wanted to miss the wedding.

They also had to make room for Nate's family, who all made the trip over from the States. Added to the mix was her adopted Resolution family, including Jed and Samara, who wouldn't miss a wedding on Resolution.

Amos and Aunty walked her down the makeshift aisle of flower petals. Her cousin, who was a pastor, oversaw the official proceedings. Kye had taken great pride in his position of best man. A massive kapmauri had followed the ceremony.

It was a hotchpotch mix of every group imaginable: young and old, wealthy and poor, black and white. All were there to witness the official joining of their families.

Regardless of their differences, it had been a successful event. Ani had taken a moment to sit back and contemplate that perhaps this was what God had meant when He referred to His church. A group of people who came together, regardless of culture, color, class, nationality, or denomination, all with one thing in common—a love and desire to serve Him.

Now, two weeks later, the Savannah was ready to leave for Cairns.

Nate had a new contract with the magazine. They wanted him to detail his trek up north to Cairns and on to the Thursday Islands. Ani was thrilled with the thought of visiting the northern islands again. The publication was keen for him to continue through to the Pacific Islands, New Zealand, and around the Asian regions. It was a life Ani couldn't wait to start.

"All set to go." Nate called down from the cabin door.

Ani took a few deep breaths. Of all the events in the last few months, leaving Resolution would take the greatest toll on her emotions.

Closing her eyes, she pushed towards the door. As she stepped onto the deck she heard a loud wolf whistle from the shore.

She stood and stared in amazement at the crowd lining the beach.

Nate came to stand behind her and wrapped his arms around her waist. "Looks like we're being given a send-off."

Kye jumped and hollered his goodbyes from the bow of the yacht.

A wave of tears flowed down her cheeks as she picked out each face amongst the crowd.

Bay and Flynn juggling Haven between them—

they had been like a sister and brother to her.

Jed and Samara, who she and Nate had taken to like old friends.

Dutch and Yvette, wise and loving like the grandparents she had never had.

Neville and Marlee, who had married on the mainland the week Ani had returned from America.

And Amos. She had always called him Uncle, but he had become like a father to her. She would miss him the most. She knew he would miss them, too.

"We'll be back. You know that, don't you?" Nate whispered in her ear.

"We'd better be," she said. "Whenever you hear me talk about home, it will be Resolution I'm referring to. It's where my family live." *It's where I found love and life.*

She smiled as she lifted a hand to wave with all her might.

Nate kissed her cheek and then moved to winch the anchor. Kye joined her at the stern as the Savannah set sail. The white canvas triangles caught the gusts of wind as they rushed through Resolution Bay.

Anika cuddled Kye to her as they continued to wave their goodbyes. He soon left her to join Nate.

Ani sat dangling her legs off the edge of the boat, enjoying the salt spray on her face and the wind gusts blow the folds of her sundress. She watched as Resolution faded into the distance.

It was like saying goodbye to an old friend. But, as she turned and saw her husband and son at the wheel of the Savannah, she knew that, although Resolution would always have a place in her heart, her real place on earth was wherever God wanted her to be.

She wanted to stay in His plan, because He knew every inch of her being. He knew every time she sat down, and rose up. He knew every failure and triumph in her life. Every hurdle she jumped, He celebrated, and every time she fell, He picked her up again. He orchestrated every beginning, and every ending.

He did this because He was her Father. He had loved her before she was conceived, and He promised to love her with an everlasting love, even to the end of time.

NOVELLA: A CHRISTMAS RESOLUTION

Breeah cringed at the state of her childhood home. "You can tell a bachelor lived here."

"Ugh." Annmarie pinched a filthy rag she had pulled out from behind a chair. "Your Gran would freak if she saw this place." She threw it into a garbage bag.

"Great-Uncle Jim certainly didn't enjoy cleaning." Breeah forced two sofa cushions apart. A musty, sick smell was emulating from the gap. "Eww." She could feel her face contort as she pulled out a decomposed banana peel.

Annmarie's eyes widened. "That's it." She pulled off her plastic gloves and placed her hands on her ample hips. "Call the cleaners."

Breeah followed her friend's lead, throwing her gloves in the garbage. "Professionals it is. Coffee?"

"Finally!" Annemarie raised her arms in full praise mode. "It is way too early in the morning for this level of activity."

Breeah laughed at her old friend's poise. Some things never change, like the way Annemarie dramatized everything.

They picked their way through an assortment of half-filled boxes, making it to the kitchen without incident. Breeah flipped the switch on the electric jug before preparing the cups.

Annemarie leaned against the counter, checking her cell phone. "My husband hasn't tried to contact me for at least an hour." She glanced up, her brown eyes wide. "I think this is a record."

Breeah measured sugar into their cups. "Did he take all three boys?"

"No way. Bailey's with my mum. An eight-month-old in a fishing boat is not fun, or wise. A six- and nine-year-old is enough for Rob. Especially in a dinghy."

Breeah poured the water. "How long do they usually go for?"

"As long as Rob's patience allows. He usually stretches to a few hours, but this is the first time in ages they've gone without me."

Her tone, combined with another glance at her cell screen revealed Annmarie was missing her boys.

Breeah passed her a mug. "Thank you again for

helping me. I know it's hard to organize life these days."

Her friend tilted her head. "My best friend's finally home. That's a small miracle, so I'm going to spend as much time with you as I can. Especially if it's another ten years before you come back."

Breeah scanned the cluttered mess on the kitchen benches. "I thought this packing up would take a few days. Who knew I'd still be here a week after Uncle Jim's funeral? He was a hoarder."

"And so dirty." Annemarie cringed. "How did your Gran and Jim grow up in the same house? I remember our childhood sleepovers here when she was alive, and this place was spotless. Talk about brother and sister being complete opposites."

Breeah sipped on her coffee. "Maybe I should have made the effort to get up here and visit with him more often. But Uncle Jim always liked to travel down to me." She peered at her friend over the rim of her mug. "He probably knew I'd freak out if I saw how he was living."

Annemarie pulled on the hem of the oversized T-shirt she was wearing. "Did your Gran know he was this bad? I mean, how could she possibly have lived with her brother without knowing he was a complete slob?"

Breeah shrugged. "I don't know. Granddad died my second-to-last year of school. Uncle Jim moved in after I went to university. They must have lived together for at least five years before Gran died. You and I are both twenty-nine this year, so what's that?" She did some quick math. "Eight years Jim lived here? The last six on his own, after Gran died?"

Annemarie nodded, making her loose ponytail shake. "Sounds about right. So we're looking at six years of hoarding." She sighed long. "Time sure does fly. Who would have thought I'd have a nine-year-old at the age of twenty-nine? So much for my dreams of Broadway."

Breeah frowned. "There's still time."

Annemarie rolled her eyes. "No, I'm afraid my physique is no longer adaptable. Unless they're looking to cast a curvy momma." She gave Breeah a head-to-toe scan. "You, on the other hand, look like you stepped off a Hollywood red carpet. How do you keep in such good shape?"

Breeah swiped some dust off her jeans and flipped the hem of her dirty singlet top. "Yeah, I'm all class right now."

Her friend rolled her eyes. "Okay, not right now, but you do look good, girl. I love your hair cut like that, all wispy with that sweeping fringe. I wish my hairdresser had that talent. Of course, there's only one hairdresser in Kiisay Point now, so it's not like I've got much choice in what I get."

Breeah fingered her streaky blonde hair. She had been happy with the style. It was a shame her new look had to make its premiere at Great Uncle Jim's funeral. "Just as well I got it done before I came. I've had enough bad cuts from Lola during my childhood to last me a lifetime." Breeah recalled some of the hideous styles she had to wear thanks to the elderly local hairdresser. If only her Gran had taken her into the nearest city like she had begged for, instead of relying on the small-town talent.

Annemarie sipped her coffee. "Oh, Lola left a

few years ago to live with one of her boys down south. Kylie's taken over the salon now and . . ." She stopped and frowned. "Sorry. You probably could do without my mentioning her."

Breeah took a sharp intake of breath, then forced it out. "That's in the past."

Annemarie bit her lip. "It's just that I always thought what she and Hayden did to you is the reason you've never come back for any length of time."

Breeah acknowledged the sick feeling inside. A week ago, when she was in Melbourne, the events that sent her life spiraling into confusion at the age of nineteen seemed so long ago. Now here she was in the house she had grown up in, a house filled with the memories of the grandparents who raised her. Flashes of teenage passion, heartbreak, and confusion stormed to the surface.

BUY NOW at Amazon or www.rosedee.com

NOTE FROM THE AUTHOR:

An adaption from 'Father's Love Letter' used by permission--Father Heart Communications.

If, like Ani, you desire the love of a father, please begin your search at: www.fathersloveletter.com

Xo Rose.

ABOUT THE AUTHOR

Rose, who holds a Bachelor of Arts Degree, was born in North Queensland, Australia. Her childhood experiences growing up in a small beach community would later provide inspiration for her first novel, Back to Resolution. Beyond Resolution and A New Resolution are the second and third books in the Resolution series.

Back to Resolution won the Bookseller's Choice award at the 2012 CALEB Awards, while A New Resolution won the 2013 CALEB Prize for Fiction.

She has also released The Green-field Legacy, a collaborative novel, written in conjunction with three other outstanding Australian authors, and has recently released the standalone novel, Ehvah After.

Her novels are inspired by the love of her coastal home and desire to produce exciting and contemporary stories of faith for women. Rose resides in Mackay, North Queensland.

BOOKS BY ROSE

The Resolution Series:
Book 1: Back to Resolution
Book 2: Beyond Resolution
Book 3: A New Resolution
A Resolution Novella: A Christmas Resolution

Other books by Rose Dee
Ehvah After
The Greenfield Legacy (A conjunction novel).

Visit Rose at:
www.rosedee.com
https://www.facebook.com/Rose-Dee-Author-172886062810998/